PRAISE FOR LAURA L. ZIMMERMAN

"Laura L. Zimmerman's YA fantasy *Keen* enthralled me from beginning to end. This present day Faerie story featuring a baffled teenage banshee and her unlikely high school friends has heart, lots of twists and turns, and a great message about using one's gifts for good. *Keen* would be the perfect next read for fans of Holly Black's Folk of the Air series and Maggie Stiefvater's *Lament*."

~Carrie Anne Noble, award-winning and bestselling author of *The Mermaid's Sister*

"A powerful story of an outcast discovering the beauty of her own voice, filled with memorable characters and vivid twists, Laura L. Zimmerman's spellbinding debut *Keen* will echo in your memory long after you've turned the last page like the eerie final note of a banshee's song."

~Kara Swanson, award-winning author of *The Girl Who Could See*

"I haven't devoured a book this quickly in a long time! Its unique premise, relatable characters, rising stakes, swoony romance, and engaging narrative style make *Keen* a perfect stay-up-all-night kind of read, complete with a beautiful message of healing and self-worth. Laura L. Zimmerman has launched herself right to the top of my list of favorite paranormal fantasy authors!"

~Laurie Lucking, award-winning author of *Common*

"A fantastic debut! Zimmerman draws the reader into the multifaceted world of *Keen*, where nothing is as it seems. I loved the characters and found myself fully invested all the way to the last beautiful page. I can't wait for the sequel!"

~J.M. Hackman, award-winning author of *Spark*

"The lure of the banshee's song is irresistible in life (and death), and it's no different in *Keen*. I was pulled into the story from the first line to the last. Laura Zimmerman's debut novel is intriguing, engaging, and hard to put down. I can't wait to see more from her!"

~Pam Halter, award-winning author of *Fairyeater* and the Willoughby and Friends Series

"A modern twist of mythical Irish folklore, *Keen* packs a fast-paced punch along with well-developed characters. I couldn't put it down!"

~Missy Kalicicki, co-author of the Sinners Series

"The modern faerie tale I've been waiting for! *Keen* grips you from the first page and pulls you into a story you won't want to leave—rife with magic, teaming with incredible characters, and filled with the promise of hope in a dark world."

~Ashley Townsend, author of the Rising Shadows Trilogy

"*Keen* weaves such a fantastical mystery, in a sense that your nose will remained glued to the page until you've pulled back every layer and uncovered every hidden clue. Nothing is ever simple for a banshee living through high school."

~Desiree Williams, author of *Illusionary* and *Sun and Moon*

"A banshee tale? So here for it! *Keen* is a powerful story of friendship, love, loyalty, and sacrifice where snappy dialogue and evocative prose paint a vivid backdrop for delightful and dangerous hints of faerie. Snag your copy ASAP!"

~Gillian Bronte Adams, author of the Songkeeper Chronicles

"A captivating story that will enchant you from the very first page. In *Keen*, Laura L. Zimmerman balances the fantastic and the everyday to give us a world that feels both profoundly relatable and strikingly beautiful. *Keen* deftly navigates its themes of belonging, vulnerability, and love, giving readers a page-turning adventure that will keep them reading late into the night."

~Catherine Jones Payne, author of the Broken Tides Series

"Fans of clean YA paranormal romance will be swept away by this brooding debut from Laura L. Zimmerman. A small-town twist on centuries-old Irish lore, a journey of self-discovery, and a healthy side of teen angst—what's not to love?"

~Lindsay A. Franklin, award-winning author of *The Story Peddler*

Lament

BANSHEE SONG SERIES

◄ BOOK TWO ►

ALSO BY LAURA L. ZIMMERMAN

Keen

Banshee Song Series, Book One

Lament

Banshee Song Series, Book Two

Coming Soon:

Silence

Banshee Song Series, Book Three

Lament

BANSHEE SONG SERIES
◄ BOOK TWO ►

LAURA L. ZIMMERMAN

Love2ReadLove2Write Publishing, LLC
Indianapolis, Indiana

Gabrielle, Grace, and Scarlett.
You are my inspiration. You are my heart.
There are no words to describe how thankful I am that
God allowed me to be your mother.

1

I AM LIVING in my own personal Neverland.

Except this one doesn't have Lost Boys or Wendy Darlings or Captain Hooks. No marbles or crocodiles. Certainly not a happy ending.

Not for me.

I am a Lost Girl. All alone.

The past few months have been . . . *hard*.

Losing my dad left a hole the size of Russia deep in the core of my soul. Can I ever be whole again? No amount of tears ease my pain. No book or movie or anything like that can truly make me happy. I'm convinced of it. I doubt whether time actually does heal all things.

At least, I won't ever be fully healed.

Still, my boyfriend, Oliver, has been as perfect as can be for a girl who just lost her only parent.

Between my moments of melancholy, he's taken me on walks, to the lake, to his house for Thanksgiving dinner. He insisted I tag along as his family went hunting for the prover-bial flawless Christmas tree. He was a perfect gentleman when he surprised me with a fancy dinner for Valentine's Day. Even though I refused to smile.

Because smiling would betray my dad's memory, right?

Oliver's not only treated me like a beloved girlfriend, but as someone who can actually make a difference in this world. Like maybe I would be missed, if I were to die. *Just maybe.*

Sharp pain lances through my chest, like a dagger delivering piercing heat through my flesh, muscle, bone. *I hope I'm not dying.*

Fire melts my skin from within. Ice has frozen my blood inside my veins. The pounding in my head is like a thousand beating drums, crashing, clanging, and thumping relentlessly. Hopelessly. Endlessly.

I fall to my knees, the sidewalk's concrete cutting my flesh. A pale house looms before me, all occupants fast asleep at the midnight hour. The fragrance of earth and frost fill my senses.

Make it stop. Make it stop!

"Caoine!" Oliver is on the ground beside me.

He doesn't remove my cloak's hood, the one I must wear whenever I sing my banshee song. He knows not to do that now. Leaving it in place is the only way I can possibly save the hearer of my song, if fate allows them to live another day longer on this Earth.

But no matter how much I try to relax, how I attempt to embrace my gift, I can't stop the pain. Can't make it go away.

Images flash through my head in fast forward. Flipping past in microseconds. I can't control them, can't focus. Can only let them flow.

Something is wrong. Why can't I control my gift?

I begin to shake, my fingers trembling, arms quaking. Sweat pours along my temples, down my back. Pebbles dig into my skin, the intensity of the dead of night freezing my insides. Still the visions invade my mind, burrow deep beneath the layers of who I am.

Go away!

"Caoine?" His voice is panicked, his hands everywhere at once. "Baby? Speak to me. Open your eyes."

He's come with me to help, to be my guide home once my banshee song finishes and I can only see the world through a rabbit hole a dozen feet away. It often takes close to an hour for me to recover after I've sung my song.

I try to groan, but my body won't respond to any of my commands. A choking noise echoes against the surrounding trees, from the solid sidewalk below me.

Wait. That's me. Why am I choking?

"Caoine!" Oliver is pounding on my back now, my face turned toward the cement.

My entire body is limp, and my hands and elbows brush against the hard ground, sending more pain through my body. The ground meets my head harder than I expect when I collapse. I can't lift my arms or legs. Can't stop the pain that radiates from every cell.

Then light. Moonlight fills my vision. I'm awake. Or—my eyes are open.

"Oh, Caoine." Oliver sighs.

I move my neck, turn my head. I've got control of my body again. My hands find the cold, hard earth, and I lurch.

Vomit spews across the dead grass, along the cracked pavement. I heave until there's nothing left, until I'm empty in more ways than one.

Finally, Oliver pulls my hood back. The images fade. Feeling returns to my body, an inferno that blazes across every inch of skin.

"Caoine," Oliver laments.

I blink. Wipe a hand across my mouth. Sit back against my boyfriend. It's over. The episode is over. *But what was that?*

Oliver repeats my thoughts aloud. "What just happened?"

His breath comes strong and heavy against my neck, his nose nuzzling behind my ear. An endearment that would normally send excited chills down my spine.

For now, it merely comforts.

My head rests on his shoulder, my body limp in his arms.

The bite of the night temperature nips at my skin, a fragrance of winter and crisp evening air drowning away the awful moment of torture I've just lived. My gaze drifts up.

I freeze. Swallow. Shiver. Burrow deeper into my boyfriend's arms.

"I have no idea. But that can't be a good sign." My finger shakes as I point to the night sky.

Bright stars dot the clear heavens above. Right in the middle is the moon. A blood-red moon, the deepest shade of scarlet I've ever seen.

There's no way a glitch in my gift and an anomaly of nature on the same night can be coincidence. I have no idea what just happened and no clue why our closest celestial being has gone wonky. But there's one thing I do know for sure.

A blood-red moon can only spell trouble. And I have a feeling I don't want to find out what kind.

2

An overhead bell sounds, and students scatter through the halls of West Lincoln High like mice evading water.

The drab walls have been cleared of artwork and replaced with banners declaring our final win of basketball season. Spring holiday is just three days away. A faint odor of old socks and cafeteria lunch hangs over the student body like a city's thick smog.

Catherine giggles at something she said, and I do a double take.

Images of the previous night hammer away at my mind, and I can't focus. At least I can blame it on the impending holiday break. A full week of bliss. At least from school.

I bite my lip to stave off the threat of tears that floods the backs of my eyes. A full week without my dad too. A week with nothing to do but think of him.

I'd rather be at school.

If Cat notices my emotional fumble, she doesn't let on. My friends are used to my pendulum-like mood swings. I mean, who wouldn't be Jekyl and Hyde after losing a parent? Still, I've got a mask to wear, and wearing it is my main priority these days.

"So I'm just not sure if I should say yes or not, ya know?"

She nudges her way past a couple of students gathered around a desk in the front of our next classroom so we can find our way to the back. Where I like it.

Even though I've been at this school for more than six months, I still get a few stray stares over my appearance every now and then. I mean, it's not every day a girl with white hair that stretches to her waist and skin almost as pale walks through the door.

Although I've finally begun to learn how to control my fae abilities and can now make myself appear like I have a more balanced diet—as opposed to my waif-like look, complete with bones jutting through jeans and arms as skinny as broomstick handles—there's just no way of hiding my odd-colored eyes.

One silver, almost simmering white, the other such a pale grass green you can practically see to my soul, they quickly became Oliver's favorite part of me. How? I still have no clue, but he loves to get lost in them. At least, that's what he tells me.

My song too. Not that I'm about to sing my banshee song to usher him into the afterlife anytime soon. But with the debacle over Halloween when the Unseelie prince tried to use me to enact a full-blown takeover of Earth, I'm finally able to control my banshee song.

I no longer sing simply to usher others into the afterlife—or at least, not *only* that. I once dreaded doing such a thing, but I now know singing them a lament is the most merciful thing I can do. It brings peace in their final moments.

But my song is so much more. With it comes images. Flashes of vision show me if their death can be avoided and how to help.

With the loss of my dad, Oliver has become my faithful companion in helping warn those who can avoid death. Helping save lives.

I've also learned to sing my special song without the threat of death and destruction. I never understood how to meld the two together before, but now I do—singing with my banshee beauty but keeping the innocence of life entangled between the notes and melody and desire.

Oliver loves to play guitar. I love to sing my banshee song. The two of us make a pretty good team, even if I don't necessarily sing *while* he's playing.

"Friends, if you could take your seats, please," our teacher announces from the front of the room, "I've got a situation in need of my attention. We'll begin in a few minutes."

She promptly turns to two students before her, one of them waving her arms wildly while attempting to keep her voice low. The other student looks less than happy.

I swing around in my chair to face Cat. "So are you going to say yes?" I still have no idea what we're talking about, but I'm taking a stab in the dark.

"Maybe. I mean, did I make a total fool of myself in front of him or what? Did he ask me on a date out of pity?" She runs her fingers through her shoulder-length dark curly hair and pushes her box-like glasses up her nose.

Oh right. Nathan.

She's had a crush on him since the Halloween dance, when he came dressed as Sonny Bono. Her own rendition of Cher earned them a prize for best costumes, even though nothing about it had been planned. Since then they've been spending a lot of time together. A lot.

I totally missed the part where she made a fool of herself, but I fumble through an answer anyway. "Are you kidding? The boy has been glued to your hip for months. There's no chance he's asking you out of pity. If anything, making a fool of yourself just gave him the courage to see you're only human." I bite my lip and lean forward. "Not that I think you made a fool out of yourself. *Your* words, not mine."

She tilts her head, the freckles across her nose scrunching together as she scowls. "I accidentally flipped my cup of soda off my table and splashed it all over the pregnant lady beside me at the restaurant. How is that not making a fool of myself?"

I open my mouth. Then foible. "It . . . could happen to anyone. Right?"

Yeah. I should've been listening to this story from the beginning.

She groans and drops her head onto her arms on her desk.

"Aww." I pat her back. Am I even doing this whole consoling thing right? It's only been a few months that I've actually had real friends. "Seriously, Cat. If he was embarrassed by you, there's no chance he'd ask you out. Like I said, he's just happy you're not as threateningly glamorous as he first thought. You're human. That's a good thing."

I bite my cheek. It is a good thing to be human. Especially coming from someone who's only *half*-human. What I'd give to feel entirely within one world or the other.

But I'm destined never to be whole. Never fully faerie, never fully human.

A sigh slips from my lips, and I mentally chastise myself. This isn't about me. I'm here to comfort a friend. "Would it help if Oliver and I came with you? Like a double date–type thing?" She lifts her head far too quickly, and I hold up a hand. "Not that I'm suggesting you need a babysitter or anything. I just thought—"

"That's totally perfect!" She squeals and draws a few looks from our classmates.

I wince and glance up front. Our teacher is still deep in conversation.

"Would you really do that? I mean, come along and keep me sane and all?" She's bouncing in her seat.

"Of course." Which is a crazy thing to say, considering just a few months ago I was terrified of even being around people. And now I'm volunteering to be a wingman on a friend's date? Who is this new Caoine and where did the old one go?

Although, I already know the answer to that. I don't want

the old Caoine back. A breath hitches in my throat as I realize I like the new me. The Caoine I've become.

I snag a stray piece of my ultra-white hair and twirl it around my finger. "So when are you going out?"

"Friday night?" She blinks rapidly when she sees my face fall. "Is that not okay? I can always ask him to reschedule."

"No, no. It's fine. I'll tell Oliver. We'll make it work." Nerves zip along my spine, and I swallow.

Oliver has something special planned for the two of us Friday night. Something about a six-month anniversary or something? I think. I can't keep track anymore. But he's kept track and is super excited for whatever he has up his sleeve. Heat pricks the back of my neck.

Worming my way out of this one might take some work.

I glance at Cat and her eager eyes, and my heart does that little melty thing like when I look at a cute little puppy. *Right*.

It's odd having friends now. And wanting to change and stuff. Actually desiring to do whatever I can to make others happy because I know they'd do the same for me.

To care about someone other than my dad.

I blink away tears. "I can't wait for Friday. Promise."

And deep down, I mean it.

Now, if I can just convince Oliver that his special surprise is worth putting off just a little longer.

3

———

THE CLINK of silverware on glass and a steady wave of chatter blanket the diner where the four of us sit: Catherine, Nathan, Oliver, and I.

Our booth has shiny, sticky seats and a table with a cracked top and grease-smeared edges. It's not our normal hangout, but it was the closest place to the movie theater where we just caught the newest zombie flick, *Heads Will Roll 3*.

Funny. I never pegged Cat as a zombie girl. Apparently it's a huge thing she and Nathan have in common.

I glance at Oliver, and he smiles back, that jagged tooth peeking from between his full lips. His kindness never ceases to amaze me. Kind of like a wave that continually crashes against my skin, over and over and over, never allowing me to fully come upright before the next one hits.

The fact that he agreed to see a zombie movie—something he's less than fond of—and was willing to delay our special surprise date make my heart do squishy things. Very squishy.

I sigh.

And sort of gag.

The fact that I'm a vegetarian hanging out in a burger joint definitely accosts the senses. I always got violently ill from eating meat, but I hadn't figured out if it had anything to do with my fae-ness until I met my best friend, Aubree. Who also happens to be full fae. Thankfully. Without her I'd be in the dark about so many things.

The feeling that I've barely scraped the surface of my faerie side gnaws at my mind every minute of every day.

A shout from a waitress comes from the kitchen, and the griddle sizzles with whatever the cook is frying up. I take a whiff of my fries and relax. Fries I can handle.

I making nummy noises as I shove another in my mouth.

"Wow. Tell us how you really feel, Caoine." Oliver chuckles and gently bumps me with his elbow. His skin, dark as night, is a sharp contrast to my almost transparent sheath.

"You know perfectly well how I feel about my fries, love. Put me in a burning building with fries and all my friends, and I'm sorry to say the fries will win." I toss him a wicked grin before dragging another beloved piece of fried goodness through my ketchup and downing it.

Oliver shakes his head. "That's harsh, C, even for you. I'd still win out over those fries, right? You'd save me from a burning building, wouldn't you?" He bats his eyelashes. "If I promise to buy you more as soon as we're safe and sound?"

I press my lips into a straight line and pretend to think. "I suppose." Then I gulp down another fry.

Cat laughs and turns toward Nathan. "She's kidding, I promise."

Her date sits beside her, his face unusually pale. Poor guy isn't used to hearing teen girls declare such undying love for food, I guess.

"So Nathan," Oliver says, breaking the tension. "What year are you? I don't think I have any classes with you."

Nathan clears his throat and glances at Cat before making eye contact with my boyfriend. "I'm a junior. I've got Orchestra with Cat, which is where we met."

Catherine's cheeks go bright pink, and she tries to hide her smile. If she's embarrassed about robbing the cradle, she doesn't appear overly concerned. Which is pretty fantastic. The notion that the guy needs to be older than the girl has always bothered me.

"What instrument do you play?" I frown at my plate as I notice I'm down to a handful of fries.

"Violin, like Cat." His light-brown skin flushes as he looks at her. His brown eyes match hers, right along with his black-framed glasses.

It's uncanny how much they look like they belong together. Warmth radiates along my arms as I glance between the two of them. I'm beyond happy for her. Like *beyond*, beyond. Being a senior and never having dated can be such a hard thing.

I speak from experience. Too much experience.

"Are your chairs beside one another?" Oliver pulls the last pickle from his burger before sinking his teeth into it, the scent of yeast and tomatoes pulling at me.

Cat ducks her head. "He's first chair, actually. I'm . . . farther back."

Nathan attempts to look humble, but I don't miss the way his shoulders straighten just a bit. Earning first chair as a junior is an accomplishment.

"Cool." Oliver nods. "I play guitar. We should hang out sometime, maybe swap techniques and such."

Nathan's face lights up. "Sure."

I have no clue if there's even a correlation of techniques between such vastly different instruments, or if my boyfriend is simply trying to find common ground so he can be kind. Like always.

Before I have the chance to dwell on the awesomeness of my amazing man, the doors to the diner fly open, and a flurry of emotion interrupts our conversation.

Aubree runs toward us, her jagged, plum-colored hair in two braids across her shoulders. Her makeup is stark, almost no color on her cheeks or lips, but a burst of hue is splashed across her eyes. Thick purple lines the top of her lids, ending in cattails, a violet smudge of color also beneath her eyes. False lashes make them stand out a mile. Her all-black leather outfit is tight, and she teeters on high-heeled black boots that zip up her calves.

She's out of breath, and my heart leaps at her approach. Aubree almost never loses her cool. And she certainly never runs. Like ever. Whatever this is, it's big.

I hop to my feet and meet her a few feet away from our table. "Hey, what's going on?"

Images of the night Seamus died in her arms in that empty field behind the school muddle my brain and swirl around like a whirlpool, sucking me into a well of guilt and regret. I shake my head to clear it and refocus on my best friend.

"We need to go. Like now."

She fiddles with one of her braids, and I furrow my brow.

"Go? Where? And why do you need me?" I try to keep my voice low enough so the others won't hear, but my back prickles with their stares.

"There's a problem. A few, actually." She licks her lips, her worried eyes settling on mine. "I need you. Oliver too, if he's willing." She doesn't bother to glance his way. She knows he'll come if I tell him it's important.

Knowing the truth of the Seelie and Unseelie Realms makes him ready to jump at the first sign of trouble.

After all, Eric, his ex-best friend *and* prince of the Unseelie Realm, kidnapped him and almost killed him in a psycho faerie spell last Halloween.

Aubree shivers, and a small whimper echoes from her throat as she glances out the window. I take her hands in mine, press my fingers into her soft, inhuman ones. Her pale skin makes me think of Seamus, how much they looked alike. How gentle his hands were, before he left our worlds.

I look into her almond-shaped eyes.

As much as I love Cat and would do anything for her, the

burning building is calling my name. And it's not French fries that have my affection. I must do what needs to be done to help my friend. And the Faerie Realms.

I don't hesitate. "Give me two minutes. Meet us outside."

She swallows and spins on her heel, heads out the door.

I turn to my boyfriend, and his gaze darkens. I don't need to say the words for him to understand.

Something has happened in the world of the fae. Something bad.

4

BLADES of dead March grass reflect red against the moonlight's glow. Although it isn't considered a full moon anymore, it still illuminates pure scarlet. The sky hangs black behind it, a curtain woven with white stars that meets the Earth behind the high school. Night air holds the lull of burned wood and dirt.

This is the same spot Eric lured me just months prior.

Halloween night. The night Aubree and I stopped the Unseelie Veil from tearing open for good. The night we stopped hell from being released in our world.

The night my dad died.

I pull in a shaky breath and dig my nails into my palms to keep another flood of tears at bay. "So what are we doing here exactly?"

A chill spring breeze drifts by, and I shiver. I should've grabbed my jacket from the car.

Aubree's bodysuit squeaks as she bends low to the ground to inspect it. "Give me a sec."

I sigh. That's the only thing she's said since the diner.

The car ride over was a long one. Long and silent. Aubree refused to tell us what was going on. As if making us wait for an explanation might make everything worse.

Or maybe she just hoped it wouldn't be true. Maybe she thought having our moral support would be enough to sway the universe from making whatever her fear is from being reality.

She gasps. I freeze.

Oliver looms like a rock behind me. He hasn't said a word since the diner, either. He's simply held my hand like the good boyfriend he is.

She trembles as she stands. I've never seen her like this. Aubree has always been the epitome of cool. Now she looks like she's unraveling faster than a spinning top.

"Give me another minute." Her voice is soft, as gentle as the breeze that blows my hair around my face.

Aubree steps away from us, toward that canvas of sky, her silhouette melting into the night. She places her hands on her hips and stares into the distance.

I glance at Oliver. His gaze is stressed, his jaw tense as he watches my friend. He absently tugs at his too tight shirt, pulling at the snugness around his biceps. His physique is on the small side, needed for a soccer player, but he's got the definition of a bodybuilder. His brown eyes tumble in my direction, forcing my heart to tumble too.

"Are you upset with me?" I ask. Because I honestly don't know.

He shoves his hands into his pockets, looks toward Aubree. Or maybe he's just looking at the heavens. "Upset?"

It sounds so . . . hollow. He's playing dumb so he doesn't hurt me. Because that's what Oliver does.

He'll do whatever it takes to please everyone. Even if it means he's bleeding on the inside, suffering from never-ending scars he won't allow to heal.

I step closer, place a hand on his cheek. The other I scratch along the tight curls of his close-cropped hair. "You know what I'm talking about. Tonight. I ruined our special date by asking you to postpone for Cat, and now I've allowed us to be sucked into some sort of scavenger hunt with Aubree. Do you feel like I'm putting everyone else before you?"

His brow pulls together, and he opens his mouth. Stops. His eyes lose their fire, shoulders drooping. He licks his lips, then leans his forehead against mine. "Nah. I'm good."

I sink into his embrace and exhale. "Oliver." I drag his name out unnecessarily long.

He closes his eyes, inhales my scent. "Really, Caoine. I'm good. Promise." He tilts his head back, lets his hands slide along my waist. "I mean, at first, yeah, I was . . . *perturbed* you wanted to postpone our date. But then I saw how much fun Cat and Nathan were having, and it felt . . . right."

Perturbed? I mouth.

The corner of his mouth curls up. "Until Aubree showed up. And, okay, I'll admit, I've been totally bummed for the last half hour. I mean, it stinks that we missed our six-month anniversary for all this"—he looks at Aubree—"stuff. *But.*" He pulls me against his body. "This is a part of your world, and I can't deny that. I'm the one who chose to get involved with a faerie. I can accept that it comes with responsibilities . . . *interruptions* like this."

"Half-faerie," I chide.

He chuckles. "Whatever, Caoine. You know what I mean. Have I been okay with us missing our six-month anniversary date? Not entirely, no. But I am now. Now that I've wrapped my mind around things. And that's the important thing." He places a gentle kiss on the side of my mouth. "We're together, at least." He kisses the other side of my mouth. "On our six-month anniversary." He kisses my bottom lip. "I'm with my girlfriend." He kisses my top lip. "I can't complain about that, now can I?"

Without another word, he gently kisses me beneath that blood-red moon, and heat rises from deep within my core, pulsing against my fingers in his hair, bursting from my heart as it beats against his. He kisses me until he takes my breath away, then he kisses me five seconds longer.

When he pulls back, I'm floating. With euphoria and desire and everything that every love story has ever been made of.

"You guys done over there?"

I whip around to find Aubree standing beside us, her face no less tense than it was moments ago. Oliver pats my sides as he turns to her.

"We've got a problem." She crosses her arms, her gaze drifting to the spot she just inspected.

"A faerie problem?" I ask, even though I already know it couldn't possibly be anything else.

"A faerie problem." She bites her lip, which is totally uncharacteristic for my fashion-queen friend.

I swallow. "Please tell me we haven't screwed up anything with the Veils."

Seriously. After everything that went down on Halloween, if one of the Veils opens or closes for good, I'm going to absolutely freak.

"No . . . and yes." She chews her lip again. "We did stop the magic of opening the Unseelie Veil. Things have gone back to normal as far as fae traveling to and from Earth. But"—she breathes in, out—"well . . . remember that spell I did, when I tried creating a barrier to keep Eric from leaving the stone circle and completing his spell?"

I nod.

She huffs. "When he countered my spell, he started a chain reaction."

Oliver asks the question I'm too afraid to ask. "A chain reaction of what?"

I take his hand, squeezing tightly.

"The magic I used to trap Eric inside the circle had to be powerful. Like, super strong stuff. He's the son of the Unseelie king, after all. And the magic he was already using was so ancient, like, paramount to anything I could do. So I went back to the Seelie Realm and asked my mom for help. She showed me a spell I could use to stop him, but she warned me to be careful. If something went wrong, it could have grave consequences."

Oliver stiffens. "Let me guess. Eric did something to the spell that caused grave consequences?"

Tears swim in the back of Aubree's eyes, and I can sense her horror, can almost feel her panic.

"What kind of consequences?" I don't want to ask, but she's gone mute.

The floodgates open, and she falls against me, sobbing on my shoulder. I wrap my arms around her, my gaze connecting with Oliver's. His look echoes the dread that pulses in my core.

This is bad.

She pulls back abruptly, wiping her hands across both cheeks. "I'm not going to worry just yet. It's possible I'm wrong . . ." She swallows hard.

"You're not going to worry about what?" I can't keep my voice from shaking. Why won't she just spit it out?

Aubree shakes her head. "I'll tell you once I know for sure." She presses her lips together. "Although, I know one thing for sure." She looks between Oliver and me, a hefty sigh slipping from her mouth. "To top it off, I've gone and lost the Book of Discernment."

Poor Oliver looks ruffled. "The book of what?"

"That big fat book of magic we used to stop Eric?" I ask.

"One of them." Aubree nods. "The other one—the Book of Judgment—Eric took back to the Unseelie Realm with him, when he defected."

I grind my teeth together. "You mean, when he went back to being who he truly is."

Aubree looks like she's about to burst into tears again.

"Okay." Oliver holds up his hands as if he's about to coach us through a soccer play. "We're going to find the book of whatever thingy—"

"Discernment."

"We're going to find it. We're going to fix . . . whatever you're afraid might be wrong. And we're going to finish our senior year. Because I didn't risk telling my parents I've decided to be a music major instead of becoming a doctor for nothing."

I hide my smile. That boy can find the silver lining in the middle of a tornado.

I turn to Aubree. "He's right. One step at a time, okay? We will get through this. *Together*. Because doing this thing solo would just be lame."

Aubree gives a halfhearted laugh, her cheeks wet again.

I give her another hug. "First things first. What can we do to help you?"

She licks her lips. "I don't want to worry you. Just . . . look along the ground for signs of—" She huffs a breath. "Well, just start looking for anything out of the ordinary."

Oliver salutes her, and I nod. We break apart, each of us taking a different corner to inspect. The night air bites harder than when we first arrived, and I shiver at the idea that my banshee song could take over at any second.

My cloak is in my purse, which I left in the car. Along with my coat. But knowing Oliver, he'll probably run down, grab my cloak, and be back before the first notes even fall from my mouth.

I slip to the northeast corner, squinting at the earth, searching for any sign of . . . *something*. It sure would be easier if Aubree would just spill already. Not knowing what to look for makes the whole thing that much more difficult.

Across from me, Oliver is bent over, Aubree to my far right. I can't see what they're looking at, but they've both found something.

My eyes fall on an object at my feet. I drop to my knees and dig into the hard dirt. I run my fingers over a cracked piece of stone, one of many left from the circle of stones Aubree used the night of Halloween.

A symbol is in the center, but it's hard to make out what it was before it was broken. The gray rock doesn't feel like anything from our world, likely some sort of fae creation, a material with the ability to hold magic.

It must've cracked when Eric counteracted the spell. I frown. Nothing here alerts me to anything off.

I stand, lick my lips in preparation to yell to the others, when there's a noise behind me. A scrape. Nothing of consequence, really. Other than the fact that there shouldn't be anything out here other than the three of us.

Before I can turn to see what it is, Aubree lifts her gaze and screams.

Oliver's head shoots up. Panic yanks him from his task. "Caoine—"

But I don't hear his next words. A hand wraps around my waist, another covering my mouth. Then I'm falling backward into an abyss of black, a liquid sea of nothing.

I fall into the Unseelie Veil.

5

I SLAM ONTO MY BACK, hard grass prickling beneath me, the breath stolen from my lungs. Pain screams from my tailbone up my spine, and I squeeze my eyes shut, biting my tongue against obscenities that beg to be released.

The air around me freezes my skin.

Someone moves behind me, a knee jabbing into my hip. I place my left hand on cold, damp earth and actually do curse. Blades of pain stab my wrist. I yank it against my chest. Agony throbs through sinew and bones. I bite my lip until I taste blood.

Did I break my freaking wrist?

Blood slams through my veins as I roll onto my right side, my arm still cradled against my body. I push up from the ground with my good hand, balancing on wobbly knees.

A boy sits on the ground where we landed, catching his breath, his gaze tentatively on me.

He's a little bigger than Oliver but not as thick. Thin light-brown arms protrude from a simple T-shirt, his jeans covered in dirt and a few rips, which look purposeful. His sneakers could be straight from 1984.

This is the person who pulled me through the Veil.

I scramble to my feet and find the closest tree to lean against, my defenses on high alert. Where are Oliver and Aubree? I need help!

My gaze locks with hazel eyes. His straight, chestnut hair falls long around his shoulders, stopping just above his chest. A dark mole rests along his right eye. He runs a hand down his face, and a single dimple pops along his left cheek when he winces. The boy pushes to his feet.

"Stay back!" I yell. As if this will actually deter the guy who just kidnapped me.

He huffs and comes to his full height. I was right. Definitely taller than Oliver. His shoulders hunch as he lowers his chin and glares at me. His fists are clenched at his sides.

I bite my cheek to keep my chin from trembling. Boy looks angry. I swallow. "What do you want with me?" My breath comes out in a fog. Just how cold is it here?

He stands there, nostrils flaring, as if he's literally trying to make my brain melt with just his stare.

"Who *are* you? Why did you bring me here?"

I don't need to ask where *here* is. I was standing in the exact spot where the Veil to the Unseelie Realm stood on Halloween night. I'm in enemy territory.

I glance around. We're in a forest, but not a normal one. The ground is cement hard, patches of paprika-hued grass and silvery snow intertwined. The sky above is a soft lavender. The trees aren't trees, either. They're puffs of pastel-colored plants straight out of Martha Stewart Christmas catalog.

And it's cold. Crazy cold.

So much colder than December in the town of Lincoln.

We're in the Unseelie Realm. The Winter Realm. The one place in Faerie where it's never spring and certainly not ever summer. Always distant, chilly.

Something moves in the foliage behind me, and I jump. What kinds of creatures even live in Faerie?

I whip my head back in his direction. "Speak!" I can't

control my shaking now, and I clutch my sore wrist even tighter.

"You. Ruined. My. Life." The boy's words are barely above a whisper. Rage balloons every syllable.

"What? I don't even *know* you. How could I have — ?"

"You don't recognize me?" A nefarious smile breaks across his face. "Can't you see through the facade of who I was for so many months? Your *boyfriend* and I were quite close, after all."

I gag on the frozen air. "Eric?" My muscles begin to shiver, and I can't tell if it's from the extreme drop in temperature or from the fact that I'm standing across from the man who murdered my dad.

The veins along his neck pulse. "I should kill you right now."

"Me?" My voice betrays me as it cracks. "You killed my dad!" I dare to allow my voice to raise in volume but remain huddled against the safety of my tree.

He laughs — *laughs* — squeezes his fists open and closed. "I killed —" He clenches his jaw and shifts on his feet. "You ruined the spell! You destroyed my chances of being the next heir of the Unseelie."

He points a slender finger at me and bounces on his toes as if he's a tiger, ready to pounce. To make his kill.

My voice is more timid than I want. "I stopped you because it was the right thing to do. I saved people."

He rolls his eyes and looks around as if I just told a joke. "You saved people? That's your excuse? I hate to break it to you, Caoine, but your job is to *kill*."

"That's not what I do and you know it." Why am I even fighting this lunatic?

He sighs. "It could've been so perfect, Caoine. I had it all planned out. You could've joined me. *Should've* joined me. I mean, why do you even care about what happens to them? The humans?" He narrows his gaze at me. "They're so . . . pathetic. Weak. Unlike us."

"I'm more human than fae, I guess. I'd rather be weak and know right from wrong than have no soul."

His nostrils flare again as he flexes his jaw. "I should kill you just for saying that." Pause. Sigh. "It doesn't matter anymore."

I take a chance and allow my attitude to peek through. "Apparently it does, or you wouldn't have brought me here."

I can't possibly pull my brow any tighter together, and I'm fairly positive I look like a four-year-old.

He snorts. "Not really. I mean, you don't mean as much to me as I once thought you did."

"What's that supposed to mean?"

"It means . . . I *thought* I was in love with you." He shakes his head. "Seeing you now makes me wonder what I ever saw in you."

I blink in disbelief. "Excuse me? You're a *murderer*. Who are you to judge?"

"Like I said, it doesn't matter anymore."

"Then why am I here?"

His upper lip curls like he smells manure. "Unfortunately, I need you."

"What could you possibly need from me?" I look past him to try to find the Veil, to see if I can dart past him and escape, but it's invisible. I'm not sure where I fell through.

"You'll find out, won't you?" His shoulders hunch as he steps toward me.

I cringe against the tree, my heart rate racing once more.

"Do you want help with your wrist or not?"

He approaches again, slowly this time. I frown but let him come close.

His touch is much more gentle than I guessed it would be. He pulls my injured hand from my chest, barely setting his fingers around it. Warmth pulses through my skin, seeps into the depths of my bones.

I squint at him but don't pull away.

His gaze flickers to mine before settling on my wrist.

Electricity fires in my flesh, and I suck in a breath. He pulls his hand away. My pain is gone.

He makes that face again, like I disgust him, then steps back.

I flex my wrist and keep my gaze on him. "What did you do?"

He rolls his eyes again. "The simplest of healing spells."

I swallow and grind my teeth. He won't get a thank you from me.

"What now?" My words are as icy as the chill breeze that ruffles his hair.

"Depends."

"On what?"

"You. Do I need to bind you for our walk, or can you be a good little girl and do as you're told?"

I scowl. "Walk where?"

"To the Unseelie castle."

He steps closer, and I can feel his hot breath along my neck.

"I'm taking you to see the king."

6

RESTRAINTS BIND my wrists and ankles. I pull against them for the hundredth time, but it's no use.

My fingers and toes are frozen.

I slump my head onto the rock that has become my pillow. I lift it quickly when I notice the familiar sign that means enslavement for the Unseelie fae etched into the surface.

The same sign was left beside each dead body back at West Lincoln High when Eric used my banshee song to murder half the town.

I grind my teeth. Okay, maybe not half the town, but it felt like it when I was the one singing my banshee lament and ushering them into an afterlife far earlier than they should've entered. I squeeze my hands beneath the restraints.

If I ever get free, I'm going to make Eric pay for what he did to me. For what he did to my dad.

I look around. How did I even get here? My memory is doing messy things inside my brain.

Bushes shaped like a hand, a face, an arm, rustle to my left, and I gasp. I'm sitting in a pile of lime-green moss, wet soaking through my jeans, my sneakers caked in mud.

Around me are trees with pink leaves, trees with blue

leaves. Leaves the size of a small car. Branches that reach high into the purple firmament. Clouds take the shape of animals I've never seen before. Scents of lilacs and strawberries swirl around my head.

Eric deposited me here an hour ago.

We walked forever, although it was probably only a couple of hours. But lack of sleep and food have made me loopy and edgy, so when I tell this story to my grandkids, we walked *forever*. End of story.

The ground is covered with a lot more snow than where the Veil dumped us. It's all I can do to convince my brain I'm not shivering. I'm not freezing to death. And I'm certainly not going to lose the freaking toes and fingers I can longer feel due to hypothermia. I've still got to graduate high school.

Another tug against my restraints is futile, but hey, what else do I have to do?

"They're not real."

I jump with a squeak at the voice that echoes from a shaggy blue bush to my right. I swallow and press against the hard slab of stone behind me. Aubree told me stories of creatures in both the Seelie and Unseelie Realms. And I'm five thousand percent sure I don't want to meet any. Like, ever.

A pair of green eyes glow from the base of the foliage. I cringe, pull my legs a little tighter to my body.

With an explosion of movement, a tiny man no taller than my kneecap jumps into view.

His pants and shirt are tattered and soiled. He's barefoot, with long, hairy toes and nasty-looking yellow toenails. His skin matches the mud around him, and hair the color of the sky sticks in every direction from his head.

Long spindly fingers curve around his waist, hands on his hips. A nose as long as his face is wide hooks to the front, eyes bulging and unblinking. His ears are double the size of normal-sized ears and droop to his shoulders.

He's straight out of a cartoon.

My heart threatens to pump right out of my chest.

"They're not real," he says again, his voice cracking like an adolescent boy's worst nightmare.

I lick my lips and stare. Because talking to the scary woodland creature will make him real, and I need this to be my imagination. *Please, please just be my imagination.*

He motions with a hand, and grime and —*holy smokes, is that blood?*—is caked under his jagged nails. "The bindings. Wish them away." He points to his temple as if the action will make me do what he says.

I wait a beat, then another. What is he even talking about?

He grows impatient and throws his hands in the air, taking another step closer.

"What do you mean, wish them away?" I say in a rush.

The little man stops, points at the ties around my ankles. "The bindings. They aren't real. Wish them away, they go away. Simple."

Wish them away? I glance at the cord around my wrists. Is it possible? Could this eccentric man be telling the truth? Or is it a trick?

Wait. Of course it's the truth. The fae can't lie. Aubree told me so. Something she and Seamus were always jealous that I could do.

My stomach clenches at the thought of my old friend, gone too soon.

I swallow, look at the little man again. He must be telling the truth. Nothing about this seems like a trick. I mean, for me to be tricked, I'd have to do something, right? This is just a wish inside my head. Harmless.

With a glance in the direction Eric fled, I decide it's worth the risk. If I can get free, I can find a way home before he returns.

I close my eyes and make a wish. I wish I could see my hands and feet as they truly are. That if the bindings aren't real, the illusion will drop.

A breath in. A breath out. I open my eyes.

The ties are gone.

My jaw drops as I pull my hands apart and stretch my legs straight. I blink in the little man's direction. How did he know that?

He chuckles. "See? Told you. Bindings not real. Wish away." He snaps his slender fingers and laughs again.

I rub my wrists, even though they aren't sore and there are no markings. The cord truly was in my imagination. "Why did you help me?"

"Doesn't pretty girl want to be free?" He frowns, confusion on his face.

"Of course. Yes, I want to be free. But why help me? You don't even know me."

"I make pretty girl happy while we wait for my prince." The man looks pleased with himself, bouncing on his toes.

"Prince?" I narrow my gaze. "You mean Eric?"

At the mention of his name, the little man bows deeply. "My prince. We wait for him. He tells us what to do."

With a grunt I jump to my feet, a little wobbly, but thankful to be standing on my own. "You can wait. I'm finding a way out of here."

I slip my phone from my pocket, and the screen glows to life. A sigh slips from my lips. At least my phone still works. I glance at the bars. Nothing. *Figures.* No cell reception in the Faerie Realms. Maybe it will come in handy as a flashlight, though.

"Where?" The man doesn't move, but his voice makes me stop.

"Excuse me?"

"Where does pretty girl go?"

I slide my phone back in my pocket. "Home. I need to find the Veil. To get home before my da—" I gulp. My dad isn't alive anymore to care where I am. "Before my friends worry."

"How will pretty girl find Veil? Find way home?"

"I—" I glance around me. Trees. Just trees. "Will you show me?"

A smile spreads across his face, and he shakes his head like this is a game. "We wait for my prince. He tells us what to do."

"You won't show me?" Why do I sound so incredulous? What did I expect?

"We wait." He's so matter-of-fact, I almost want to plop right back down.

Instead I roll my eyes. "Really? You set me free only to keep me captive?"

He waves a hand, that confusion back. "Pretty girl not captive. Free. I help free."

"Yeah but—*grrr*. Never mind." And I plop back down. Because my legs ache and I'm tired. And hungry. Visions of fries dance through my head. I grump in my spot.

I huff. Grab a fistful of grass. Toss it aside. Repeat.

"Why so upset? My prince returns. Then he tells us—"

"What to do. Yeah, got that."

He sits beside me. "Why so sad?"

"I just told you. I want to go home."

"Go home soon. Need to help my prince first."

I blink in surprise. "Did Eric tell you this? That he'll let me go home after he does . . . whatever he's doing?"

"Overhear my prince talk about plan. This is what he says. You go home. Eventually."

"Eventually?" My heart sinks. Eventually could be a very long time.

And Aubree mentioned something about time working differently between Faerie and Earth. What if I returned to find my friends old and buried? Would the Earth even be standing, after that blood moon thing and all?

"Just wait." He pats my leg. "My prince has important book. Finds other book. Then king is happy, and you go home."

I straighten. "Wait, what? Eric has a book? The Book of

Discernment—did he tell you this? Aubree was looking for that book! The little sneak took it from her?"

Heat flares up my core. The jerk lured us to that stupid field. He'd planned to kidnap me all along!

The little faerie nods. "He find Book of Discernment, yes. Wonderful news! Especially after losing Book of Judgment." He glowers again. "That book his but someone take it. So he take other book."

"But why? The spell was broken. Why would he need them?"

"My prince returns. He tells us—"

"—what to do." I say the last words along with him. "Yeah, got it."

That's all the information I'm getting out of him, apparently. My only question is why Eric needs me for this whole thing.

I don't have much time to reflect, though. Before I can form another question, loud crashing bellows from the woods in front of us. I tense, jump into a squat, ready to sprint away.

Little man toddles to his feet, a pleasant look on his face.

A bush rattles, then rips to the side.

Out of the brush comes Eric, face red, panic screaming from every limb. "Run! They're coming!"

Before I can move, he has my arm.

"The king's men are after us. We need to hide!"

7

———

Eric's fingers wrap like spiderwebs around my shoulders, guide me into the deep, dark woods. I despise his closeness, the way he looms behind me as he directs me through dense rainbow foliage.

I misstep and stumble, my ankle crying out in agony. As I glance over my shoulder, I search for the little man who set me free, a fact I'm quite thankful for now. Would Eric have let me loose before his escape, or would he have left me for dead?

The little man is in the same spot as before, now just a speck in my vision. He raises his eyes and meets mine, a strange smile on his lips.

He disappears with a pop.

My feet falter, and Eric practically rams me over.

"Run, Caoine!" he yells in my ear.

I grind my teeth and press the muscles in my legs even harder.

He's still close, but I don't feel his body heat any longer, something both comforting and regretful. His presence makes my skin crawl, my hands begging to rip him apart and leave him for the king's men, after what he did to my dad.

33

But the air around us is so frigid, I need him to get wherever we're going. Somewhere warm.

"Where are we going?" My voice shakes as I shove a bush aside. It swings back too quickly and gashes my skin beneath my sweater. My feet find solid ground even though I can't see our path very well.

Despite the lavender sky above, it's still night here in Faerie, just like on Earth. When will dawn come? Will I even be able to stay on my feet long enough to find safety?

"Does it matter?" Acid lines his words. "We're about to die. Just run."

I barely hear his footsteps behind me, even though he's twice my size. How can he be so quiet?

Oh right. He's fae.

I really need to learn a few things about stealth. And magic. Magic would help too.

A shout rattles the forest to our left, and Eric instinctively swings his arm around my shoulder, aiming me in the opposite direction.

My breaths come in gasps. "How many are there?"

"Do you truly want to know?"

That many? "Never mind."

"Just run."

For once, I'm happy to do exactly as Eric tells me.

To our right is a gathering of rocks, and he aims us there. The formation looks unnatural, as if someone — or something — piled them on one another to form a sort of mini-fortress.

Of course, the thing that did that would need to be huge — like, twice the size of a house — to lift such big rocks and place them so accurately. Or maybe it's just natural.

Either way, an unnatural fluorescent pink vegetation grows along the exterior, making it look like cotton candy.

I nibble my cheek, and my stomach growls.

Pastel bushes grow around the structure, claiming it as

their own, as if a monster from the deep is pulling it to an early grave.

A new smell emerges, something other than cold and dirt. A rotting scent, putrid, musty, filled with death. And metallic. Blood?

My throat tightens, and I fight a shiver. I don't want to know what kinds of things have died around here. Or what killed them.

Voices float on the breeze, farther away than the last echo.

Eric yanks me around the back of the formation, his back flush with the stone. Only one hand is wrapped around my wrist, but I have no doubt his thin hand could keep me in place without a struggle. He's so much stronger than I remember from Lincoln. His fae side?

His chest rises and falls as he catches his breath, his gaze still behind us. I can almost see his pointed ears straining to listen.

I blink.

I hadn't even noticed his ears were pointed when we first arrived. Had he glamoured himself not to freak me out? Or did he lose concentration as we ran for our lives?

A minute passes. Then three. Neither of us moves.

When we haven't heard a noise for at least another four minutes, he releases me, shoulders slumped. He runs a hand through his hair before bending at the waist, hands on his knees, slowly breathing.

My heart races as I glance around. He isn't holding me, and he's distracted. Should I make a run for it? This could be my only chance. Electricity buzzes through my fingertips.

My gaze settles on one brightly colored tree to the next. Then the uneven ground to the canopy of leaves above, symmetrical, floating beneath the purple sky like I'm under-water looking at the surface from below.

I have no idea where I am. No clue how to find the Veil.

And soldiers intent on hunting us down are just a matter of feet away. I'm trapped. Eric is my only salvation.

Heat pulses up my neck, falls down my spine. Fantastic. How did my greatest enemy suddenly become my ally?

I smack my hands together, trying to get feeling back into them. "Where were you? Before?" Because there's nothing else to do while I wait for him to recover.

He doesn't look at me. "I met with the king."

My arms snake around my waist, shielding my body from cold and fear. "You didn't take me?"

He straightens. His eyes finally find mine, and my heart hammers in my chest so much harder than necessary. "I couldn't. Not until I could trust his words."

"What's there to trust? You're his son. You literally killed people to try to take over the world for him." I dig my fingers into my side.

A sarcastic snort tumbles out. "His *son*." He mutters under his breath, looking away. "Being his son has nothing to do with trust. I wasn't about to waltz into his castle with a prize without knowing his true intent."

I roll my eyes. "Let me guess. I'm the prize?" My belly bubbles with anger.

"Of course. What else would you be?" He sneers, looking me up and down.

I grit my teeth but let him go on.

Eric sighs. "I tried. Tried to please him, to do exactly as he asked. But it was all a farce, as always."

I shove my hands in my pockets. "If he's so hard on you, why don't you ask your mom for help?"

"My mother?"

"Yeah, the queen."

His face is stoic. "I never said the queen was my mother."

Whoa. So Eric is illegitimate. Interesting.

He huffs again. "There's no way I'm letting him have you. Not without guarantees. And he can't have the book, either."

"The Book of Discernment?" I hunch and look around, lowering my voice. "Where is it?"

He tenses. "Someplace no one else can find it. Not unless I want them to."

Aubree's tear-streaked face flashes in my mind. How distraught she was when she told Oliver and me that she lost the book. And Eric had it this whole time.

I clench my hands, dig my nails into my palms. *Jerk*. I nibble on my lip. Do I tell him what she said right before he kidnapped me? About how he may have started a chain reaction on Halloween night?

He narrows his gaze at me in challenge.

Nope. Not sayin' a word. I'll let her deal with him. And it won't be pleasant. I almost smile. At least he can't read my thoughts.

I shrug and look around, as if the forest is so much more interesting than our conversation. "So now what?"

"I'm working on it."

My gaze is back on him in a millisecond. "You don't know?"

His fists clench. "I hadn't planned on my father flipping out and sending his men after us. I suppose we should go get the book, although I need to be sure we're not being followed."

"What about the little man? Could he help?"

"Little man?"

"The one who helped free me? You know, little, hairy, with a pointy nose? Looks like he stepped out of a storybook?"

Eric shakes his head. "Nym? He's harmless. And not much help."

"He told me how to get free. Aren't you mad about that?"

He snorts. "Where would you go?"

I press my lips together. "It wasn't a very good spell, you know."

"Never intended it to be. I just needed you to be quiet and to stay put."

I look around. "We can't stay here forever. Can we at least find shelter? It's freaking freezing out here, if you haven't noticed." I cross my arms over my chest. "I mean, what are we doing? Can I please go home now that I'm no longer the king's prize?"

He surveys the area, opens his mouth to speak, but stops. A grin spreads across his face. "I've got something better."

I lift my brows.

Eric turns and walks deeper into the woods. "Follow me. It's time to eat."

8

THE BOY WALKS AWAY. *Right in the middle of a conversation.*

I throw my hands up and follow, because what else can I do? My belly grumbles. Yeah, I'm actually pretty hungry. Sustenance sounds like a nice change of scenery. And my trembling body just wants to be inside, *out* of the cold.

Eric snakes his way through the trees like the serpent he is. It takes two minutes, maybe three, before a small cottage appears. I do a double take, then glance behind me. How is that thing hidden so well? Glamour?

The cabin is complete with a wood pile on one side and a small pond on the other. The roof has seen better days, but a couple of super comfy-looking chairs are on the porch, so score.

The forest's unnaturally dyed foliage grows right up to an imaginary line that circles the house about fifty feet in diameter. The house can't have more than three or four rooms.

I lick my lips and pause. The place is welcoming. Cozy. The kind of house I'd want to visit while vacationing in the mountains, if my dad and I ever did that kind of thing.

Eric walks right up to the door and pushes it open, disappearing inside.

39

I stop and blink. Does he even know who lives here?

I debate following him. What would Oliver do? My heart clenches. Why can't he be here with me?

A high-pitched echo of an unknown fae animal ricochets through the trees, and I jump. Then I run to catch up with Eric. Taking my chances with a guy I *know* is dangerous is a better option than subjecting myself to a plethora of creatures that could tear me apart in seconds, thanks.

The inside matches the outside to a T. It's sparsely furnished, and everything is made of wood. Handmade. The front door opens into a living room with a small kitchen off to the left. Two doors along the back wall lead me to believe those are bedrooms.

Where is the bathroom? And do I really want to know?

I pull in a breath and note the stale air, as if no one has been here for days. I bite my lip. "So, uh, what is this place?"

Eric rummages through a cabinet. "Don't worry about it. We're safe here."

My eyes bounce around the cramped living room, a layer of dust coating every object. "Erm, are you sure?"

"Positive." His voice is monotone, and he doesn't face me while he sifts through the cabinets.

"Right," I mutter as I find a spot to sit.

The sofa poofs up a cloud of dust when I plant myself. I cough and wave at the air. Eric doesn't respond.

Awesome. I fidget with my shirt sleeve as I glance around. Nothing on the walls. A small shelf of books in one corner. We could literally be sitting in the house of a witch that eats children. This is Faerie, after all.

I look at the front door, then to Eric. Could I make it far if I ran?

If only I knew where he'd hidden the Book of Discernment. If I could get it, I might be able to use the book as leverage to get out of Faerie. *If* I found someone who knows of its importance.

Eric turns around, and I startle. He holds out both hands.

"I've got nuts and some dried fruit. Hungry?"

Instinct tells me to spit something malicious at him, but the way my stomach gnaws yells at me to hold my tongue.

"Sure," is all I can manage. I refrain from asking for French fries. Will I ever eat my beloved comfort food again?

He tosses me a pouch and slides into a seat at the table. I loosen the strings on the leather pouch and find dried prunes inside. *Yum.* Without a second thought, I shove three in my mouth, close my eyes, savor the flavor. A nummy noise rumbles deep in my throat.

I freeze. Open my eyes.

He's staring at me, contempt in his gaze.

I finish chewing and swallow against my dry throat, looking down at the remaining prunes. "Oh no. I'm bound here for all eternity, aren't I?"

I know my fairy tales. Eating or drinking anything fae is the last thing you'll do of your own free will.

"Relax. You're part fae. Most sustenance won't affect you. Unless it's been specifically spelled to."

I crinkle my nose.

"It's fine. I didn't spell it. I can clearly kidnap you with zero problem without magic." He rolls his eyes as if *I'm* the one being unreasonable.

"Oh."

He nods to a wooden barrel on the counter. "Cups are in the cabinet if you want a drink."

I hide the tension in my body as I stand, cross the room, and snag a clay cup from the cabinet. I have no reason to trust him, but I'm thirsty.

I force my body to relax as I take a sip. It doesn't taste spelled, but honestly, how would I know? I hold back a sigh.

The water glides down my throat like the cool cascade of a waterfall. My body immediately confirms how dehydrated I am.

Three cups later, my belly finally feels full. My head spins a bit from drinking so fast.

And then my bladder joins the fun. *Crud*. "Um, so, know if there's a bathroom around here?"

He takes a bite of a cracker and glares at me.

Where did those come from?

Then he points to the room on the left. "There's one off that room."

"Thanks." My tone totally isn't thankful at all.

I step into the room to find exactly what I expect: a wooden chair, a single nightstand, and a few hooks on the wall for clothing. Simple. Concise. No bed. Because the fae don't sleep.

A door stands to the right, and my heart rate picks up as I pull on the handle. I prep my brain to encounter spiders and other creepy crawly things. But none of that awaits me.

Inside is a regular twenty-first century–style toilet and sink, cleaned and scrubbed for a king. Or queen, in my case.

I sigh and shut the door.

When I return to the front room, I ask, "Are you going to tell me whose house we're in?"

I plop on the sofa. Another layer of dust bursts into the air.

He finishes chewing whatever he's eating and glares at me. "Get some rest. We've got a long journey ahead of us."

"We're sleeping here?" My question is more of an accusation.

He shrugs. "Would you rather sleep in the woods?"

No. I pinch my lips against the sour words I want to spew. I hate that he's right. "Fine. Where do I sleep?"

"I don't care. I won't be sleeping." He laughs, as if being a fae that needs no rest *ever* is funny.

I huff and lie down on the sofa, his soft laughter the last thing I hear as I drift off to sleep.

———

When I wake it's light. Much lighter than before we arrived. How long was I out? I sit up and rub the sleepies from my eyes, look around. Eric is gone. Like, really gone.

My heart hammers in my chest. My captor is gone. I'm free. Free to run. Free to go home. I swallow. Is it possible to survive if I make a run for it?

My blood pounds inside my veins as I race for the door, stop, turn around, and head to the kitchen. Who knows how long this trip will be? I might need to eat again.

I grab another pouch of something and crackers wrapped in paper and cram them in my pocket, take time for a quick drink, then I'm out the door.

The frozen air slams into me like a freight train. I shudder, curl my arms around my body. Everything looks the same. Which direction did we even come from?

I gather my courage and run into the trees. Maybe if I just start moving I'll see something familiar?

Crash. Crunch. Yeah, I'm crazy loud. I hold my breath as I run, afraid Eric will hear me. Until I see spots. Bad idea.

Snap. A branch beneath me breaks, and I stumble, fall to my knees. Ouch!

Then I'm back on my feet and running again. I've got to get away from Eric. This might be my only chance.

Slap, slap, slap—my feet pound the ground. Something flashes in front of me. I come to an abrupt stop, my breathing pulsing in and out of my lungs like a tidal wave. The flash flickers across my vision again before disappearing.

Then it's back. Bright. Radiant. Blinding. I raise my arms to shield my face, but a second later, its brilliance fades to a small dot of light, hovering midair.

The blood in my veins turns to ice, and I remain still. Some unknown fae creature is before me.

Why did I run from Eric? This is so much worse than being with him.

I pull in a shaky breath, step back. Is it even possible to outrun a faerie?

The tiny light pulses once more, grows an inch, then two. In the next blink, the ball of light is no longer a ball of light.

It's Oliver.

9

OLIVER. *Oliver.*

Before my brain can speak any kind of logic to myself, I run. I sprint into my boyfriend's arms. He's real. He's flesh. And so, so warm.

I can't stop the tears that well up, overflow on my cheeks like I've never cried in my life. A never-ending cascade of fear and uncertainty and joy.

"You're here," I whisper. My voice is muffled against his strong chest.

A low rumble of a chuckle echoes from him, his arms rubbing my back tenderly. "Did you think you could get rid of me that easily?"

I pull back, stare into his perfect face. "You have no idea how badly I've been trying to lose Eric. I just got free."

"Eric?" He sucks in a quick breath.

I nod. "He took me. He looks different, but it's definitely him."

Oliver's arms drop from my waist. He looks uncomfortable as he looks around.

I look too. "We should get back to the Veil. He could be close."

45

Oliver licks his lips but stays silent as he looks around.

I embrace him once more, unwilling to ever let go of this man of mine again. I breathe him in. Breathe him out.

He smells . . . sterile.

I crinkle my nose. "Have you showered since I disappeared?"

His gaze finds mine.

I stutter out an explanation. "I mean, I know it hasn't been long, but you're in the same outfit from last night."

"Caoine, we should go." His voice is strained, his eyes back on that ridiculous forest around us.

Heat crawls up my core. Why won't he look at me? Hasn't he missed me as much as I've missed him?

"I agree," I say, "but where is the Veil?" I pause. "How did you even get here? Through the Veil, I mean?"

Oliver's eyes lock with mine. I swear they flash red for an instant.

I blink. Nope. Same regular beautiful brown I've come to love. Faerie is seriously messing with my brain.

My boyfriend just looks at me, doesn't bother to answer.

"Oliver?"

He sighs. His arms loop around my waist. "I've been going out of my mind with worry."

I can't contain the groan that spills from me. "Seriously." I roll my eyes. "If I could kill Eric before heading home, I'd totally take the time to do it. But I just need to get home. Can we go?"

"Of course we can." He smiles in that way that makes my heart flutter.

Except . . .

For the fact that his tooth . . .

"Hey." I frown. "When did you get your tooth straightened?"

Oliver stops smiling immediately.

A rock the size of the moon plummets in my belly.

This isn't Oliver.

I step back, but his fingers dig into my side, holding me in place much tighter than my boyfriend would ever dare.

I swallow, my palms slick with sweat. "What's the first song you ever sang to me?"

His brow furrows. "That is not important right now, Caoine. We need to get you out of here."

We? I squash my fear down to my feet. "Answer the question first, *babe*."

His eyes really do turn red now, and his voice drops a whole octave. "I said, you are coming with me. *Mortal.*"

Emotion lodges in my throat. "What are you?" I can barely get the words out.

Oliver's face begins to morph, his hands wrapping like ropes around my upper arms, squeezing the way a boa constrictor would kill its prey. He raises me inches from the ground, my legs dangling like a rag doll's.

I inhale, ready to scream. But that could draw something even worse. Why didn't I stay with Eric?

The Oliver-that's-not-Oliver grows fangs, saliva dripping from the tips, its skin suddenly a putrid green. A stench that rivals the dump three blocks from my house wafts from the creature that holds me.

Now I do scream.

"Let her go!"

I blink. Freeze. The voice came from behind me, so I can't see the owner. But I would know that voice anywhere. Eric.

The creature that holds me scowls, grumbles.

"I said, put her down."

The thing watches Eric over my shoulder. Waits.

"I do still have a title here in Unseelie, do I not? Would you like to face my father?"

Fake-Oliver sniffs. Grunts. His fingers slowly release me, those fangs retracting into the mouth of the boy I love.

"Step away from her, and I'll forget this ever happened."

I wish I could see Eric. My feet meet ground, and I scramble to regain my balance.

In a flash, Oliver is gone. Replaced by that small white ball of light that entranced me from the start. I exhale in a huff. *That* had me so scared?

"We would not have hurt her." A disembodied voice swirls around the light.

"I have no doubt." Eric is by my side, hands clenching and unclenching. "Leave. *Now*."

The light flickers, dims, then flies into the trees, disappearing in seconds.

We stand in silence, the only sound that of our breathing. Guilt floods my limbs as I check myself over to assure I'm not missing anything. Like fingers or toes.

Eric turns to me, furious. "Why would you leave like that? Do you have a death wish?"

"I—I . . ." Are there even words to explain?

He shakes his head, looks in the direction of the cottage. "I was behind the house for ten minutes. Ten minutes, Caoine. And you try to get lost in the Unseelie Realm? How smart is that?"

Why does this feel like I'm being interrogated by my dad right now? "I don't . . . I wanted to get away." My cheeks are hot. It *was* a stupid plan.

"Well, congrats. You succeeded. And bonus, you almost got yourself killed."

I grind my teeth. "Got it. It was a dumb idea. I won't leave again." Until I have a better plan of escape.

He presses his lips together. "Let's go. We're going to get that book. Before my father finds it."

I scowl but follow him. We don't walk for long before he stops. I open my mouth to ask why we're stopping but don't. It doesn't matter.

Eric has brought me to the most beautiful sight I've ever seen.

We stand on a precipice. The edge of eternity.

At least it feels like it.

The forest has come to an end. The rocky earth extends only another twenty feet before it ends, plummets into nothing, hovering above a valley filled with lush pink and orange vegetation, a large lake right in the center.

Snow-covered evergreens in pastel colors line the edge of the water, a vision of macarons popping in my head. The water is so clear and still, I can see the reflection of every cloud in the lavender-tinted sky.

I lift my chin, a scent of lilacs invading my senses. The heavens are a canvas: the clouds are turquoise and shaped in perfect spheres, spaced evenly apart. Each cloud is a cotton ball, fluffy and velvety. Longing stirs deep in my belly.

The far end of the lavender sky kisses the tops of the trees. I sigh, tension draining from my shoulders. An eerie silver hue lines the snow-laden leaves. The color almost matches my eyes. I could bask in this view for days.

A nip of a breeze sends a shiver across my skin, bringing a scent of strawberries and freshly baked bread along with it. That's the scent of winter here?

We're definitely not in Kansas anymore, Dorothy.

Eric clears his throat. "Want to rest?" He gestures to a small crop of rocks behind me, shaped a bit like a chair.

I open my mouth to ask why I would need to rest when we just came from the cottage, but I close it. My upper arms suddenly ache. I guess that encounter with the evil faerie sort of took it out of me.

I glance at Eric. Frown. How did he know?

"Sure," I say instead.

He nods. "I need to take care of something before we go any farther. Wait here." He looks around. "I don't sense any other creatures nearby, so you should be safe." His gaze finds mine. "Try not to get into any trouble."

I resist rolling my eyes and plop onto the rock that isn't a chair. Only after settling my legs does it hit me just how exhausted I am. And we haven't even walked very far. I turn to ask Eric how much farther we'll be going, but he's gone.

Humph. He could've at least said goodbye. How long am I going to be here, anyway?

I look around. A set of caves stands off to my left. One literally looks like the face of a tiger, it's mouth open wide with razor-sharp teeth jutting from below and above. A few mustard-hued bushes are on my right. Otherwise it's just thick forest and that abrupt drop-off.

The cold begins to creep along my skin, and my throat wants to close. I shut my eyes, count to ten as I inhale, exhale. I need a distraction.

The sight before me is beautiful, but thinking about the certainty of death should I misstep warns me *not* to focus there.

I rub my arms to help with the chill, and my hand stumbles over my watch. I glance at it. *10:45.* Is that the time in Faerie or on Earth? Daytime or nighttime? Eep.

I sigh. One thing I haven't done since entering the Faerie Realm is checking what resources I might have brought from home. I empty both jean pockets. Then frown.

My haul is abysmal. Then again, I hadn't planned on getting kidnapped right after date night.

Aside from the food I brought from the cottage, I've got three things going for me. My cell phone is still functioning, although no bars. I've got fifty-five cents to my name and Aubree's lucky rabbit's foot.

I rub the latter between my fingers, smiling at the memory of the day she gave it to me.

The idea of a rabbit's foot had been completely foreign to her. Why would a faerie need luck when they've got magic, right? But we spent the day thrift shopping and stumbled upon a small basket of them at the cash register.

Aubree was enamored with an earthen item being "lucky."

She bought it immediately . . . and then had her purse stolen. And discovered her car had a busted taillight.

She declared nothing about the rabbit's foot could possibly be considered lucky and tossed it my way. I gladly accepted it, since any kind of gift from a best friend is precious. But I hadn't considered the luck factor until now.

Maybe it is unlucky.

I scowl. If I ever make it home, I'm setting this thing on fire and asking Aubree for a new gift.

A chill breeze ruffles my hair, and I shiver. Something orange moves out of the corner of my eye. I look to the tree line. Then I do a double take.

Was that a cat?

I rub my eyes, squint into the abyss of branches.

Nope. Nothing. Faerie is odd.

I clench my fingers tight around the rabbit's foot and miss Aubree. At least I've got something from home. Something of *her*. And luck or no luck, it's my lifeline to sanity. I press the soft fur to my cheek and sigh. I'll take whatever reminder of home and the people I love I can get.

Eric stumbles into view, and I scramble not to look like a nostalgic fool, cramming my goods away.

Except he probably wouldn't have noticed anyway. He's freaked. Like totally panicked as he runs straight for me.

"Hey," he whispers like it's no big deal, even though his eyes tell a different story.

I jump to my feet. "Eric."

A growl echoes in the distance, not at all far enough away for comfort.

My eyes go wide. "What was—?"

He grabs my arm. "Do we really want to find out? We've got another friend behind us. And this one isn't human or fae. A creature's picked up our scent. Run."

WE HEAD BACK into the forest. Bushes the height of an NBA player loom over me, in bright shades of red and royal blue.

Branches snap like toothpicks beneath the behemoth's weight. Eric's in the lead as we zigzag through foliage.

His lean frame crashes into limbs, knocks at loose branches, and smashes flat blades of grass as he lumbers through the Faerie wilderness.

My legs are shorter than his, so I need to take twice as many steps just to keep up. My gaze is locked on his back, right between his shoulder blades. His back is wider than it was as redheaded Eric.

A grunt sounds from behind us, and I chance a look over my shoulder. I trip, fall. Pain shoots through my knee, and I stifle a cry. I look behind us again.

Nothing. I see nothing. But the footsteps are still coming. The monster still pursues us. I can hear it.

"Quick," Eric whispers in my ear.

He slings one of my arms over his shoulders, his arm firmly around my waist, and hauls me to my feet. We run together. Or rather, he runs while dragging me like a sack of potatoes.

My feet barely touch the ground. Under normal circumstances I would protest. A freaking murderer is carrying me around on his hip like it's no big deal!

A growl. The sound is far too close.

I gasp. *Never mind.* I'll play damsel in distress if it means escaping the *scary* that follows so close behind. I tighten my grip around Eric's shoulders, grab his shirt, my knuckles white. My other hand instinctively wraps around his neck, pulling myself closer to his frame in an attempt to gain speed.

It works, and we take off even faster than before.

Our breaths are heavy, unsteady. Sweat gathers along my back and underarms. My knee screams in pain. I swallow. Has the creature seen us? Does he know where we are?

Eric ducks below a low-hanging branch with an end like fingers, but he doesn't have time to warn me. It grabs for my face, slicing with a vengeance. My cheek throbs, stings. I barely contain my cry.

He stops, puts me down, although I don't put weight on my bad leg. "You okay?"

I nod, one hand holding my newly acquired injury. Pain stabs my temple, echoes toward my eye. *Fantastic.*

I glance at Eric. He still breathes like a thousand pounds of weight is on his chest, his gaze on mine. He looks concerned.

Concerned? A matter of hours ago, he was about to present me to his father, to kill me.

"Can you move?" he asks as he glances over his shoulder.

Why? Why is this boy being so caring when he's so . . . *not?*

I lick my lips. "I'm fine." My eyes snag on a solution. "Wait. There. We can hide there." I point.

Eric pales. "Um—"

Something crashes not far behind us.

"Go!" I yell this time. I shove him toward the place of refuge with all the force I can muster.

He actually stumbles in the right direction as I limp painfully after him. He attempts to regain his footing, to turn us around, but I push him right toward the tree.

"There's something I need to—" He teeters off balance as he tries to talk to me over his shoulder.

"Just go," I order again.

In seconds we're standing before a giant redwood.

At least, it looks like a redwood. Its bark is a vibrant plum, so there's that. The tree is large enough to hold four smaller trees, with roots that extend far and wide. On one side, a human-sized fissure extends from the ground.

Eric has to duck to make it in, but I push against his back. There's plenty of room for the two of us.

We both turn as we enter, his back pressed against the inside of the ancient plant, mine barely touching his front. And suddenly we're out of space.

Is it my imagination or did the space in here just decrease?

I dig my fists into my legs to stop them from shaking, clench my jaw against the tremble in my chin. There's maybe five inches in front of me, just enough room to envelope us in shadows. Just enough room to hide us from the beast. I hope.

I hold my breath and listen, try not to put weight on my throbbing leg.

Eric begins to gasp. His breathing is out of control. Is he having a panic attack?

My eyes widen as I twist around to look at him. But there just isn't enough room for either of us to move.

I can feel him shaking at my back, hear his muffled cries as he tries to bury them inside himself.

"Eric?" I whisper. What happened to the overly confident guy who literally just carried me through the forest?

His only response is to grab my hand. *Hey!* I yank it away and smack it on the tree. Ouch. Guy who murdered my dad *doesn't* get to touch me unless I say so.

But he doesn't give up. I hold both hands in front of me to keep them out of reach. He may be crying like a baby, but he isn't getting any sympathy from me.

I gasp when he reaches around my waist and pulls my left

hand into his. If I had the room, I'd jump away. Instead I freeze like I'm solid stone. A grunt echoes a matter of feet outside our hiding spot, and my blood turns to ice.

Eric's fingers dig into my hand with zero gentleness. I clench my other fist and silently beg the tree for a few more inches to pound the guy. How dare he touch me! I attempt to lift my leg so I can stomp on his foot, but there's just no room.

He's still trembling. Both his hands squeeze mine, crushing bones. A gag lodges in my throat.

"Eric." I want to yell, but I need to control my volume.

"I'll be fine." But his voice wobbles.

He presses his head into the base of my neck. I cringe and pull forward, aching to get away from him but trapped like a rat in a never-ending wheel.

He quakes again, even stronger than before.

He's freaked. *So freaked.* I can hear him trying to regain control of his breathing, can imagine the way his eyes are shut tight, his jaw flexed to capacity.

Discomfort squirms its way along my skin, up my back. Why is this dude touching me? I squeeze my eyes shut and try to force the image of him stabbing my dad from my mind.

Outside the tree, the noise grows louder, footsteps, right on top of us. I hold my breath. Eric's fingers dig deeper.

The monster walks closer. Eric breathes. I stay frozen.

Step. Step. Step.

Eric's fingers dig. Dig. Dig.

Breathe, Caoine. Breathe.

Please don't let me die. I need to see Oliver again!

The noise outside recedes. Rose-gold sunlight filters through the trees, calm, peaceful. Chirps of nature return as if nothing is out of the ordinary. As if a massive threat to every living creature hasn't just passed through, looking for a half-fae chick and traitor prince to consume.

I exhale. Swallow. Count to ten. Is it safe to come out?

Eric still hasn't budged. I have a feeling he won't until I do.

My belly lurches as I make the decision to take a chance, to step outside.

In slow motion, I limp into the daylight. Each step I take sends a ripple of waves through the orange vegetation along the forest floor. As if everything around is more than alive. As if it's waiting. I shiver.

Blessed fresh air drowns me, and my lungs bask in its glory. Scents of strawberries and cassia settle along my skin, and I relax. Eric follows me step for step but still hasn't let go of my hand.

Wait. The boy hasn't let go of my hand!

"Hey!" I almost shout—remembering to soften it at the last moment. I shove his chest. "What's the deal?"

His eyes are closed, his face pained. Without looking, he reaches out and grabs my hand again.

He doesn't hold it like he *wants* to hold my hand. It's more of a need, a frantic grasping for sanity.

It's bizarre, but I let him. What the heck is happening right now?

"Give me a minute," he says between clenched teeth.

And for whatever reason, his holding my hand doesn't seem creepy anymore. It feels . . . *desperate*.

I wait. Look around at the ridiculously tall bushes and trees the colors of a crayon box, assuring myself the creature is gone.

Eric's breathing returns to normal, his chest rising and falling in a regular rhythm. He releases my hand and opens his eyes.

He looks around us like he's just now realizing we're in the forest. I stare at him, waiting for an explanation. He avoids my gaze and walks in a slow circle.

I clear my throat. He ignores me. So I step toward him . . .

And stumble with a hiss.

This gets his attention. "Here. Let me help you."

Eric bends down, one hand on my knee. A familiar warmth

spreads across my leg, the pain immediately receding. The same warmth floods my cheek. My fingers brush against smooth skin, the scratch now gone.

Without another word, he stands and resumes his brooding.

"Thanks," I whisper. I cross my arms. "Mind telling me what that was all about?"

He sighs and turns his hazel gaze to mine. "What *what* was all about?"

I roll my eyes. So we're playing this game, huh? "Well, for starters, when you went all psycho inside the tree? And what was with all the handholding?" I shiver, because *ew*.

His shoulders slump, and he stares at his feet.

My heart sinks. I've never seen him like this. Like, ever. Not even as redheaded Eric. He looks . . . defeated. Lost.

"Eric?" My voice is softer. Less judgmental.

He keeps looking at the ground. "Sorry about that."

A minute passes, and I wait. I give him space. Because no matter what's happened between us—even though he totally freaking killed my dad—somehow it feels right. Now is not the time for holding grudges. It's time for listening.

A feeling that goes against all rational thought blooms deep within my belly.

He swallows. "So I sort of have a problem with small spaces." Finally, he glances up, his gaze catching mine. "Like, a real problem with them."

"Why? Did you . . . ?"

He shakes his head, his old demeanor returning, gaze hard. There's no messing with this Eric. "That's not important. Not right now. Maybe I'll tell you later, but for now . . ."

I hide my gasp. *Later?* How much later? I need to get home.

He huffs a breath. "As for the *handholding*." He chuckles, even though nothing about his laugh sounds humorous. "Yeah, let's just say, I needed a little help."

"Um . . . ?"

He rolls his eyes. "I forgot. This is your first time here. You don't know."

"I don't know . . . what?" I raise my brows and try to appear patient even though I'm anything *but*. What is it with faeries forgetting I'm not full fae and need a little explanation?

He crosses his arms. "Faeries are unique. We each have a special gift, something that sets us apart from the rest."

"Gifts? Like magic?"

He shakes his head. "No, not faerie magic. There are different levels of that too, but for the most part, all faeries have the ability to do magic. And magic can be done in the Mortal Realm too." He bites his lip. "On Earth, I mean."

A pause. "What I'm talking about can only be done while in Faerie. We each have a gift. Something that makes us special. Something we learn to control and perfect over the years. For a time such as this." He holds out one hand, indicating the direction the beast fled. "For protection. Survival."

"Your holding my hand made the monster miss seeing us?"

He laughs. For real this time. "No. Losing the creature was all you, Caoine. Good thinking, by the way, ducking into the tree. Your plan worked. *Surprisingly*."

I ignore his rude comment and shake my head. I'm still lost.

He flashes a cocky smile that isn't actually meant for me. "So I just told you I can't do small spaces, yes?"

I nod.

"When faced with said small space, I tend to . . ."

"Flip out?"

"Yeah. Pretty much. I'm not sure I would've been able to control myself without you. I needed your help to get through the panic attack."

"You needed *me*?" I point to myself like an idiot, then throw on a look of defiance as I toss my hands on my hips.

His look turns gentle. "Yes. You." He holds out both hands. "See, my gift is physical empathy. I can sense what others are feeling with just a touch."

"Um, so you could feel how crazy scared I was while we were hiding from the monster, and you couldn't wait to have twice the amount of hysteria to control?"

None of this is making any sense.

Again, he shakes his head. "No, I don't feel what the person is feeling. I can sense their *essence*. Their true . . . self-worth."

"My what?"

He steps forward, reaches out and touches my sternum. I should back away, but again, it doesn't feel weird. I don't even flinch.

"I can feel who a person truly is. Inside." He taps my chest again, then steps back. "I've sensed it before, Caoine. Which is why I knew it would work."

"You sensed my *self-worth*?" It's so hard not to allow my sarcasm to take over this conversation.

"Peace. At your core, you're filled with peace, Caoine."

I snort. "Wait, what?"

"I knew you wouldn't accept it." He shakes his head. "You're peace, Caoine. Whether you believe it or not."

I begin to protest, but he stops me, his voice harsher than before.

"Don't fight it. There's no fighting it." He scratches a hand through his shoulder-length hair. "I mean, think about it. You sing humans the most beautiful lament they've ever heard moments or hours before they pass into the afterlife. How much more peaceful can you get?"

I blink at him. "But I'm surrounded by death."

"No, you're not. You are *peace*. And you pass that peace on to others, despite what you want to believe about yourself. Others can sense it in you. I mean, *I* can."

He swallows, inhales. "Which is why I needed to be touching you when I panicked. Your skin, specifically. I needed direct contact so I could pull from that peace. To calm myself and stop the terror building inside me."

I open my mouth but shut it just as quickly. Me? Peaceful?

A shiver tumbles down my back. Now that I'm no longer running, the cold is finally catching up to me.

"Thank you, by the way. You saved us."

His nostrils flare like this is the hardest thing he's ever had to say. He presses his lips together.

"And now you know the truth about yourself. If we're ever in a situation like that again and I need to stay calm, I'll probably look for whatever exposed skin I can find on you so I don't lose it altogether."

His laugh is awkward, but somehow, I feel sorry for him. Sorry that he needs someone like me around to make him feel better. To feel whole.

How is it that I've only been under my kidnapper's control for a few hours, and already I'm empathizing with him?

I chew on my lip and nod. "So now I know. That's cool and all, but can you please ask next time? Instead of just grabbing my hand?"

He sighs, nods.

"Awesome. Think we can find our way out of these woods? 'Cause I'd love *not* to run into that monster again."

I don't mention what's truly on my mind. *Home.*

"Yeah. Let's get moving. Before he returns." Eric pins me with his gaze. "Or something worse finds us first."

11

We walk for hours.

Okay, maybe it's barely an hour. It's impossible to tell in a place like this.

Besides the fact that it's Faerie and I still haven't gotten used to how different it feels on a physical level, there's also the whole "I'm in the most beautiful place not on Earth" thing. Like, really, truly beautiful.

So far we've passed a waterfall with water plunging in hues of pinks, purples, blues, and greens, being swallowed into dry ground. A pond with lily pads the size of an SUV.

I have no desire to meet the frogs that inhabit those.

And chunks of ground wide enough for a few houses and landscaping float in the sky a few hundred feet above. How they got up there, I have no clue.

And the trees? Some appear to move right along with us. No joke. I whip my head around and swear I catch the branches on one still shivering from jolting to a stop so quickly.

We weave our way in and out of foliage, under canopies of plum-hued leaves the size of my dining room table. The sky has lightened to an almost white, even though a hint of purple is still leftover.

If I weren't so terrified of what's around every turn, I might stay forever. I take in a deep lungful of crisp, lilac-scented air.

But it's still crazy *cold*. I blow hot breath into my cupped hands in hopes of regaining feeling.

Eric and I walk in silence.

Images of Oliver and Aubree invade my brain. What are they doing? Are they totally freaked that I've disappeared?

Heat fills my chest. If I could just feel Oliver's arms around me one more time, I think I could make it through this. I bite my lip to stop the tears.

I can't tell how deep into the woods we are or if we're a safe-enough distance from the castle yet. But Eric knows. He seems to know everything.

Much more than he's willing to share with me.

He turns abruptly and holds up a hand. "Let's stop for a rest."

Without waiting for my response, he plops onto a rock and pulls a bottle of water from his backpack.

I stare at him. Okay. I settle in on another rock close by.

"Are we lost?" I almost flinch at the way my voice bounces through the forest.

"Of course not." He tosses me a look like I'm being ridiculous. "I'm a woodsprite."

"A what?"

"It's a kind of faerie. Basically, I'm sort of one with nature. It . . . talks to me." He shrugs. "I thrive in the outdoors."

"So we're lost but we're not lost?"

"Something like that."

I bob my head. "Cool. So can you do kooky stuff like make plants grow on command or entice vines to wrap around someone's legs, like in the movies?"

He averts his gaze. "There are limits to all fae powers."

His sour look ends the conversation. I huff. He offers me a sip of his water.

I take it eagerly. "Well, where are we going?"

His face twists. "What's it matter to you? You don't know where we are, and you know nothing of Faerie. Trust me, you'll see soon enough."

"Trust you? Are you serious? Give it a rest, Eric. You had your little *moment* back there, and I didn't tease you or make a stink about anything that went down. The least you can do is answer a few questions."

Eric grunts and snatches his water back, guzzling the whole thing at once.

Heat bubbles inside my chest like a mountain of lava ready to spew. Dude doesn't even have the courtesy of using words?

My gaze narrows. "You killed my dad."

Eric freezes.

The compassion I felt for him earlier is long gone.

He glares at me. "You still don't know?"

"Don't know what?" I throw my hands in the air. "I've been in this place for twenty-four hours and still have zero answers why you ruined my life just to bring me here!"

He frowns. "Your dad's not dead."

Now I *know* I've been punched in the stomach. My throat closes, and I can't breathe.

Can't breathe.

Can't breathe.

"What did you say?" I whisper. My entire body is shivering.

He almost rolls his eyes but sighs instead. "He's not dead, Caoine. He's perfectly fine. Well, sort of." He tilts his head. "I mean, my father's got him, so there's that."

"What?" My voice is shrill. I blink rapidly.

"When I stabbed him . . . back on Halloween night, well, the wound wasn't fatal. We fell through the Veil and . . . . I healed him."

"My dad . . . he's not . . ." I swallow. "Dead?"

Eric shakes his head.

Something courses through me. Euphoria and calm and relief

and elation and a billion other feelings I can't begin to describe. Tears flood my eyes, and I can't stop the deluge that falls down my cheeks. I grab my middle and bend at the waist. I blink again.

My dad is alive!

Dizziness tugs at my head, and I fight to stay upright. I can't stop crying. I can't breathe. I can't think. How can he be alive?

I gasp for air and straighten. I need answers. "How did your father get him?"

Eric huffs. "As soon as your dad was able to be moved, I took him to the king."

I flinch, but he goes on before I can lay into him.

"I still had a job to do, Caoine. Even though the spell failed, I knew if I could present your dad to the king, then maybe he wouldn't kill me."

My jaw drops like it's filled with lead. "You used my dad as leverage to keep yourself *alive*?"

"Will you shut it and listen?" He looks at me like I'm a child. "Yes, I brought your dad to the king. I was still . . . under his influence, all right? I figured he'd be happy I had something we could use as a bargaining chip."

I hiccup from my sudden change in emotion. "My dad isn't a *something*."

He ignores me. "But my father was mad. Like, furious. He couldn't believe I'd failed the spell. Went on and on about how many years he'd waited." He shakes his head. "He told me to bring him both books and to find a way to get you into the Unseelie Realm, then he'd consider forgiving me."

I wipe at the tears drying on my face but hold my stomach, a wave of nausea filling it. "The Book of Discernment and the Book of Judgment? Didn't you already have one of those?"

Eric nods. "But did my father need to know that?"

I rock back at the impact of his confession. "You never trusted him."

He pauses, looks away. "On my way back to Earth, the Book of Judgment disappeared from my bag. I was in so much trouble if—when—my father found out." He sighs. "So I did the only thing I could. I sneaked back to Lincoln, stole the Book of Discernment from Aubree. Then I grabbed you. I hoped my father would be true to his word, that he'd forgive me and give me a chance to recover the other book."

I squeeze my hands together. They're still shaking from the sudden realization that I'm not alone any longer. I've got my dad back!

I exhale. "But you played it safe?"

He pauses. "If I brought you and the book to his castle and he refused to forgive me—if he tried to have me killed . . ." His hands open and close at his sides. "Yeah. I played it safe. I chose to keep you and the Book of Discernment away from the castle until I'd spoken to him. If he acted rationally, I'd retrieve you and go from there."

"There's nothing rational about the Unseelie king though, is there?"

He looks away, pounding his fist on his thigh.

I scratch my hand through my ratty hair. *Great.* "So what's the plan? How do we get my dad back?"

"We're not."

"*What?*" My hands still shake from the adrenaline of learning my dad is still alive. Now they tremble from fury.

"We're going to retrieve the Book of Discernment, then we'll find that other book. If my father gets either one, things will grow exponentially more complicated."

"And?"

"And . . . I'm taking this day by day." He shrugs.

"So that's it? You're no longer working for your father? You're changing sides, just like that?" I snap my fingers. "It doesn't bother you that an innocent man is sitting in a jail cell and needs to be freed?"

He glares at me. "I didn't plan on this happening. I'm sort of winging it, if you hadn't noticed."

"Well, could you do me a favor and not wait a full day before telling me something major again? Like the fact that my dad is alive? Like, *alive* alive? Living and breathing and holding entire conversations with *your* father somewhere back in a fairyland castle?"

He scowls. "Sorry I didn't clue you in since we were *running for our lives.* I'll make sure I stop to tell you things while my father's men put arrows through our heads next time."

"See?" I roll my eyes. "That's exactly what I mean. He already deceived you, but you still trusted him. He made it perfectly clear he used you, tricked you, lied to you—"

His nostrils flare, and pink spots appear on each cheek. "Yeah. Got that. I don't need a rehash of how much I mean to the guy."

"Yeah, but that's my point, Eric. He already showed his true colors. Yet you trusted him again. Why?"

"Because he's the only family I've got! What else do you expect me to do?"

"Even when you realized you were on the wrong side, you still trusted him and did what he said anyway?" I cross my arms.

"I didn't . . . I was . . . confused."

"So you're saying you're still on his side? Will you betray me the next time he pretends to love you again?"

His neck goes a deep shade of crimson. "I never said that."

"You just said your father wants to kill you. Are you telling me you've really done a one-eighty in a matter of minutes? That you're willing to help me?"

"Yes!" His voice vibrates through the air, echoes between the trees, weaves its way into the void around us.

I suck in a breath. Our gazes connect.

Seconds pass, then a minute. Still, our eyes remain on each other. My heart beats so loudly, it drowns out the sounds of nature all around us. His breaths are choppy, coming in waves, short and stunted.

"Why?" I finally whisper.

His jaw tenses. Then his shoulders slump. "Because . . . because . . ." Eric wipes a hand down his face, our connection broken. He sighs like the weight of all of Faerie is on his shoulders. "Because of the feeling."

"The feeling?" My brow pinches together.

He scratches the back of his neck and looks to the side. "Yeah. I don't know how to explain it, really. But for whatever reason, I *feel* it. I couldn't feel it before, but now I do. I can feel his betrayal. In here." He touches his chest. "I know who my father is now. For real. And I'm not really sure how I was duped in the first place, you know?"

He swallows, frustration pinching his features.

"I mean, it's almost like I was in a dream or something, before. Back when I first found out who he was, what he wanted me to do. It's like, yeah, I totally wanted a father. I'm not gonna deny that. I *wanted* to be wanted. Wanted to be a prince, right? But then . . ."

He shakes his head. "Things got peculiar. And I'm not sure why or how. They just did. One second I saw the guy as an opportunity, a way to have a father in my life for the first time. The fact he was king was just a neat bonus."

I raise my eyebrows. "A neat bonus?"

He ignores me. "But then I suddenly felt like I would do anything to please him, anything to *be* him. All I could think about was finishing his mission, doing whatever it took to complete what he asked. I couldn't think of anything else. Nothing."

He opens his mouth to say something else, but his eyes travel over my face, and he stops abruptly.

"I honestly can't tell you why I went along with everything he said. I mean, I didn't necessarily disagree with what he was trying to do—opening the Veil and all—but I definitely wouldn't have been on board with . . . the way things went down."

The deaths—that's what he's talking about. All the people who died for the sake of the spell he enacted back at high school. Was that only a few months ago?

"But I'm thinking straight now. I know that. I am making my own decisions now." He looks me right in the eyes. "Yes, Caoine. I will help you get your dad back."

Before I can reply, a loud thud sounds behind me. His eyes are immediately scanning the trees, his body tense.

"What was—?" But I never finish.

Something crashes through the bushes. From behind a tree pops a familiar face, attached to a tiny body.

"My prince?"

"Nym?" Eric stands from his rock seat.

"My prince!" The small man scuttles forward, a lopsided grin on his face. "Been searching for you. Afraid my prince caught. Or worse." His beady eyes grow wide.

"We're fine, Nym. Thanks for your concern." Eric puts his hands over his head and stretches.

"On a journey?" The little faerie rubs his hands together, a grin on his face.

Eric doesn't look at him as he takes in our surroundings. "Something like that."

"Hello, pretty girl."

I blink as his attention turns on me.

"Any idea where my father's men are?" Eric interrupts.

I bristle at this. Even if I had no intention of responding to Nym, it's beyond rude for him to assume I wouldn't.

"Not close. Not far." Nym watches Eric in awe.

Eric nods. "We should get moving, then."

"Wait," I say. "You never answered my question. *When* will we save my dad from your father's prison?" I stumble into step beside him as he trails away.

He glares at me. "After we find both books."

I stifle a growl. "So far your plan to gain the king's favor has completely failed, we've been chased by soldiers and monsters, and it appears you have no clue what we should do once we retrieve the other book."

"*Monster*," he says, his gaze firmly on the brush before us. "There was only one."

"Right." I roll my eyes. "Mind telling me what we'll do once we've got both books?"

He swats aside a low-hanging, fuchsia-colored branch without checking to see if it will swing back and hit me. It doesn't, but still. Nym hops along at my heels.

Eric glances at the lightening sky. "I've got an idea or two."

"Meaning, you've got no clue." I trip again and almost face plant. Nym makes a noise of caution.

"Chill, Caoine. I've got a clue." He glances at me, every bit of that softened boy who needed my *peace* long gone. "More than you, anyway. The most important thing is that my father not get his hands on them before we do."

I press my lips together and follow him blindly. Because . . . what other choice do I even have?

Prickly leaves and pointy bushes reach out to grab me, snag my clothing, do everything they can to slow me down. I mutter a few curses under my breath and swear I hear Eric chuckle. He's totally enjoying this.

This . . . torture I'm enduring.

Nym skitters around my feet and catches up with Eric, mumbling adages to his *prince*. Whatever history they have is beyond me, but it's obvious Eric couldn't care less about the poor guy. Nym treats Eric like some sort of demigod.

There's no sun here in the Unseelie Realm, despite the fact I swear I saw two moons hanging in the distant sky last night. No sun but double moons? So bizarre.

Still, the temperature rises quickly with the breaking of day. Thus far I haven't lost any fingers or toes, but another few hours in the frigid temps could've done the trick.

Is Eric using magic to make sure I don't freeze to death? I frown. I don't want to be indebted to him in any way.

I rub my nose. It's numb from the cold but somehow still tickles, no doubt bothered by the new scent of fresh leather and linen. How do these dragon-sized flowers grow in the middle of winter?

I eye Eric as we walk. Is he really leading us to safety or into another of his father's traps?

No matter what Eric's past shouts at me, I have to believe he intends good. His butt is on the line too. I swallow. The alternative is too dark to handle.

"So, uh . . ." I clear my throat, which has a frog stuck deep inside. "About my dad . . ."

"Yes?" Eric plows forward, pushing aside another door-sized bunch of leaves.

"He's there. In your father's castle."

"Yeah."

An insect of some sort whimpers from under my foot, and I jump to the side. If an insect can whimper, it's probably not a good sign.

I suck in a breath. The thing isn't large but would frighten even the bravest knight in shining armor. Covered in thick magenta hair, it has ten legs, four bulging eyes, and responds with a catlike hiss. Yikes.

I skitter after Eric. *Ask nicely, Caoine.* "Um, well, is there a reason we can't just go save him first? I mean, you've already got one book. You have no idea where to find the other. Will it really delay things to detour to the castle to free my only living parent?"

"It's not that simple." Eric's voice is monotone. He squints ahead as if he's trying to get his bearings.

"How so?"

He stops abruptly, and I almost run smack into his shoulder.

"You do realize we just escaped, right? There's, like, zero chance we'll be able to get close to the castle anytime soon."

I blink at the way he sounds so human. Sometimes I forget just how many years he spent on Earth, following me around, attempting to blend in with humanity. He's like a regular teen.

My gaze travels over his long, dark hair, the way it tumbles across his shoulders but looks like it's been perfectly styled. The brown of it in contrast with his hazel eyes, so different from his eyes as redheaded Eric. I swear he could've stepped off the soccer field at West Lincoln High.

Soccer. My thoughts travel to Oliver, and my heart sinks.

How much is that boy going insane right now? Knowing I'm in Faerie, that I've been captured by the fae? Are he and Aubree attempting to find me? My throat closes.

"Caoine? Did you hear what I said?" Eric tilts his head, those hazel eyes narrowed.

I sigh. "Yes. I did. I get it. You're right. But when do you think we can get in there? I need to see my dad again. When will they let their guard down?"

He runs a hand through his hair. "Honestly? Never."

My eyes pop out of my head. "Never?"

"Well, my father knows you're here. He knows you'll come for your dad. I think there's zero chance you're going in there undetected."

"Not without a plan, yeah, but—"

"Even with a plan." He frowns at the way I *pfft* in his direction. "Seriously. I'm fairly certain they're going to be on guard, *forever*. I'm not sure all the planning in the world will get us in there and your dad out."

I throw my hands in the air. "Thank you so much for the confidence!"

"What? Do you want me to lie to you? Something I can't do, by the way. But I'm pretty sure we've established I'm here to help you. That means declaration of all the things. Even the ones you don't want to hear."

"Yeah, but . . ."

"But what? You want me to pretend we're going to get your dad out without a problem? Fine, I can do that. But more important things need to be attended to first."

I huff. "More important than my dad?"

"Yes, Caoine. More important than your dad." He puts his hands on his hips. "Look, we need the books to get him out of the castle anyway. As morbid as it sounds, your dad is perfectly safe where he is. The king wants to use him. He can't do that if he's dead. Which means we can focus on other things, like making sure we get that other book before my father does."

"Why would we need both books to free him?"

"It takes magic to beat magic."

Sure. Whatever that means. I open my mouth but freeze. "I have your word that you'll help me get him back?"

His gaze narrows at me. "We need to get those books."

My heart pounds. What if the king decides he no longer needs my dad before we find both books? "So the books are more important than a person's life?"

"Right now? Yeah. He's under the protection of my father and is safe as a kitten. At least until *you* show up again."

I grind my teeth but don't say anything else out loud. Because every single thing Eric just said is absolutely true. My dad is safe. And if Eric won't help me until we find both books, then we need to get busy finding those books.

How is it possible we're working toward the same goal?

The bigger question, though, is how we're going to do all the things he just said.

Before I can voice it, a new distraction slams into us. Or rather, Eric.

As we stand there staring one another down in a silent power struggle, an arrow springs from the dense foliage and plants itself right in Eric's shoulder.

13

I DON'T HAVE time to react. Eric shoves me to the ground.

A second arrow zips through the air in the exact spot where his head was. Panic becomes my cloak as we roll through dead leaves and patches of melted snow.

The sound of another arrow *thwaping* into plum bark just above us jolts Eric to life. He pulls me to my knees and yanks me behind the nearest snow-covered bush. Then he knocks me to the ground in one swift motion.

I'm seriously going to puke.

Before I can blink, he's got his upper body on top of me. His good hand is crammed over my mouth, which is actually a good idea since I squeal the minute my head smacks the ground. A second passes, then five.

I buck against his weight.

The man who tried to kill my dad has me trapped. Who cares if it's to keep me safe? My fingers curl into the hard earth beneath me as I fight the urge to bite the boy.

His bad arm is tight to his side, what with the arrow sticking out and all. Cobalt-blue blood dribbles down his sleeve, blossoms along the fabric like spilled fruit punch.

The smell of cassia hangs heavy in the air, but I can still

74

pinpoint the scent that is uniquely Eric. Smoke and aftershave mixed, neither overpowering the other.

He twists his head to look behind us, his heart pounding like bass at a dance club. And then the urge to hit him is gone. Peace trickles through my body like I'm safe. Which is weird.

My throat closes. *What am I thinking?*

This guy is a full-on sociopath.

Twigs crack and snow crunches beneath purposeful footfalls as our enemy moves slowly around us. Clearly he doesn't see us hidden under whatever kind of bush this is.

And my heart is torn. On the one hand, whoever this mystery person is wants Eric dead, which is totally fine by me, since he deserves it. On the other hand, Eric's sort of my only acquaintance in the realm, the only one who might be able to help me get my dad out of faerie jail. So, yeah.

I sigh. I definitely need him alive.

The footfalls pause, prowl a bit more, then move away, the pastel-colored forest going quiet.

Eric relaxes and slowly moves to the side, only now wincing in pain. His face blanches white, and he squeezes his eyes tight, the muscles along his jaw clenching.

I sit up and crawl over, lifting my hands to try to help. He opens his eyes with effort, looks at me with a hooded gaze. He shakes his head as if to say there's nothing I can do.

Crap. We lost the psycho hunter, but now we've got a bigger problem. What in Faerie are we going to do with a freaking arrow in Eric's shoulder?

An idea forms in my mind. I take the back end of the arrow. Whoa. The thing is twice as thick as any arrow I've ever seen. Then again, I only took that one archery class.

But the wood is rigid and flexible at the same time, carved from a pink-tinted wood. There are no feathers to guide its direction, but the end is carved into a star pattern.

I wrap one hand around it.

Eric's eyes go wide, and he flinches.

"I saw it in a movie," I whisper. "I need to break off the end so I can pull it through."

"You *what?*" His voice is dangerously close to regular volume.

I glance over my shoulder. "Just hold still."

He angles away from me. "No, thanks. I'd rather bleed to death."

Even though I'm on my knees, I plant my hands on my hips. "Seriously? That's not an option."

"Well, you performing minor surgery on me in the middle of the forest isn't an option, either."

I roll my eyes. "Got a better idea?"

Before he can answer, his gaze slips over my shoulder like rain melting down a window. His face stills, a vein along one temple pulsing with his heartbeat.

Air catches in my throat, and I jump to my feet, careful not to put too much pressure on my weak ankle.

Then I whip around to face whatever is at my back.

A girl.

My age, although she's probably a few hundred years older, considering she's fae.

She's medium height with dark curls that shimmer down her back and over her shoulders. Her white skin complements every part of her, from her hunter-green pants and matching tunic, to her knee-high leather boots, buttoned up the sides.

In her hands is a bow, arrow notched and pointed right at my chest.

She looks . . . familiar. I blink.

The girl narrows her gaze at me. A faint white line stretches from her right ear over her brow, a scar from years past.

"Move out of the way, mortal. My fight is with the coward prince behind you."

This is the person who shot Eric? A *girl*, not a guy.

Why had I pegged her as a male this whole time? My feminist side does an internal fist pump for *girl power*, even though she's totally pointing an arrow at me.

I hold up my hands. "Whoa. Let's slow down here. There's no need to shoot the coward prince."

"Excuse me?" Eric whines from behind.

"Funny." She sneers. "I didn't peg you for an idiot."

Now it's my turn to do a double take. Where do I know her from?

Her brows raise. "The guy almost killed your dad. Why defend him?"

I nod. "You've done your homework."

She relaxes a bit, and only now do I see that her bow hand is cocked at a strange angle, her fingers almost seared together, neatly manipulated around the bow so the brunt of the weight rests on her palm.

Her left hand is deformed. How can she hold that position for so long?

"Of course I did." She waits another few seconds. "I'm here to save you, Caoine Roberts. I'm the best chance you have of surviving."

I breathe. Count one, two, three. A winter breeze sends chills across my skin. An image from West Lincoln High flashes in my head, a memory of working on the *Black and White*. A friend, laughing.

White skin. Dark curly hair. Glasses.

Catherine.

The girl who has an arrow pointed at me is my friend, Cat.

14

"CAT?" My voice is a whisper, my insides running wild.

The girl shakes her head. "Close. But not quite. Her sister." She sniffs, but her arrow stays perfectly aimed.

"Wait. You're *not* Catherine?" I shove my trembling deep inside, down to the place where it will be safe and sound until I choose to deal with it. Which will likely be never.

"My name is Aibell. Cleona's my twin."

"*Cleona?*"

"Technically *Clíodhna*, but it's easier for you to pronounce Cleona. And yes, I'm talking about Cat."

My insides twist and writhe like snakes that have suddenly been set free. "Cat's *fae?*"

"Of course. It would be impossible for my twin to be human when I'm full fae." Aibell looks at me as if I've lost my mind.

My cheeks heat. "No, I mean, she's been fae this whole time and never told me?" Blood pounds in my ears. "Does Aubree know?"

She shakes her head. "Some fae are able to cloak their true nature even from those like them."

"But why? Why wouldn't she tell me who she was? Why

78

didn't she help me?"

My belly clenches. If I'd known Cat was fae, it would've made the whole Halloween thing so much easier. How could she have betrayed me like that?

"Um, can we discuss this later? I'm sort of bleeding to death over here." Eric looks both pathetic and cocky at the same time. How does he even do that?

Aibell's gaze shifts behind me. "Oh good. The traitor wants to die sooner. Shall we get this over with?"

I push aside my feelings. "Uh, yeah. Could I get you not to shoot him just yet?" I shift. If she looses another arrow, I'm not convinced I'd be willing to jump in front of it.

She frowns. "The boy *did* try to murder your father. Am I correct in this?"

"Yes. Yes, you would be correct, but—" Am I so silly to defend this dude? "I need him to get my dad back. And, well, he's proven to maybe have had a change of heart."

"A change of heart?" She raises her eyebrows.

I nod.

"Well, the fae cannot lie. So as long as you are sure he stated it in such a way that's trustworthy . . ."

She leaves the last word hanging, as if I couldn't possibly be smart enough to assure such a thing.

I hesitate. I honestly didn't pay attention during our conversation. Did he include a loophole to be a double agent?

I swallow. "Yes. I'm sure he's telling the truth." I don't look at him to gauge whether I've made the right decision or not.

She lowers her bow. "Fine. Let me get you two out of here. The way you've been stomping through the woods—I'm surprised you haven't been attacked by a scarlet reynard or eaten by a wild gowher already." She eyes Eric. "You sure you're still fae? You've spent far more time in the Mortal Realm than is good for you."

He huffs and struggles to his feet. I give him a hand, but he swats it away. Aibell snorts and starts in the opposite direction.

Her lithe form glides through the forest as if she's part of creation. I sprint to catch up, my sore ankle working through the pain with each step. Not broken, at least. Eric lags behind.

I bite my lip. "So you're taking us somewhere safe? Somewhere the king's men won't find us?"

"Sure. We'll go with that." She looks me up and down. Her attitude is so different from her sister's. "Although, I'm not sure anyplace within the Unseelie Realm is truly safe for . . . someone like you."

I frown. "Someone like me?"

Her lip curls. "A half-fae who doesn't have control of her fae powers to shield herself."

I press my lips together. *Fantastic.*

We walk in silence. None of us appear to mind. Aibell is less friendly than her counterpart, and Eric is in the worst mood ever. Which I guess he's allowed, considering the arrow tip sticking through his flesh. He hasn't even complained that we're no longer headed toward the book.

I clear my throat. "So how has one of my closest friends been fae this whole time and I've never known?" My chest aches like I'm the one who has taken the arrow.

"Cleona didn't want you to know. That's how." Her response is monotone.

I bite back a sarcastic reply. "But why? I mean, is it because you're both Unseelie?"

Aibell stops in her tracks and looks at me. "Cleona and I aren't Unseelie."

"Oh. But you're here, so I figured—"

"Do not assume things, Caoine. Not everyone here is Unseelie, and even then, not all Unseelie are bad. The fae are *tricksters*. Do yourself a favor and don't trust anyone. Ever. It might save you someday."

I sigh. "Right. Except for the fact that I'm trusting you and Eric right now. I mean, I sort of have no choice. Otherwise, I'll never get out of here."

She starts walking again without a response.

"So you and Cat are from the Seelie Realm. Why wouldn't she tell Aubree? She's Seelie too. Why all the secrets?"

"Cleona was sent to your school for a different purpose. It's her story to tell. Ask her the next time you see her. For now, I'm here to help you."

"Cat sent you?"

She dips her chin. "As soon as I heard what happened, I knew I needed to find you." Aibell does nothing to hide the glare she plants on Eric.

He rolls his eyes.

"Great." I pretend not to see the exchange. "Think you can help me spring my dad from faerie prison and take me to the Veil?"

Aibell laughs. "It's not even close to that simple. There are restrictions on the Veils. The fae can only use them with special permission, and even then, the king usually has to go behind the Seelie queen's back. And freeing someone from the castle prison isn't something you do on a whim. Until we figure out a way to get you out of here, you're here to stay."

It's my turn to whip around and wither Eric with my glare. Why didn't he tell me this sooner? I've been asking to go home for hours, and he just kept saying he wanted to get us away from danger. Couldn't he have clued me in that my escape home was going to take longer than I thought?

He curls his lip and looks away.

Nice. Hours. I've been here hours and hours. In fact, nighttime is over.

I stop in my tracks, Aibell only stopping after a few more steps. "Wait. My song. Why haven't I sung my song? I've never gone this long without singing."

She tilts her head. "Poor, Caoine. Not used to the ways of Faerie? Your song doesn't work in the Unseelie Realm, dearie. You will never sing again. Unless you can find a way home."

15

MY HEART STALLS in my chest. "I can't sing my banshee song inside the realms?"

Aibell lunges forward, her right hand firmly across my mouth. "Shh! Do you want to get yourself killed?"

Eric tenses and steps closer. I blink as Aibell loosens her grip and puts space between us.

"Did I say something wrong?" My gaze darts to Eric and back.

She exhales as she surveys the area. "The hideout isn't much farther. Do me a favor and don't talk until we get there."

Aibell stalks off, leaving Eric and me standing in a circle of confusion. What I wouldn't give for a little more of Cat's sweet attitude from that girl.

The rest of the hike isn't far—she's right about that. We push through a tight copse of story-high trees and come to a dead stop.

The ground before us is nonexistent. A massive chasm engulfs the soil, a hole the size of half a football field waiting for one of us to misstep. I swallow.

"Let's go." Aibell trudges ahead toward a thin, twisting branch that extends to the other side of the abyss.

I fumble for words.

Eric nods at the pint-sized bridge. "Go on. You're not afraid of heights, are you?"

"It's not the height that has me worried." I scowl. "It's the falling to my death part."

He snorts and follows Aibel.

The two of them are like tightrope walkers. Perfectly light on their feet, impeccable balance. Not a single worry.

My belly writhes in protest. I slowly step to the bridge. Why does the branch look so much thinner than from a few feet back?

I glance over my shoulder. Nothing but giant pastel trees that look as if they'd like to swallow me whole. Gulp. Aibell and Eric have already crossed to the other side and stare at me.

Waiting.

Right.

I place a foot on the branch, take a full breath. My other foot joins it, exhale. Right, left. I concentrate on each foot's placement and not the impending doom that awaits me below. Right, left. My heart beats erratically. This is actually easier than it looks. Why do I always think I have two left feet?

Seconds later I'm standing beside Eric and Aibell. I give an exaggerated huff.

Aibbel gives me an impatient look and walks away.

The corner of Eric's mouth tilts up. "Not bad. Maybe your fae side is catching up to you."

He follows Aibell. I frown. I hadn't thought about that. Will my faerie side become stronger?

I run after the two only to stop several feet away. In front of a gigantic mushroom. An honest-to-God mushroom the size of a skyscraper.

Or a tree, since that's what it is. But it's the size of an ancient redwood I saw in a vacation brochure last year. The kind of tree five people can stand around with arms outstretched, fingers barely touching.

The tree reaches so high, clouds touch the tippy top. Turquoise-colored clouds, in this case. Except this tree has an entirely white bottom half and a massive mushroom canopy.

It's not the only one. Mushroom trees dot the landscape every dozen feet all around us. But none are quite as colossal as this one.

Aibell is still. She stands before the tree as if something should happen.

Nothing does. An uneasy knot grows in my belly, and Eric's shoulders go rigid. Have we made a huge mistake?

Snap! Something shifts. Or *somethings*.

The mushroom canopy begins to quiver like the most fantastical earthquake ever. Then a loud splitting sound makes me jump. The base of the tree gapes open, a deep fissure breaking open in welcome.

A whine rustles against the wind, and I narrow my gaze.

It's as if the thing is alive.

Wait, this is Faerie. It probably is.

I swallow. Is this happening of the tree's free will, or is Aibell doing some sort of magic?

As everything comes to a halt, a sigh that encompasses relief and joy spills from the ground surrounding it. I breathe easier.

Aibell steps into the tree, her entire figure disappearing. I pull in a shaky breath and follow. It's only after I'm across the threshold that I remember Eric and the fact that she hates him.

What if she closes the hole before he makes it across?

But I don't need to worry. In seconds he steps through the invisible magic wall, his warmth a constant against my back.

I raise my eyes to the sight before me. We're no longer in the forest, and we're certainly not inside a mushroom tree. The room is large with high ceilings. The walls are a muddy brown. The floor, ironically, is a glossy hardwood.

And the ceiling—if it can be called that—isn't actually a ceiling. It floats above us, and the wall has no definitive ending as it fades into nothingness. Above hangs the night sky. Literally.

Not the delicate lavender that belongs uniquely to Faerie, but the night sky from Earth.

My home.

Black and liquid and filled with a million stars that I can count but can never touch. Constellations jump out at me, reach for me in a smoky whisper, as if their fingers will wrap around my soul, will never let go.

I suck in air and force my eyes to the rest of the room.

A gathering of cushioned chairs sits in a circle at one end. A smattering of ancient and ornately decorated tables and chairs fill the middle space. Toward the opposite wall is a single bed, clearly unused, since the fae don't sleep.

But none of these things catch my attention, not really.

Warmth cocoons me like a tight blanket, and I almost squeal in delight. I scrunch my fingers open and closed. It's been too long since I've felt anything but cold.

But what's more urgent—the thing that demands every ounce of my attention, warm or not—are the three faeries who stand dead center of us.

Aibell steps forward. "Caoine, welcome to my home. These are your new best friends. They're going to help get you out of Faerie."

16

MY HEART RACES. "You can help me get home?"

One of the fae, a woman at least six feet tall, offers me a gentle smile. "It would be our honor, Caoine, daughter of Saoirse."

She's dressed in a stark white gown that flows to her bare feet, her hair cropped short, a muted green framing deep-brown skin. Her silver eyes glow with the same radiance that surrounds her, making her appear partially transparent.

A faint outline of wings hangs behind her, but when I blink, they're gone. But her ethereal appearance isn't what has me reeling. That name. *Saoirse.* My mother.

I gasp. "How do you — ?"

"Welcome to the Unseelie Realm." The faerie drifts forward and offers a slender hand. "My name is Laoise."

I marvel at the fact that she's even thinner than I am.

I take her hand. Her skin is cool, and my own has no memory of having touched her once we've parted. She disappears, only to reappear seconds later across the room.

A noise escapes my lips, and my face heats. Eric doesn't even flinch. There is so much about the fae I've yet to learn.

"Did you . . . ?" My heart thuds faster inside my chest.

86

Aibell chuckles as if amused by my reaction. "Laoise has the Gift of Evanescence. She can turn invisible." Her grin falls. "She's also a wisp, so be kind. Someday she might lead your children into the woods never to return if you disrespect her."

Ice fills my veins, and I glance at Laoise. She looks at me with delight. The kind of look a grandmother would give a child before offering a cookie. Except now I envision those cookies laced with poison.

I make a mental note never to cross the fae, especially her.

A short, squat male faerie beside her lifts a spear over his head and holds the position with precision. He's aiming at Eric, who continues to huff and puff beside me from his injury.

My eyes go wide, but I don't move to protect him.

"Hold, Gar. We're not done with the traitor just yet." Aibell's command is only halfhearted.

He's covered in hair: long, knotted strands that fall down his back, eyebrows thick and bushy, a beard that covers most of his face, extending to his navel. His skin is a haunting gray, his face pocked. His hands are small, barely large enough to wrap around the weapon. He looks like a child, if said child could grow a mass of hair and deep wrinkles.

"Why keep him alive?" Gar's voice is gruff and deep, exactly what I'd expect from such a figure. "Our orders were —"

Aibell's eyes flash. "I'm aware of our orders, goblin."

He growls and stays rooted to his spot.

"Plans have changed. Lower your spear."

Gar hesitates, and I get the distinct impression he doesn't like taking orders from a female. His gaze travels over me, and that same icy sensation tumbles along my skin.

Finally he lowers his weapon, and I exhale. Wait. Was I worried he would kill Eric?

Gar grunts. "Just know, when I loose this in your direction, I won't miss. I never miss."

Aibell waves him off with a roll of her eyes. "Yeah, yeah.

You're good with a long, sharp projectile. Got it." She looks at me. "Meet Osgar, resident goblin and angry little man."

A rumble sounds from the depths of his chest, but she doesn't react. Instead, she gestures toward the last remaining fae. "That is Killian."

The faerie barely drops his head in welcome, his features soft and tender.

"He's Seelie as well, but he prefers to live in the Winter Realm."

I frown but don't ask the obvious question.

A bow is slung across one shoulder, a quiver of arrows around the other. He's tall—so much taller than Seamus or Aubree or any other fae I've met. And just as thin. His elegance drifts around him, and I feel like I'm standing near royalty.

His clothes are simple, camouflage to match the forest, with supple leather boots. His light skin is accented by long, blond hair. Locks are braided and twisted together, the rest hanging loose around his shoulders. His jaw is strong and square and totally clean shaven, as if he couldn't grow a beard if he tried.

The boy could be a supermodel.

The heat in my cheeks returns. I clear my throat. "Hey. I'm Caoine."

Aibell snorts.

Right. Of course they know who I am. They're here to save me. "So . . . what's the plan? When can we spring my dad?"

When can I go home to Oliver?

Gar's voice is so low I feel it through the floor. "What is the situation with your father?"

Aibell answers for me. "Brent Roberts was taken hostage by the king."

I swallow as color drains from my face. Hearing the words out loud hits me hard.

Killian's voice is smooth, mesmerizing. "Your father is safe as long as he remains under Raghnall's care." He looks at me as if offering comfort. "Should we not use the time at hand to discover why the king brought Caoine to the Unseelie Realm?"

Laoise tilts her head. "Wasn't it to complete the spell that failed on Samhain Eve?"

Eric shifts beside me. "Um, can I get a little help here first?"

Aibell flares her nostrils. Laoise glances at him as if she's just noticed his presence. Gar's fingers tighten around the spear at his side.

Disgust pours from Aibell. "We're here to help Caoine, not you."

The eyes of every fae in the room weigh like an anvil on my back. I should let him suffer for what he did. I should demand that we save my dad, that they get us out of this place before they move on with their plans, but . . .

Sigh.

I will always be more human than fae. And my humanity begs for mercy. Even for the slime of a man who tried to kill the only family I have on Earth.

My gaze falls on Aibell. "Heal Eric, and I'll do whatever you think's best. As long as we can free my dad."

Gar groans, and Cat's sister clenches her jaw.

I lift my chin. I won't be budged.

"Fine," Aibell spits. She glances at Killian. "Do your thing, elf. Make it quick so we can get to work."

Without hesitation, Killian places his weapons on the ground and leads Eric to the table. For once, Eric keeps his snarky mouth shut, something I'm thankful for.

I don't know why I asked them to save him. I don't know why I'm here or what I'm going to do next. But one thing I do know: I'm still human. And I won't watch others suffer.

Even if it kills me.

17

HIS SCREAMS COULD WAKE the dead. I don't know what Killian does to remove the arrow, but the way Eric suffers burrows under my skin and takes root.

I shiver with guilt as I sit in a chair and endure Gar's heavy stare. Laoise assists Killian in his efforts to save their mortal enemy. Aibell has disappeared to realm knows where.

Tears burn my eyes. Worry for my dad invades my thoughts with every scream Eric releases.

Is he suffering like Eric is?

Finally the fae finish tending to Eric's wound and retreat to another part of the tree.

Laoise kindly offers me a plate of nuts, dried fruit, and cheese, and I receive it far too eagerly. When was the last time I even ate?

Four minutes later, my belly twists in protest as I attempt to fill it beyond capacity. My fingers tingle as I debate if I should force myself to eat more—in case I don't see another meal for a while—or if I should listen to my body and avoid puking.

I glance at Eric and catch a shudder rocking his body. His eyes are closed, but I sense he's still awake. My fingers curl around the wooden plate as I consider the remainder of my meal. None of the other fae offered the prince anything.

A heartbeat passes, then two. My gaze flickers across the three faeries huddled together in their soft chairs. I look back at Eric, lying on the table alone and in pain.

My chair scrapes the glossy floor as I stand, drawing the eyes of only Laoise, who gives me a slight smile. Does she know what I'm about to do? I cross to Eric swiftly, just in case one of them tries to stop me.

I don't even know why I do this. He tried to kill my dad. And Oliver. My back tenses as I lean my hip against the table, the plate of food beside me.

His hair sticks to his skin with sweat, his cheeks pink. Heat rolls off him like he's a heater in the middle of winter. Which I guess he sort of is.

Another shiver tumbles across my arms. The cold of the Unseelie Realm has returned. I've almost grown used to it.

He tosses his head to the side, his face pinched. A groan barely escapes his throat, only loud enough for me to hear.

The arrow was burrowed in his shoulder too long.

Extraction was harder than it should've been. They removed it without any pain meds, and I get the feeling their bandaging was only enough to suffice, not enough to aid in the healing process.

I hesitate. This boy is my enemy. He deserves to suffer.

Except . . .

Except.

What if Oliver were in his place? What if it was my boyfriend who suffered, who needed an ounce of compassion to ease his agony?

I suck in a quick breath. Reach toward Eric. Touch his hot skin.

His hazel eyes pop open, connect with mine. I slowly pull up my sleeve and give him a small nod. With effort, he reaches across his body with his good hand and grabs hold of my forearm. Then he sighs.

The crease along his forehead disappears, and his entire body visibly relaxes as he soaks in my peace or whatever he gains from my touch. I feel nothing, physically. We sit like this for a full minute. He lets go.

His eyes remain closed for another few seconds before he opens them. "Thank you." His voice is hoarse, and he coughs.

I bob my head. "Hungry?"

Eric laughs and winces before indicating no.

We sit in silence for a moment. Then I ask, "How long does it last?"

"How long does what last?"

"My . . . comfort. Or whatever you get from me when you touch me."

He breathes. "Thirty minutes? Maybe an hour? I can't remember. I've only pulled from your essence once before."

Right. I glance at Laoise as her gaze flickers in our direction. The other fae ignore us. "She has a gift, too."

"Yeah. They all do, probably."

"Probably?"

"Well, it's possible for a faerie not to have one, but that's pretty rare. Most fae have at least something different from the others."

"Sort of like me being a banshee?"

He bites his lip. "Not exactly. I mean, your job is different than a gift. I'm a woodsprite, which is my job. It's what I was born to do. But my gift didn't become apparent until I was a child. Every faerie's gift appears at different stages of their life, but most know what it is by the time they reach their fifth or sixth decade. If it doesn't come by then, it's likely they don't have one."

"Oh." I pause. Think. "So what does it mean that I haven't sung yet?"

"You mean that you aren't a banshee here?"

I frown. "Yeah. Aibell said something about that. She said I couldn't sing in the Unseelie Realm. Why not?"

"Remember how Aubree and I told you that your singing for Seamus was rare?"

My stomach clenches, and I force my anger down. Yes, I remember that day. It was only a few months ago, but it was also when I thought Eric was a friend. Not evil incarnate.

And we're discussing Seamus's death as if it had been done by someone else, not *him*.

"Well, it's true," he continues. "A banshee's sole purpose is to sing to humans, to predict their deaths and usher them into the afterlife peacefully. Banshees don't sing for other fae, unless there are special circumstances. So, no, banshees don't sing here."

"Okay." I take a beat. "So what will I do?"

Eric's brows pull tight. "What do you mean?"

"I mean, I don't have a job. What's my purpose?"

I literally just figured out my real purpose in life right before this dumb boy whisked me away to the Unseelie Realm. What am I supposed to do now?

He shrugs. "It's not like you'll be here that long, Caoine. Just enjoy the break, I guess."

I blink. Enjoy the break? "What's that supposed to mean?"

"It means, chill. So you don't sing for a few days. Is it that big a deal?"

Annoyance stabs across my chest like wildfire. "Easy for you to say. You're a freaking woodsprite. Apparently you're all about woods and sprite-ness and stuff. You never stop being that. And you've got some crazy-cool gifting you can access anytime you touch someone. I'm sort of feeling a little useless here."

He huffs as if I'm being a touchy teen girl. Which I totally am, but ugh. I've got a point!

"You'll be fine. Once you're back in the Mortal Realm, your banshee side will return, and you'll be back to your old job." He eyes me warily. "I thought you didn't like doing that, anyway."

I press my lips together. "Let's just say I've grown used to the responsibility."

"Well, give it time. You'll get it back."

"But I don't have a gift like other fae?"

"I didn't say that."

"How can I know?"

He looks to the other fae and back. "You don't. If it comes out while you're here, then so be it. Otherwise, you might not have one. You are only half-fae, after all."

I stifle a retort.

Without another word, I throw the plate of food onto his lap and ignore his flinch when he's forced to move his shoulder. I stand and stomp away.

With or without a gift or a job, I will be useful in this realm. Somehow, some way.

18

"WAKE UP!"

A chair screeches across the floor, rousing me from my dreamless slumber. I blink a few times, take in my surroundings. My heart sinks.

Still in the Unseelie. Why did I think I'd actually wake to find Oliver near?

My belly grumbles, and I sit up in the oversized chair I fell asleep in. Eric is in the bed to my right, his face twisted in agony, but awake.

Killian, Laoise, and Gar are seated on the sofa in the corner. Aibell stands at the table, her hair still flying from her swift entrance. Her cheeks are pink from the outside chill. She sifts through a linen bag, pulling out fruit and bread.

I stretch my knotted neck and frown. Am I the only one who slept? I bite my lip. Of course I was. Fae don't sleep. I keep forgetting the little things. Little but important.

With a final stretch, I stand, brushing off my two-day-old clothes. Ew. I stink. I don't even want to remind myself of my lack of toothbrush. Faeries probably snap their fingers and magically clean themselves.

"Up and at 'em, Caoine. We need to talk." Aibell holds out

a piece of lime-colored fruit I've never seen before. "First, eat. I don't need you fainting while we trek through the forest."

I stride toward her and take the fruit, feel the soft give of its flesh beneath my fingers. "Are we going to save my dad?"

Her hazel eyes hold mine. "Like I said, we need to talk." She turns to her friends. "Hungry?"

Gar grumbles. "I had some beetles earlier."

My eyes go wide, and Killian chuckles. Laoise gives me that mysterious smile that makes my insides crawl.

"Fine. I don't care." Aibell throws down the rest and steps away so she stands between the table and the seating area.

I shift uncomfortably with that fruit still squeezed in my fist. Aibell places her good hand on her hip.

"I have some news." Her gaze is on the other fae, but I know her words are for me. "It turns out Raghnall needs Caoine for a reason, and he won't let her cross to the Mortal Realm until he gets what he wants."

Eric snorts, then hisses in pain. "I could've told you that."

She glares at the boy. "It's more than what you think, silly prince."

His only response is a second hiss that has nothing to do with his injury.

Cat's sister turns back to the group. "Raghnall sent Eric to retrieve Caoine under the pretense that he wanted to finish his spell to open the Unseelie Veils for good. This was only half true."

She pins him with another look, and his shoulders slump, contrary to the way he looks at her. I can almost see redheaded Eric, his temper barely contained.

"He wants something more." Her leather clothes squeak as she straightens. "I believe it has to do with his wife —"

"That's enough!" Eric scrambles up from his bed, his chest heaving, fist clenched.

Aibell rolls her eyes. "Fine. We won't talk of your beloved father —"

"I didn't say he was be —"

"*But* the fact remains that Caoine's purpose here goes deeper than even you believed, *prince*."

She pauses long enough for my nails to dig into that sweet-scented fruit, for the juice to dribble down my hand.

"Something happened during that stunt you pulled on Samhain. Something . . . not expected."

Killian tilts his head. "Not expected by whom?"

She sighs. "By anyone. Even King Raghnall didn't know this would happen."

I finally find my voice. "That what would happen?"

Laoise's eyes glint. "Raghnall seeks the books for more than just completing his original spell. He has a greater purpose in his quest for the pair."

"And for Caoine," Killian says.

Aibell nods. "Getting Caoine out of the Unseelie Realm might not be as simple as we first thought."

My heart trips over an invisible current. "Why?" Also, I'm not leaving here without my dad.

Gar strokes his beard. "The spell Eric enacted on Samhain unleashed something that could affect the king's wife? What would this entail?"

Eric's face is red. "I said, don't talk about her."

Aibell glares at him. "Afraid Caoine will find out your dirty little secret?"

He lunges at her but stops as Gar matches his movements. "It's not my secret to tell! I just want nosey outsiders to keep their business out of my family."

"What?" She huffs. "That *family* wasn't even yours until a few years ago. You have as much claim to them as I do, *princeling*. Get off your high horse and either join our efforts or leave." She scowls. "I thought you said you'd changed sides, anyway. Or does your allegiance still lie with your father?"

"I feel no love for my father, I can assure you." His jaw

clenches. "Whatever event you're referring to has nothing to do with the past. There's no reason to bring it up."

She chortles. "Like I said, afraid."

He narrows his gaze. "From what I know, Raghnall wanted Caoine here to complete the spell I began on Samhain. Her dad was kept here simply as assurance that she would comply. What new information could you possibly have beyond that?"

Aibell crosses her arms. "That spell you did that night? The one that failed, I might add? Aubree used magic to try to prevent you from succeeding. Strong magic. Magic that literally holds the threads of our worlds together."

Laoise's voice is calm. "But it failed just as Eric's magic failed."

I step forward. "Aubree told me this before Eric—" I clear my throat. "Before I came here."

Killian gazes at me in curiosity. "So you already know, earthling?"

"What happened?" Eric asks.

"I—I don't know. Not for sure." I shrug. "Aubree wouldn't tell me the whole story until she was sure. I, uh . . ." I clear my throat. "I never got the full answer before I arrived here."

Eric's cheeks pink.

Aibell's mouth pulls down at the corners. "You know nothing more?"

I shake my head.

Killian turns to Aibell. "Were you not able to learn more of the consequences of the failed magic?" He continues to look like a supermodel, despite how vexed he looks.

"Unfortunately, my informant refused to share any more of the situation. The only thing she would say is we need to retrieve both the Book of Judgment and the Book of Discernment if we're to correct what's been done."

I blink. "Eric has the Book of Discernment." I look to him.

His shoulders fall, and Aibell's jaw drops.

19

AIBELL WHIRLS ON ERIC, her eyes on fire. "You have the book?"

His nostrils flare as he glares at me. I swallow. Oops. Was that supposed to be a secret?

"Yes," he says. The pulse along his neck thrums. "We were on the way to retrieve it before Gimpy here gave me her present." He gestures toward his bandaged shoulder.

Aibell snarls under her breath.

"This is wondrous news!" Laoise floats onto her toes as if she can truly levitate. Which, come to think of it, she probably can. "We only need to locate one of the two tomes."

I nod. "Eric had the other book, too. Until it was stolen."

"The Unseelie prince possessed both tomes for a time?" Killian's gaze is filled with awe and something else. Worry?

Eric shakes his head. "Not exactly. The Book of Judgment was taken from me just before I procured the Book of Discernment. I never actually had both in my possession at the same time."

"But why?" Killian asks. "Why would you need such books?"

Aibell answers Killian's question without taking her eyes

off Eric. "Because he is his father's son. Why have one book when you can have both?" She tilts her head. "Or was your real plan simply to hand both books over, along with Caoine, the minute you had them all?"

The prince curls his hands into fists. "Haven't you heard a word I've said? I have no intention of allowing my father to gain possession of those books. That's the reason I was trying to get them both in the first place."

Aibell crosses her arms. "So says the son of the Unseelie king."

Red flushes across Eric's cheeks, and I know he's about to do something he'll regret.

"I believe him." My heart pounds against my ribcage.

"Why, human?" Gar's voice is gruff but echoes the look reflected on each of the faerie's faces.

"Because . . ." I nibble on my lip. "Because he had every chance to hand me over, to give me to his father, but he didn't. He saved me. More than once, actually."

Eric's gaze drops to the floor, and the steam leaves him.

I continue. "He really did intend on obtaining both books simply to keep them safe from his father."

Aibell nods. "Well, now he's got a new purpose." She steps forward. "We need to get both books, but not simply to keep them from King Raghnall's possession."

I glance between her and the other fae. "But first we save my dad, right?"

"Obtaining the books is more important."

My eyes go wide. This again? Why does my dad compare so little to those dumb books?

Killian's chin lifts, his stance majestic, his face proud. "Aibell has been tasked with the job of delivering both books to Queen Faílenn of the Seelie Realm."

Aibell releases a breath, her shoulders tense.

"Is this true?" I ask.

"Queen Faílenn is indeed looking for both books." She

motions to those around her. "We have pledged to fulfill the task."

"No." Eric's stern voice makes me jump.

I blink. "Why not? Won't delivering the books to the Seelie Realm put them as far from your father's reach as possible? Isn't that what you want?"

His jaw flexes in anger, and the crimson color returns to his face. "Not if it means giving the queen even more control over us."

Killian's voice is steady and soft. "King Raghnall has broken the Laws of Necessity. He must be punished."

"This is exactly what I mean!" Eric scrubs a hand through his hair. "The Unseelie are already under her control, already prisoners in our own realm. Why should we give her any more power over us?"

Aibell spits to the side. "Your father knew the law, and he broke it. What more would you expect from the Seelie queen?"

I swallow as my eyes bounce from faerie to faerie. I have no idea what they're talking about, but now is clearly not the time to ask.

Laoise almost sighs her reply. "The queen demands to possess both books in the Seelie Realm. To keep all the realms at peace."

Eric splutters. "But that will make the Fae Realms unbalanced. This isn't fair!"

Aibell rolls her eyes. "Your father should've thought of that before he attempted to lock the Seelie Realm up for good, making the Mortal Realm his new playground."

Eric's upper lip curls like he smells something bad.

Aibell ignores him. "Our orders are clear. Queen Faílenn wants both books in her possession as recompense for the misguided actions of the king. He'll regain the right to hold the Book of Judgment in the Unseelie Realm once she deems his punishment lifted."

Eric grabs his head and spins away. "This is unbelievable."

"Decide now, Unseelie prince." Aibell glares at the back of his head. "Will you join us in our quest, or are you against us?"

My heart speeds away as Eric stays planted in his spot, silence his only answer.

"Eric," I whisper. I step toward him, our bodies close, a waft of that earthen scent tumbling in my direction. "Please, Eric. They're right. There's no better place for the books if we want to keep your father from getting his hands on them."

I can almost see the sour look on his face, even though he still faces away from me.

"We can't save my dad until we do this. Please?"

He drops his head. Fear stabs through my core as I think he's about to walk out the door, never to return. But then he does the opposite, surprising me.

"Fine." His face is no longer red, but now his shoulders droop. "I will retrieve the Book of Discernment for you. I will assist in the recovery of the Book of Judgment." He lifts a finger at Aibell. "But I want the queen to remember this. She owes me."

Aibell doesn't hesitate. "Done."

The other fae gasp. My eyes grow large. Making a deal with a faerie is no light commitment. Especially one not considered carefully.

How can Aibell speak for the queen in such a way?

"It's settled then?" Killian asks. "We're on a quest?"

Aibell nods, makes eye contact with each of us. "Our quest has begun."

Spirited music carries on the evening breeze. Woodwinds and strings and even the *thump, thump, thump* of a drum.

Laughter spills around our group where we sit along a bank of pink grass that lives during winter. Bits of snow cling wet to my pants. The sky hangs lavender and waning above. The scent of burning wood and strawberries drifts from the camp of faeries just a few yards away.

A chill works its way down my spine. Have they seen us? Do they care?

"That one there." Aibell peeks above the mound of earth that conceals the six of us. "She's the one we want."

Laoise simply nods before disappearing into a ball of light small enough to fit in the palm of my hand.

I gasp, in awe of her pint-sized wings that flutter as fast as a hummingbird's. Her glow is brighter than a star yet doesn't hurt even a little to look at.

The same ball of light that pretended to be Oliver. Or another wisp, that is. I assume it wasn't actually Laoise who tried to lead me astray.

She zips toward the few dozen fae who dance and sing the night into existence.

"I still say this is a bad idea," Eric grumps from his spot, his bad arm slung across his body in a kerchief I fashioned from a spare shirt.

None of the other faeries wanted to help him, and they certainly didn't want him hanging around their lair while we were on our mission. So despite his pain and the fact that he isn't done healing, he came along.

Aibell is not in the mood to play nice. "I'll let you know when your opinion is wanted."

She doesn't look at him, her gaze firm on the spot where Laoise hovers near three female faeries.

"I'm telling you," Eric says, "I grew up in these woods. I know these backcountry fae better than you. They won't like a wisp spying on them, and they won't give us what we want without payment."

Gar grunts.

Killian's gaze finds Eric. "We're fully aware of how our kind function, shamed prince."

Eric shakes his head. "It's not enough—"

"Shut it." Aibell sniffs. "You'll make us get caught, and then I'll have to kill you."

He rolls his eyes and looks away. I return my sight to the party. My heart races and my palms sweat regardless of the dropping temps.

The boy is right. Making deals with the fae is tricky business, and something in my gut warns me to run. But we need this information.

I swallow and focus on Laoise, who flits from faerie to faerie.

"Why did you do it? Why did you decide to join us?" I whisper to Eric.

His gaze meets mine. "I'm not letting you leave my sight."

I nibble my lip. "Fair enough." He did work really hard to get me here. "Tell me again how this is going to work?"

He doesn't look as annoyed as I expect him to. "There's a

faerie at that party who knows things. Laoise hopes to fly close enough to whisper in her ear, ask her where the Book of Judgment resides. If the faerie believes one of her friends has posed the question—and if she's consumed enough faerie wine—her lips should be plenty loose."

"And she'll spill the beans on where the book is hidden?"

He dips his chin.

I blow out a steady breath. "As long as we get that thing before your father does." Tears prick my eyes. "Every day that passes with my dad in his care freaks me out."

"The king has plans, Caoine. Big ones."

I nod, my heart heavy. "Which is why he needed me."

"Which he doesn't have." Eric shifts forward. "He needs you and both books. Your dad is safe. I promise you this."

I close my eyes, exhale. What if he's wrong?

"If all goes well, we'll get the location of the missing book from that fae down there." Eric nods toward the party.

"Right. Then we can save my dad. One step at a time, I guess." I pause and look back to Eric, my voice low, only for him. "Thank you again for helping me. I get that you could easily hand me over to your father."

He shakes his head, his face clouded. "No, that's no longer an option. In fact, I don't understand why it ever was."

"What do you mean?"

"My relationship with the king. It's . . . strained at best. I never knew him as a child, only met him a few years back. I still don't quite understand why I was so eager to please him." He squints, his gaze directed at the blue-tinged mountain range basking in the distance. "It's like it was a dream. And now I'm out of it. You know?"

I nod, even though I don't know. Not really. The dreams I encounter while in my banshee song are different. Deadly. But also filled with hope at times.

"Well, for what it's worth, thank you." I pause, lick my lips.

"Um, so, question . . . about my song. Aibell said I shouldn't let anyone know I'm a banshee. Why not?"

Eric frowns, begins to reply—

Until Aibell tosses me an evil look that says to be quiet.

Oh crud. Did she hear? The last thing I need is to be in trouble with that chick.

We sit in silence another few minutes, waiting for Laoise to do her magic. The sky grows more purple, the air around me colder, the music louder. How much longer can this take?

And then . . .

"She's found her." Aibell's voice is hopeful. "Wait. What are they—no!" She grabs her sword in her good hand. "They have her."

My heart pounds in discord with the faerie drums, my gaze searching for any sign of Laoise.

There is none.

The fae took Laoise. And it doesn't look like they have any intention of giving her back.

21

EVERY FAERIE in our group is on their feet in seconds. I warily glance to the party below, sure we'll be seen. Killian's height alone will give us away.

"This is unfortunate indeed," he says.

Gar pulls his spear from behind his shoulder. "Obnoxious faerie scum! I'll make them—"

"You'll make them nothing, Gar." Aibell's lips are pressed tight. Despite her tough-girl act, it's obvious she cares for this troop of oddball fae. "I'll try to speak sense to them."

"Sense?" Eric cradles his arm as his face grows red. "Are you kidding? They're completely wasted, and the party hasn't even started! There's zero chance—"

He grabs her bare arm but immediately recoils as if she's burned him, disgust splashed across his face.

Aibell jumps in his face. "Oh and I suppose they'll listen to a traitor princeling like you?"

Gar has her back, his whiskers trembling even though he stands a full head shorter than she. He shouts something I don't quite comprehend. The language of the fae?

Then Killian joins the fray, his gentle voice a peaceful mix amid the chaos. His words are definitely not English.

Yep, they've switched languages.

Eric and Aibell are practically nose-to-nose. His neck bulges, shoulders thrown back. She appears to have grown three inches to meet his eye.

I glance to the dancing in the field below. Not a single faerie has veered from their jumping and hopping around that bonfire. The three faeries Laoise was spying on are gathered together, giggling. One holds a glass jar with a crude lid made from a leaf. Inside is a bright dot, flying in circles.

Laoise. *Crud*.

Another faerie grabs the jar and shakes it, smacking Laoise against the sides. The three laugh harder. My insides clench.

This is all my fault. These faeries—Aibell and Killian and Gar and even poor Laoise—are here because they're trying to help me find a way home. Out of Faerie. Back where I belong.

I bite my lip and skirt around the huddle of flying words and boiling tempers. It takes me four-and-a-half seconds to stumble down the winter-grassy hill, and none of the party fae even look my way.

Wow, when a faerie's drunk, they're drunk.

Then I'm standing before the three female faeries who kidnapped Laoise. All are taller than I am, something I'm not used to. I swallow as three pairs of eyes fall on me.

One faerie is plump with a large nose and whiskers on her chin. Her yellow hair has twigs stuck inside dreads, her gnarled fingers yanking at a stray lock.

Another has cerulean hair, cropped tight to her scalp, a tattoo splashed across one side of her face. One edge of the tattoo is the Unseelie symbol of enslavement.

My stomach twists in knots.

The last faerie—the one who holds Laoise—is beautiful. Her glossy nut-colored hair tumbles over delicate shoulders, eyes as blue as a summer's sky, sparkling, a perfect accent to her smile of too white teeth. Her cheekbones are high, her neck long and elegant. She literally could've stepped out of a major motion picture.

"Well, hello human," she says.

My heart stops beating.

She knows I'm not full fae. But how? Is it *that* obvious?

Her eyes rake me over like I'm her next meal, and a shiver scuttles across my back.

I take a deep breath. "That's my friend. I'd like her back." Swallow. "Please."

I wince. Should I have been so polite? Aren't faeries unkind to those who appear weak? Dread pools in my belly.

The beautiful faerie considers me. "What do you say, Elan?" Her gaze falls on the plump faerie. "Shall we give the play toy back?"

Elan giggles, her double chin jiggling right along with her body.

I eye the glass jar, internally pleading with Laoise. Why won't she just change back into her full-sized self? Or disappear?

The beautiful faerie looks at me, head cocked. "Do you think we should give her back, Einin?"

Einin shakes her head. "What would be the fun in that?" Her tattoo crinkles with her smile, an open rose that now closes. "We found her. We earned our play toy, fair and square, Eithne. Surely even a *human* can understand that." Her eyes glitter with delight. "Finders keepers, right?"

Anger and fear burn behind my breastbone. What will they do with Laoise?

Before I can respond, all three of their gazes flick over my shoulder, landing on something far more interesting than me.

The others have joined me.

It's only in that second I recognize the lack of sound. The way the music has stopped, all commotion at a standstill, every bit of reverie now in complete silence.

I glance around. The entire party has stopped. Every faerie

eye is trained on me. The only sound is the fire crackling in the breeze. A puff of smoke wafts my way, making my eyes water. Did one of the faeries do that on purpose?

"Let her go." Aibell's voice is strong and clear at my back.

I freeze.

Eithne puckers her lips. "I don't think so, *neamini*. But thanks for playing."

An audible gasp comes from behind. I refuse to turn around, though.

"That's enough!" Eric's voice booms with authority, and I jump. Elan and Einin both scowl.

Eithne doesn't lose her smile. In fact, it grows. "It's an honor to have a *prince* among our ranks tonight, ladies." Someone near the fire chuckles, but everyone else stays quiet. "It's good to see you. Handsome as ever, I see." She licks her lips. "Bored of daddy's silly commands already? Come to join some real fun?"

"That's King Raghnall, to you, *Eithne*."

Her voice drops to a low purr. "Or . . . did you miss me?"

I can't help but make eye contact with Eric, his glance lingering on mine a beat too long.

He looks back to her. "Give the wisp back. Now."

She shakes the bottle, the soft ping of Laoise's body banging against the sides. Aibell starts. Gar growls.

"What will you give me?" Eithne's tone is taunting.

"Nothing. Give her back!" Eric takes a step toward the group, next to me.

Einin hisses. Elan clenches her jaw so those jowls wiggle again.

But Eithne just smiles. "Come now, princeling. Have you been away from Faerie for that long? Have you forgotten how this works? Faeries make bargains; we do not bow to demands."

Heat invades my ears, my cheeks, my neck. "We have nothing to give. Please."

Eric winces. *There I go pleading again. But what else can we do?*

"Please," Elan mimics. At least she doesn't giggle. She reaches out and strokes my cheek.

Something sharp stings my skin, and I flinch.

"Don't touch her," Eric warns.

The corner of Eithne's mouth curls up as she glances at him, then looks at me. "There's always something to give, human. Trust me."

"How about this?" Aibell raises her sword. "You give our friend back"—she glances around the partiers with ease—"and I won't tell *them* the real reason you're at this party."

Eithne's eyes flash, and her face pales.

Aibell nods. "I know the truth."

A few murmurs break out, but most of the fae stay silent. Elan and Einin look like they want to jump across our little circle and rip Aibell's throat out.

Eithne's grip on the glass jar tightens, her nostrils flaring. "You think you know me?"

"Nope. Not even a little. But I know a secret." Aibell wags her brow. "And I'm guessing you don't want it shared with the rest of your"—she glances around—"*friends*."

Eithne's face crumbles into pure hatred. She pulls in a shaky breath, and without warning, tosses the jar to Eric. "No matter. We've had our fun. I didn't have any grand plans for the stupid ball of light, anyway."

Eric doesn't take the lid off the jar but carefully holds it close to his body like a treasure.

Aibell spits to the side. "It was nice doing business with you."

I crinkle my nose. *I will never understand the fae.* The world tilts as a bout of vertigo forces me to fight to regain my balance.

Eithne crosses her arms. "Staying for the party? Or can we

get on with our fun without the grandparents hanging around to scold our every move?"

This draws laughter from the fae by the bonfire, and the music suddenly kicks into high gear.

The standoff is over. I exhale, finally.

A faerie not taller than my knee does a backflip right in front of me before running off to join a maypole dance by the fire. Laughter fills the air once more, not a single glance in our direction.

Elan and Einin remain frozen, their demeanor that of cats ready to spring on their prey. Only Eithne looks relaxed, although my guess is, beneath the surface, she's nothing of the kind.

"Until next time." Aibell nods and walks away, Gar and Killian in her wake.

Eric waits for me, his eyes on the beautiful faerie. My feet feel sluggish as I walk toward him.

She takes one last look at him. "Nice seeing you, Eric." Her gaze flitters over me before settling back on him. "Don't hesitate to stop by if you ever get bored. I always welcome an old . . . *friend*."

He clenches his fist as she rejoins the party, tucking the glass jar close to his side before motioning me to move ahead of him. Someday I might ask what all that means.

But not today.

22

WE DON'T STOP MOVING until we're far enough from the party that we no longer hear music. We rest among a grouping of rocks near a drop-off to a valley, clustered together in a formation perfect for seeing the view below.

Dots of white scatter the expanse beneath us, trees displaying their pastel colors in a most regal manner. A slender creek brimming with fuchsia water winds its way uphill through the mass of colorful foliage.

I sigh. My head pounds, and my blood feels too thin within my veins.

Aibell slumps on a large rock, her withered hand resting on the hilt of her sword neatly tucked against her side. Gar grabs a rock short enough to sit on, and Killian chooses to stand, his keen eyes trained on the woods around us. Eric ceremoniously squats to release Laoise from her captivity.

A whoosh of air rockets from the glass, and an explosion of light brightens the world around us, before it plunges us back to the growing darkness of night.

The dark-skinned fae lands on her feet just before her knees give out. Eric is close enough to get a hand under her arm before she falls flat.

I shift uncomfortably, once again the half-faerie who doesn't belong.

Laoise gasps as if each breath could be her last. Her hands go out like her world is spinning. Which it probably is, considering how Eithne shook the container before we were able to retrieve it.

"Are you all right?" Aibell doesn't even look at Laoise, her words muffled into the arm where her head rests.

Laoise nods. "I am. Just shaken."

I bite my lip against the obvious pun.

Eric helps the wisp get steady on her feet. "What were you thinking, getting so close?"

She sighs as she brushes dirt and twigs from her clothes. "I attempted to whisper multiple times." She lifts her palms. "I wanted her to think one of her companions had spoken."

I frown. Why did they believe those faeries would have that information in the first place? I close my eyes from a wave of dizziness before I can voice my question.

"What's done is done." Aibell pushes off the rock. "We'll just have to find someone else we can get the information from."

Irritation squiggles in my chest one second too long. I'm so tired of being told only half the plan. "Why did we need that faerie anyway?"

Aibell swings her gaze to me, as if it's the first time she's seeing I'm even present. "We didn't need her. We needed what she knows."

"Eithne is a Seer," Eric says.

Aibell huffs and walks toward the cliff's edge.

"Which means?" I ask.

Laoise's silver gaze is steady on mine. "A Seer is what humans would call a fortune teller."

Killian grunts. "Not those who would deceive just to make money, mind you." He sets his bow and arrows on the ground beside him. "One who truly sees the future. And the past."

I nod. "So a clairvoyant? Wouldn't she have known we were coming?" My stomach sours, and I suddenly have the urge to wretch.

Gar grunts. "Not necessarily. Sometimes Seers get visions of their own accord, see things past, present, or future, no matter if they intend to or not. Otherwise they need to know what event or person they're looking for."

Laoise smiles. "Or object."

Eric's gaze finds mine. "The Book of Judgment."

Laoise tilts her head, not one piece of her green hair out of place. "We needed a Seer to learn its location. If my question was posed correctly, it should have triggered her abilities, making the location clear to her."

Aibell purses her lips. "If that's even possible."

Eric throws her a glare. "It is."

Laoise explains when she sees my confusion. "Aibell questions the ability to find such a magically powerful object through a Seer. She believes the books may have protection to prevent them from being stolen by any fae who has access to a Seer."

I nod. Makes sense. I look at Eric, at the crinkle in his brow, the way his eyes are narrowed at Aibell. Why does he believe it will be so easy to find?

"No matter," Aibell says. "It was worth a shot. If we can't use a Seer, we'll just have to figure out another way."

"And we definitely need both books?" I ask. "The queen was clear it had to be both?" I don't voice my concern that I just want this part over so we can save my dad. Pronto.

My pulse quickens, and I feel sick. I place a hand on my belly. Why is my heart beating so fast, and why is my body suddenly spiraling?

Eric nods. "We need both books."

Aibell crosses her arms. "Which would've only been one if you hadn't lost it."

His eyes flash red before melting back to their usual hazel.

"I told you, I didn't . . . I wasn't—" He grimaces and places a hand to his head. "Since I've been back, I haven't been thinking straight. I can't explain it. I just don't know what happened."

Aibell snorts. "Says the son of the king with the master plan."

Killian, Gar, and Laoise stare at Eric.

An urge to defend him swells in my belly, but how can I? What she said is true. How can any of us believe he's innocent? That he had no control over his actions?

I don't know what to say, don't know what side to take.

But it doesn't matter.

Spots float before my eyes, and I sway. Before I can put another coherent thought together, I tumble to my knees.

Then everything goes black.

23

I'm a block of ice. I can barely get my eyes open, and I cannot move my fingers.

Sky, a deep plum, hangs above me. I suck in a lungful of air. Shards of glass rip apart the flesh inside me; I push it out with force. A thick cloud of white bellows from my lips, dances along my sight, before racing into the ether.

The crisp air shocks my lungs, and I cough. And cough.

The action alone racks my body into convulsions, but somehow I find the strength to sit up. A blanket covers me, so I push it aside.

My head spins. My belly lurches. And I vomit.

Fantastic.

Freezing, sick, and—wait, where am I?

My belly emptied itself down the side of a large rock on which I sit. I tremble, but it has nothing to do with the cold. In fact, I can't even feel the chill anymore. My body is growing accustomed to the Unseelie Realm.

"How do you feel?" a low voice lilts in the darkness.

Oliver? Maybe I've finally woken from my nightmare and I've simply finished singing my banshee lament, my boyfriend ready to hold me tight and never let go.

I glance up. My heart sinks.

Killian sits on the edge of the rock where I lay. We're in the same spot we were earlier, just *on* the rocks instead of *beside* them. Someone moved me.

With a wince, I place a hand across my stomach. "I feel just peachy."

Killian's gaze narrows, his brow pulls slightly.

My other hand finds my forehead. *Stop spinning.* "What happened?"

My gut continues to bubble, and I swallow back bile.

I must've made quite the face because he holds out a water pouch. I hesitate only a second before accepting it, the cool, clean liquid a blessing on my throat.

"Poison." Killian shifts but remains seated, his back perfectly straight, attention at the fullest.

I frown. "I was poisoned?"

He nods. "One of the three from the party."

He motions along his jaw, and a soft throbbing suddenly comes to my attention on my own face.

I feel the skin along my cheek where Elan touched me. Pain ricochets from my ear to the top of my head. A muffled cry escapes, and I squeeze my eyes against the sting.

"We don't believe it to be serious. Merely a faerie prank." Killian takes off his bow, sets it beside him as he rests back on one elbow.

"Great, a prank." I roll my eyes. "I'd love to see how it would feel if they meant to kill me."

He flinches. "You would?"

I sigh. *Sarcasm and fae don't mix.* "No." I glance around. "Where are the others, anyway?"

"Aibell and Gar escorted Laoise back to the mushroom tree so she can recover. They were unsure if they should move you. I was confident the poison was merely topical and would work its way from your system in a few hours. I volunteered to remain with you until it had done so."

"What about—?"

"The son of the Unseelie king searches for a plant to aid in your recovery. He'll likely return soon."

"Eric's looking for medicine? For me?" Heat fills my cheeks.

"Well, he's looking for a medicine he believes will heal you." Killian shrugs at my confused look. "I may have sent him to search for a plant that doesn't exist."

I bite my lip against a laugh. "You sent him on a snipe hunt?" A smile breaks my façade for the first time in days.

"A snipe hunt?"

I shake my head. "It's basically a wild goose chase."

Killian remains flummoxed.

I sigh. "You sent him on a meaningless quest. For what reason?"

He blinks. "To send him away from me, of course. Otherwise he and I would've been the only two awake."

Now I do laugh. "And conversing with the son of the Unseelie king would truly be that bad?"

Killian's gaze turns hard, and his jaw flexes. I continue to laugh. Forgiveness is not a strong suit of faeries.

I stretch. The sick in my belly has subsided, and my head is finally sitting straight. He's right. The poison did work its way out of my system.

"So it's just you and me?"

I pull that blanket back up over my shoulders now that the night chill is sawing into my skin again.

The faerie nods. "Until the others return, yes."

"And then what? Are we still looking for a Seer?"

"Or something similar."

I huff. "Peachy."

He purses his lips. "You keep referring to that fruit. Does it have great significance to you?"

I open my mouth. Close it. "I just like peaches." Since I have no idea what to say to that.

Killian nods, satisfied with my answer. We sit in awkward silence for a minute. Or maybe ten. But . . . so much awkward.

I clear my throat. "Any chance you and I could take a quick trip to the castle to save my dad?"

A sharp pain sticks deep in my chest as I consider what he might be going through right now.

Killian's only response is a raised eyebrow.

Right. I suck in a breath. "So will Eric be back anytime soon?"

"The son of the Unseelie—"

"Wait, wait, wait." I wave my hands like the dork I am. Killian stills. "Why do you keep referring to him in such a fancy manner? Is saying his name all that bad?"

Killian's nostrils flare. "You may have befriended the young man, may have chosen to trust him, but the rest of us will not follow in your footsteps. The boy is a traitor to our realm and doesn't deserve the privilege of a name."

I shake my head. "I'm confused. Eric's a traitor because he followed a job his father gave him, the *king* of the Unseelie. Apparently, a plan that was against the better judgment of the rest of the realm. Why do you say King Raghnall's name with reverence but hate his son so much?"

"The king of the Unseelie is still the king, regardless of his actions or character. He deserves respect from his subjects until he's removed from the throne."

I snort. "So you totally disagree with everything King Raghnall stands for, so much so that you hate the son who enacted his plan, yet you still respect the mastermind behind the whole thing?"

"I don't expect a daughter of Earth to understand the ways of the fae."

Daughter of Earth? I blink. "And I don't get how you can hate one person for something and not hate another for exactly the same thing."

Killian doesn't flinch. "Like I said, I don't expect you to understand my logic."

I shrug. "Fine. We agree to disagree."

We sit quiet for another minute. I fiddle with my blanket. Bite the inside of my lip. Look around the darkness of the trees for any sign of movement. There is none.

Then I huff. "Is it because Eric's not a legitimate son? Because the queen of the Unseelie isn't his mother?"

Killian only shows his annoyance by tilting his head. "Please don't speak of the late queen in such a fashion."

I grimace. "In what fashion? I only said she's not Eric's mom. You hate Eric. Shouldn't that make you happy?"

He sighs.

"What is it with you fae and not speaking about the queen? Eric pretty much flipped when Aibell mentioned her yesterday. Why does no one want to talk about her?"

Killian's gaze bores into mine. "Can we kindly change the subject?"

"But—" I slump where I sit. "I just want to understa—"

"You will not understand our kind. You're not one of us."

My insides turn to ice. Of course it would come down to this. I'll always be more human than fae, simply because of where I grew up. But that doesn't change the fact I'm not one or the other. I will never truly belong.

Tears sting the backs of my eyes. If only Oliver were here. He would understand. He would hold me and make me feel wanted. The pain of missing him burns my chest like hot coals.

I clench my jaw and look away. "So what? You're loyal to Aibell? Your only interest in getting me home is to please her?"

"Why would you think that?"

"You just said it yourself. I'm not one of you. I clearly don't understand your ways. You hate that I'm friends with Eric, although I think *friends* is too strong a word." I pause. "Aibell is helping me get home because her sister is one of my best friends. Does it pain you to help me at Aibell's word? Even though you can't stand the sight of me?"

Killian frowns. "I never said such a thing, daughter of Earth. I don't hate you, nor have I ever hated you."

Warmth cuts through the cold air, tickles along my skin, inside my chest.

His face softens. "I am committed to aiding you because I choose to, Caoine. You are important, and I have a role to play in your story."

I open my mouth to protest but fall silent. He has a role to play? What does that even mean?

The faerie gives me a gentle smile. "As long as you're under my care, you will be protected, Caoine Roberts. I will defend you to the end."

My eyes go round. The end. The end of what? And why does this suddenly sound like the climax of a movie where he's about to run into battle to save me?

I swallow. "Erm . . . thanks?"

He nods. "You may not understand our ways, but know I'm faithful. Even when no one else keeps their word."

A chill spills along my spine. As much as this heart-to-heart has helped me get to know him, he's slightly creepy. Maybe *not* being alone with this guy is a wise choice from now on.

"Thanks," I say.

Before I can pick his brain about anything else, a cry pierces the night, a wail that sounds remarkably like a banshee song.

Killian grabs his bow, and my heart sinks to my toes.

24

ERIC LEAPS onto the rock inches from my side, his hand across my mouth before my ridiculous girly scream can escape.

Instinct is to claw the boy's eyes out for touching me, but I refrain. Killian's gaze narrows, but he doesn't loose an arrow at my protector. Thankfully.

Another banshee-like cry echoes in the purple night, and we tense collectively. Eric slowly removes his hand as the three of us look around.

I narrow my gaze to see into the darkness, but the action is futile. "What—?"

"Shh," Eric warns, his finger on his lips.

"A scarlet reynard?" Killian asks, the string of his bow still taut.

Eric gives a quick nod. "A pack of them. Probably a mile or so out. Still . . ."

Killian purses his lips. "Too close."

"Too close," Eric confirms.

"We must leave at once." Killian hops to the ground.

Panic floods my chest. "What about Aibell? And the others? If they come back, the scarlet . . . *whatever* might eat them!"

Eric's brows raise to his hairline, the rest of his demeanor unusually calm. "They might tear the others to shreds, but they won't eat them."

My jaw hangs open.

He shrugs. "Scarlet reynards don't have a taste for the fae. It's a shame they're stuck in our realm."

He winks before holding out a hand to help me up.

I attempt to bat him away, but he grabs me anyway. I sputter as he ushers me to the ground, his hands brushing my arms. I forgot how fast the fae can move when they want to.

He sucks in a quick breath, his eyes closing for a split second as he absorbs my power. Of peace. Of calm. Of *whatever*. A chill spreads across my arms. So odd.

Both his arms are free, and there's no sign of the sling or even an injury. He's clearly better. I open my mouth to ask but reconsider. Killian looks around us with urgency.

I dust off my clothes, then look where I sat. "What about the blanket?"

Eric absently holds my elbow as if to move me along, his eyes on the same spot of forest where Killian looks. This does nothing to ease my concern of scarlet reynards eating *me*.

"Leave it. We should move."

"But Aibell. Where — ?"

"The others will meet us Tumblecreek. I sent a message, securely." This last part he directs toward Killian, who nods.

"A message. How . . ." I bite my lip. "Wait, do you mean Nym?"

Another shriek splits the night air, this one followed closely by a second, then a third. None of the calls sound as far away as they had when they first broke the quiet gloom.

"Daughter of Earth," Killian whispers. "I suggest we listen to the traitor and finish this conversation at Tumblecreek."

I don't miss the nasty glare Eric gives him.

But we move as one, my footsteps the only sound breaking the calm around us. I trip over a clump of roots, and Eric catches my arm, righting me just as quickly. I *so* don't deserve the title of fae. If I hadn't sung my banshee song almost every night of my life, ushering death to humans whose time had come, I wouldn't believe I was even remotely related to faeries.

Well, besides my white hair and skin, not to mention my freakish eye color. But I don't have to stare at them all day, so they're easy to ignore. Sometimes.

As we carefully tread patches of snow and mud, I sigh. How many days has it been since I last sang my banshee song? I dig my nails into my palms and blink away tears.

It's curious that something that has plagued me my entire life is now something I miss.

The song is part of me, after all. It defines me. Without my song, what am I, really? I have no role as a faerie. And I've never been very good at being human.

I swipe at a tear that threatens to spill over my cheek, look away from the fae who walk beside me so they won't see this bout of emotion that has decided to rear its ugly head at the most inopportune moment.

Will my song ever return? Will I make it back home? A spike of fear pierces my heart, and I concentrate on *not* falling flat on my face. What if I return home to find Oliver like, old? Married? *With children?*

I stifle a gag, and Eric gives me a confused glance.

Oh my gosh. I've got to stop obsessing. *Stay alive, Caoine. Concentrate on running from the scarlet reynards.*

One thing at a time. "Your arm's better," I say after walking for a few minutes in silence.

Eric nods. "The fae heal quickly, just as we have the power to heal others."

"Why didn't Killian just heal you when he took out the arrow?"

"The arrow was spelled. He did what he could, but it still took my body some time to heal itself."

"Spelled?"

"Faeries aren't like humans, Caoine. We don't die easily. One of the few ways to kill us is with a weapon that's been spelled."

"O-kaaay." I drag out the word because this seems obvious.

He sighs. "The law in Unseelie is that the only weapons that can be spelled are those used by the king's guard."

"Oh." I blink. "So why was Aibell's arrow spelled, then? Did she mean to kill you?"

"Appears that way."

Huh. No wonder he hates her so much. "Couldn't she get in trouble for spelling a weapon without the king's permission?"

"It would seem that way, but . . ." He shrugs.

"Wow." I nibble my lip. Yeah. She's definitely not Cat. But that should make me feel better that she's willing to do whatever it takes to save me from the Unseelie, right?

I pull in a hard breath, release it. "Thanks for trying to help me, by the way."

His brow crinkles. "With what?" His low voice grates against the silence of the night.

"The, um, plant you were looking for. To help me." I avoid his gaze so I don't give away Killian's secret.

Eric snorts. "I wasn't looking for a plant."

My eyes go wide, frozen on the prince.

He shakes his head. "Don't you remember, Caoine? I'm a woodsprite. I grew up in the forest. I know every plant in existence."

He keeps his voice low, even though I know Killian can hear him with his supersonic faerie hearing.

My eyes trail over Killian, then back to Eric. "So you knew?"

He nods. "I knew."

I look back to Killian, but he doesn't flinch. Is he even embarrassed that he hadn't tricked Eric in the first place? And how exactly had he worded it, since he can't lie?

So many questions I would love answered about this species I belong to.

"So what were you doing?" I duck beneath the canary-yellow leaves of a tree with a trunk the width of a chair leg but with branches as big around as telephone poles. The mysteries of Faerie will never cease to amaze me.

"Working on exactly what we're doing right now." At my narrowed gaze, he goes on. "I needed to find Nym. He doesn't often come around when others are with me."

"He doesn't?"

Eric shakes his head. "He's shy like that." He chuckles, and I can almost see the old Eric, the redheaded one from West Lincoln High. "I was shocked he appeared to you, honestly. He must trust you."

"He trusts me? Why?"

He shrugs. "Who knows? Faen are weird."

Oh. Sure. Because I totally know what a faen is.

I clear my throat. "You trust him? Nym, I mean?"

He nods.

"But I thought you said not to trust anyone in Faerie."

Eric chuckles. "No, I told *you* not to trust anyone in Faerie. I've lived here my whole life. I've got better judgment when it comes to that type of thing."

I bite my lip, hesitate. "And you don't trust Aibell."

At this he clenches his hands, looks away. "I don't."

An image of Cat flutters through my mind. Warmth spreads across my chest. I'm not wrong to trust her, though. "Did you sense something? When you touched her earlier?"

He shrugs. "I feel something every time I touch someone. Why would that be any different?"

But he avoids looking at me.

Fine. Change the conversation. "So you found out something during your *not* search for the magical plant?"

"I did."

I wait a beat, but he doesn't elaborate. I growl under my

breath. *Why is Eric suddenly so cryptic? Almost like he enjoys watching me squirm.*

"Aaaaand?" I draw the word out to annoy him.

"And what?"

"And what did you find? Is there a Seer who will help us?"

"No." He steps over a large branch and holds out a hand to help me over.

I bat his hand away, then practically fall on my butt attempting to scale the thing by myself. But I *do* it. So there.

"Elaborate please," I gasp as I struggle to catch my breath.

"No, there is no Seer. Yes, I learned something helpful." He pauses, a smirk pulling at his lips. "It's not a person, but it should help us figure out where that book went."

"Awesome. What is it?"

"A well."

I lick my lips, blink. "A magical well?"

"Yep. And it happens to be near where I hid the other book. Two birds, one stone."

I swallow back the snarky comment I'm dying to make. "A magical well in Faerie. How . . . convenient."

He tilts his head but keeps his gaze ahead. "You'd be surprised just how rare they are."

I resist rolling my eyes. "Great. So you found a way to solve our problem and sent Nym to give word to Aibell—" I stop in my tracks. "What's that?"

A small pile of fur rests just off the path to our right. I bend down to investigate.

Eric cringes. "Caoine, not a good idea—"

"What has Caoine found?" Killian backtracks to us.

I flip the animal over. I'm not one for touching dead things and *definitely* don't trust any kind of animal in this desolate land, but something about it beckons me. Almost like it's calling to me.

It looks like a rabbit, but not. Its hind legs are too large, its ears far too small. My heart patters faster as I check the animal over. Is it hurt? And if it is, what can I even do?

Eric shifts. "Caoine, what are you doing? We don't have time for this."

Killian nods. "Much less the poor judgment on her part for touching an unknown creature within the realm."

I grumble but continue searching for a heartbeat on the poor pile of fluff. My hand tingles as I pick off a few leaves stuck to its fur. The thing is still warm—no way it's dead.

There's still no sign of a wound or reason for it to be unconscious when—

The thing snaps alert, eyes open, ready to bounce away. Which it does when I finally allow it freedom.

"Poor thing." I watch it hop with a frown. Something about it makes me want to keep it for a pet.

"What was wrong with it?" Killian asks.

I shake my head. "No clue. But it wasn't dead. Maybe it was in a deep sleep?" I turn to Eric. "Do creatures hibernate around here?"

He shrugs. "Does it matter? Come on. We need to get moving."

I huff but follow him, Killian taking the lead again. We walk in silence for another five minutes, a delicate breeze causing a chill to cling to my skin.

I twist my face into a scowl, weary of the constant march through the woods. "So . . . when do we get to this . . . Tumblecreek place? I've gotta pee."

Eric stops short, and I almost run into his back. "Really, Caoine?"

"What? It's true."

"Classy." He sighs and looks at me. "In answer to your question . . . now."

"Now?"

"*Now* is when we get there." He pulls back a low-hanging branch. "Welcome to Tumblecreek."

25

THE SMALL TOWN bustles with life, despite the fact that it's past midnight. I suppose this is how the town always looks. Or maybe it comes to life at night.

Either way, I feel as though I've crossed a portal into the faerie version of New York City.

The buildings are made of clay and mud with thatched roofs, but somehow stand nine, ten, and even twenty feet tall.

Faerie magic, for sure.

Some have glass panes, others have reflective glass like those on skyscrapers. A few of them have the symbol that signifies they are enslaved etched into their sides. Not like graffiti, but like it's art, a symbol of pride. I swallow.

The roads are dirt, shared by horse and wagon, bicycles, mopeds—do they run on gas?—and even some fae bopping around on skateboards.

Scents of food, sweet and fried, drift along with us—a waft of patchouli, a niggle of horse dung too, but a damp, briny smell tampers it down. Are we close to water?

The style of clothing is varied, too. A few faeries sport what I'd expect to see out of a fairy tale: plain neutral-colored pants and tunics, soft leather shoes, fabric hats.

Yet the rest look like they've stepped right out of my high school, with the latest jeans, designer shirts, and boots.

One kid skates by with a mohawk, ripped jeans, chains, and facial piercings.

Although, to be fair, he's probably a few hundred years old. All faeries look like teenagers, no matter their age.

My gaze shifts to Eric. Aubree told me she's over one hundred, Seamus closer to two hundred. How old is Eric?

A sharp pain stabs below my heart as I think of Seamus. Our friendship had been brief but fierce, his life cut short by the man who protects me now.

Eric glances at me, and my belly clenches. How have I grown to trust him? Knowing he killed Seamus and countless others? And how he tried to kill my dad.

My palms go sweaty, and I distance myself from the boy by a few feet. Faeries are good at deception. Staying focused on freeing my dad and getting home are my top priorities.

"Stay close." Eric sidles back up to me.

I bristle but stay where I am.

"You remember what happened at that party. Faeries can see right through you. They know you're part human. Believe me, they'll pull out every trick they've got."

Right. Stick close to a madman's side. A classic Friday night. I snort at my own sarcasm, but we move on, Killian in the lead.

Most of the faeries ignore us, merchants with small stands lining streets and crowding corners. Voices hawk their latest "wares from Earth," a few faeries even standing on small makeshift stages for more attention. One guy holds a pair of sneakers, totally not brand new, scuffed and muddy.

A lady calls for an asking price on a cell phone. I do a double take. Stuff from Earth apparently is in high demand.

I shrink closer to Eric's side. He's right. If they're this nuts about selling objects from Earth, I don't want to think about how'd they react to me. I swallow and duck my head.

We press through the crowd, moving just a few streets into town before Killian motions to a shop with a picture of a glass of beer and a half-naked woman on the front.

Awesome. Looks like my kind of place. I roll my eyes but follow them in.

The joint is a conundrum. To the left is an old-fashioned pub, straight out of *Lord of the Rings*: simple wooden tables and chairs, clay mugs filled with ale, sconces along the walls, and faeries dancing on tabletops.

To my right is a bar scene straight out of the twenty-first century: crisp, clean tables, a dart board on one wall, jukebox on the other, a bar that wraps around a large-screen TV, and a flashing neon sign advertising some brand of beer.

On this side is even more laughter and a fight tumbling around in the background.

I hide a smile. My dad would love this place. My smile fades.

Killian chooses the old-fashioned side. My heart settles a bit. But only a bit. Nowhere feels remotely safe. Eric slinks to a table along the wall and waves a server over. I dip my head once again.

A tall, lithe female arrives, ears pointed, skin the shade of a clementine, sapphire gaze. Her dress is simple; the way she looks at me is not. I swallow and avoid eye contact. But even from my position, I can see the way she looks at me, as if she wants to eat me alive.

Eric places a hand on my knee to steady me, but I slip away from his grip.

"What nectars do you have in season?" Killian asks, drawing her attention.

I release my breath.

"Bollenberry and nainspere." Her voice is musical. Light, airy, childlike.

I tilt my head in an effort to hear better.

"May I trouble you for a mug of the bollenberry?" Killian

graces her with a smile, something I've rarely seen since meeting him.

"And for the handsome couple?"

Her gaze burns my skin, her voice calling to me. I pull in a breath and lean an inch toward her.

Eric flashes her a smile, his dimple making an appearance. "Nothing for us, thanks."

"Such a shame," she lilts. "The pretty girl looks like she could use some refreshment. Perhaps some wine?"

Her voice—*that voice.* My head spins, and I close my eyes. I want to look at her, to stand and follow wherever she leads. The edge of my vision goes wonky.

"I have just the thing. The most delicious batch we've seen in years."

My body lurches, my legs filled with lead as I attempt to stand. I need to be with her. Now.

"No thanks." Eric's voice is loud and forceful as he makes me stay seated.

I flinch at his rudeness. Why is he being so mean to the beautiful faerie whose only desire is to see me satisfied?

She snorts and walks away. His fingers are back on my leg, digging deep into the fabric of my jeans. He pinches me.

I yelp. The spinning in my head comes to a halt, the haze around my vision gone. Pain shoots through my leg. "Ouch!" I glare at Eric.

"Better now?" He looks more aggravated with me than concerned.

I hit his hand away. "I'm fine. I was fine."

"She was enchanting you." Killian's faint smile is still in place, and I swear he giggles.

"She was—" My words lose steam, a crinkle forming along my brow.

Eric nods. "Her voice enchants humans. She wants you to drink the faerie wine. Way more mischief if you do."

I slump, hurt.

He pats my hand like I'm a child. "Like I said, everyone knows. Everyone will try to trick you. Stick close, Caoine."

I pout for thirty seconds. "So what are we doing here?"

"This is where we're meeting Aibell and Gar, maybe Laoise, depending on how she feels after her . . . accident."

"So we're stuck here for an unknown amount of time, I'm not allowed to eat or drink, and I shouldn't leave my babysitter's side. Fun night out."

Eric actually laughs. For the first time since West Lincoln High, the laugh actually reaches his eyes.

War rages inside me. I should hate him for killing my friend. But he looks so different, not at all like the faerie who wanted me dead.

I purse my lips. "What if they don't show?"

"They will show," Killian deadpans in his usual way.

Sure. I look out the window. My gaze lands on one of the hawkers on the street, waving an Adidas bag filled with who knows what above his head.

Eric follows my gaze. "They pay a pretty price for things from your world."

I look at him. Is it really *my* world? He lived there too, once.

The server swings by and tosses Killian's drink on the table. I'm careful not to look at her but can definitely hear her laughter as she walks away. My cheeks burn.

"It didn't used to be this way." Eric leans back in his seat. "There was a time when faeries could cross the Veils whenever they wanted. Markets like these were unheard of because the fae could have mortal goods in abundance."

"That symbol . . ." I glance at Eric's wrist, the spot where the enslavement symbol glowed on his skin Halloween night. The night he tried to kill me.

His wrist is clean, not a mark to be seen. Where did it go?

I lick my lips. "Aubree told me about it. It means to be enslaved, right?" Or revenge.

He nods. "The Unseelie believe they are slaves to the Seelie Realm."

"Why?"

"Because of the Laws of Necessity."

There's that phrase again. I sit a little straighter.

Killian glances at us but looks back to a raucous group of faeries dancing on a table across the room.

"The what?" I crinkle my nose.

Eric sighs. "I won't bore you with the history, but awhile back, King Raghnall and Queen Faílenn were allies. He messed up, made some bad decisions—decisions that could have ended life on Earth. So the queen put a plan in place before he could stop her. Powerful magic called the Laws of Necessity. Magic *we* feel enslaved by."

"Wow." Pause. "So what do they say? The laws, I mean."

He shrugs. "They basically say what I told you: Unseelie faeries aren't allowed to cross the Veils unless they're royalty and have permission."

"But you did. Your dad got you through without permission."

"Yeah, I'll bet the queen is still scratching her head over that one." The corner of Eric's mouth tilts up, the jester I remember from high school. "That's why it had to be me, since I have my father's blood in my veins. Only I could do it. As to how he did it without permission? I have no clue. I just did what he asked, and it worked." He shrugs again.

I look at him, closely. His face is soft, not at all what I remember from Halloween night.

His brown hair is messy. Hazel eyes watch me, and I'm struck with a memory, one of a deep shade of plum. The only thing obviously fae are his pointed ears.

"Why do you hide your appearance?" I lower my voice, but Killian can still hear.

Eric fiddles with a crack in the table. "Does it matter?"

"I've seen what you truly look like. Your skin glitters and

you have purple eyes. At Lincoln you had red hair and green eyes. Why bother to change? Why not be yourself?"

He swallows, his jaw flexing. Hardness envelops his face. "I just do." Then he smiles. "Don't you like the way I look, Caoine?"

That dimple digs into his left cheek, making him look younger than when we first met. Flirty Eric.

I hesitate. "You look fine. It just . . . seems like you go to a lot of trouble not to look like yourself."

Cockiness flits into his gaze. "I've got my reasons."

"Alert, friends." Killian straightens. "We have company."

My heart skips a beat, and I turn to the front door and lock eyes with Aibell.

She doesn't look happy.

26

"I'VE GOT THIS." Eric makes a face like he sucked on something sour as he stands.

I glance at the fae around me, dancing on tables, pulsing with laughter, spinning in conversation. My vision shifts, strangers coming in and out of focus. Like I'm the lone white gumball in a machine filled with rainbow skittles.

My gaze settles on our server, the one with sapphire eyes, who looks right at me. Her lips curl into a deadly smile. Every nerve in my belly quivers, and I fight not to swallow.

To show weakness.

A sense that I'm underwater clouds my brain, and I fight to stand. "I'll come too." My voice is too forced.

Killian blinks but shows no other emotion.

Eric turns to me. "I can —"

"No, thanks. I'd rather come with you."

A pungent puff of smoke, scented of licorice and mint, drifts from the table beside us, making my eyes water. But at least it clears my head from all the toxins and enchantments from the last few hours.

He gives me a hooded look but nods. Killian drains his

mug, then sets it on the table along with an . . . acorn? He leaves no other form of currency.

We head toward the front of the pub, me sandwiched between the two towering male faeries. My protectors. For now.

Aibell sees us coming, spins on her heel, and exits.

A chill slithers across my skin as we leave the warmth, both from the splash of frigid temps outside and because I leave the terror and uncertainty of a race of people who want nothing more than to play with me like a toy.

As if I deserve every minute of torture. All because I'm not like them. I am *other*.

I push the frustration that's been my life since birth away and follow the group around two corners and into the alley behind the pub.

Gar leans haphazardly against the clay wall, his fingers gripping his spear with enough tension to make me pause.

What do they know that I don't?

Eric and Aibell immediately begin to argue. Shocker.

"A faen?" Aibell growls at the prince. "You sent a faen to give me the message?"

"Do you have a better way of communicating with you?" Eric demands. "If you didn't understand the message, those were scarlet reynards back there." He points in the direction we came from. "There wasn't much time to warn you not to come that way, and I had to decide. Would you rather I allow you and shortie here to walk into a trap, to fend off those things by yourselves?"

Gar grunts at Eric's cutting words but doesn't engage. I swear I see his eyes flash red, though.

"That's not the point," Aibell spits. "He knows where we live now. You gave him the location of our shelter. Anyone could show up at our door now. The point of a secret hideaway is for it to remain *secret*."

"He's loyal to me. There's no danger—"

"Loyal?" Aibell snorts. "Just how thick are you? Do you truly believe he won't stab you in the back? There's no such thing as a loyal faen, you idiot."

Killian and I stay frozen, Gar seething with all the hate a fae can have toward another fae. Eric barely trembles, his gaze locked with Aibell's. Something shifts within him, and unease spills across me like sightless fog.

The only other time I saw him like this was Halloween night. The night he tried to kill Oliver. To kill my dad.

I squeeze my hands together so they won't shake, nausea my companion once more.

Please don't kill Aibell. I need her to get home.

We stand in silence, the two in a silent stare down.

Finally Eric breaks the tension. "That's *Prince* Idiot to you."

He shoves past her, walking deeper into the town, deeper into the darkness and noise of this unique part of faerie land. The others quietly fall into step.

I snake my way past Aibell and Gar and Killian to catch up with Eric. Despite the anger he wears like a crown, it's safer beside him. Why I know this, I have no idea. But I do.

"Where are we going?" I whisper.

A glance over my shoulder shows Aibell rolling her eyes, the other males walking stoically behind us. I stumble in the darkness but stay close to his side.

"Don't worry about it." Eric walks with all the confidence of an MMA fighter and the drive of a psychopath.

"Why all the secrets?"

"Well, first off I don't want her all up in my business." He tosses his head in Aibell's direction as he stalks forward. "Also, I just don't like people knowing everything about me."

"Oh." I can totally respect that. Being a hardcore introvert, I value my privacy above a lot of other things.

I walk beside him in silence. We turn another corner and head down a street of cottages, the road quiet and not a soul to be seen. I count each heartbeat, every awkward moment of my life crushing in on me all at once.

"Once we find the well, will we be done?" I finally squeak, just to break the silence.

Eric's shoulders tense as he walks, his eyes straight ahead, and I think he's not going to answer.

Until he does. "No."

"What else do we need to do?"

"You'll need to stop me."

My heart races inside my chest, and I fight to keep my blood pressure from skyrocketing. "Stop you?"

Finally, he pauses in his tracks and looks me square in the face. "You'll need to stop me from killing her."

He jerks his head toward Aibell.

I gasp.

He winks, a grin not far behind, before he begins walking again.

27

WE WALK until the sky awakens with tangerine swirled with rose, smeared across a pallet of lavender.

The streets go still, the air around us muted and sleepy. I yawn, my nose filling with a new scent of stringent plant I've probably never heard of and definitely don't want to touch.

By the time we reach the edge of town, my imagination has run wild, believing the ground will fall off abruptly, taking me along with it into the pits of nothing.

But it doesn't and I don't. Not into a pit.

My legs go weak, and I yawn again, this time unsuccessfully keeping my eyes open. Someone picks me up and carries me, and I don't even care. A warm hand finds its way to my wrist, pulls up my sleeve, touches my skin.

A gentle pulse of serenity flows through my arm, spreads over every inch of me. I allow myself to drift, drift, drift away.

My eyes open and close so slowly, the scenery is vastly different with each blink.

I turn my head toward the tense chest that carries me. Scents of wood, fire, soap, and aftershave all register before my world goes obsidian and my memory fades.

My dreams are filled with days past. Football Sundays

spent with my dad. Late-night dates talking with Oliver. Hanging at the coffee shop with Aubree.

Melancholy seeps into my bones as I slowly awake and remember my reality.

I open my eyes. I'm in a makeshift bed of straw and blankets on the floor of a one-room cottage I don't remember seeing before passing out. My joints complain as I sit up and stretch, my neck properly cricked, my back and legs sore from poor circulation.

Curse these faeries and their lack of proper beds.

A quick fingering of my hair loosens a few tangles, but I'm thankful not to have a mirror. I can only imagine what kind of rat's nest my bedhead looks like at the moment.

I smack my lips and move my tongue around my mouth, then grimace. Also, I need to ask Eric for a toothbrush. Being kidnapped and trapped in the Unseelie Realm is no excuse *not* to have some sort of hygiene.

"Feel better?"

The voice startles me fully awake, and I instinctively pull the blankets to cover me, even though I'm clothed.

Eric sits at a square two-person table alone. Murmurs echo from the other side of the door, and someone laughs. I assume the others are outdoors, waiting for me to wake.

I look at Eric. It's creepy that he's been sitting here watching me sleep.

I don't say that, though. Instead I say, "I'm fine."

He gestures to the space before him. "Breakfast?"

I glance at the fading light out the window. "Wouldn't this be supper for me?"

He shrugs. "If you insist on remaining human."

A *pfft* tumbles from my lips as I shove aside the blankets and stand. "What's that supposed to mean?"

"It means there's a whole other side you refuse to accept." He raises a brow and lifts something from the plate.

I huff again as I cross the room and yank the wood chair

from under the table, plopping on it with more effort than necessary.

The plate is filled with nuts and berries, a saccharine scent of petals and hunger. Any chance I can order some French fries? I sigh and give him a pointed look that asks the question I don't say aloud.

He chuckles and nods. "It's safe to eat. I picked them myself."

What's he laughing about? He scratches a hand through his hair and leans on his elbows.

Silence hangs in the room like a weight. I pick at a nut. "You put me to sleep, didn't you?"

"Not really. I just gave you a little help. You were already on your way."

"What I mean is, you touched me. You did something with that gift thing of yours."

He snorts. "It's not a mystery, Caoine. That's how our fae gifts work. It goes both ways. Just as I can draw from you, I can also transfer whatever emotion I choose to give you."

My arm tingles where he touched me earlier, and I can almost feel the same sense of serenity as before. "Well, whatever you did, thanks."

I pick up a berry and roll it between my fingers.

"Sorry there's not more. Our host is presently occupied, which leaves little nourishment in the place." He glances out the window, brow furrowed. "Hopefully they won't return anytime soon."

I cough mid-chew. "We slept in someone else's house who isn't even here? Who doesn't *know* we're here?"

"*You* slept in the house."

My jaw drops. Way to throw me under the bus.

His expression is aloof. A nerve in my cheek twitches, but I go back to eating.

My gaze lands on the chair beside him. A large, thick book sits on it. A particularly ancient-looking book. "Is that—?"

He grins. "The Book of Discernment. I retrieved it from its hiding place."

"It was here the whole time? This is where you were taking me from the beginning?"

"It took us a while to get here, but we made it." He winks. "If Aibell hadn't gotten us off-track, I would've been able to retrieve it days ago. But we're good now. We just need the Book of Judgment, and we're golden."

Huh. Maybe I should've listened to Eric in the first place. I don't say this out loud, though.

A minute goes by. Eric watches me eat.

I avoid his gaze. "So this is our backup plan for finding out what we need to know?"

He nods. "It works out since this is where I needed to be anyway."

I lick my lips and concentrate on my food. "And Eithne? Do you think she would've helped us?"

Eric scowls. "It was a stupid idea. Chances are slim we would've gotten the right information anyway."

"She, um . . . seemed to know you."

He doesn't answer. Just breathes.

I swallow. "Were you two, like, together or something?"

"Why would you think that?"

I twist my lips. "It was sort of obvious from the way she said goodbye. I do have a boyfriend, you know."

A sudden wash of melancholy seeps into my soul at the thought of Oliver. *I'll be home soon. I promise.*

Eric sighs, nods. "Yeah, I guess you could say we were . . . together. At one point."

Finally, I look at him. "You don't seem happy."

He shrugs again. "Let's just say it didn't end well."

Interesting. I stop eating, sit back in my chair, cross my arms. "I'm listening."

Eric groans. "I don't want to get into this."

But I want to hear it. "Come on. Spill."

Why do I even care?

The chair creaks as he leans back, scratches a hand through his hair. "It was . . . nothing."

I pummel him with a glare.

"Fine. It was something. But it's over."

"Why?"

"Why what? People break up sometimes. Does it need to be some big mysterious thing?"

I narrow my gaze. "I didn't think so until you started acting all . . . weird." I flail my hands around.

He pauses too long. "Fine. We broke up because . . . because—of *you*, all right?"

I flinch like he's hit me. "Me? What does Eithne have to do with me? I never even met her until today."

"Yeah, except we were dating right before my father started his plan to use you for the spell. Right before he sent me to tail you through high school."

"Okaaay."

"So . . ." He rubs his eyes, rests his head in his palms. "Don't you remember how I felt about you? Back at West Lincoln?"

I bite my lip. "You liked me? Like, really liked me?"

He huffs. "You can say it, Caoine. I was obsessed with you. I'll admit it."

"Yeah, you were slightly freaky. You even said you loved me." I laugh nervously.

Eric nods. "I tried to tell you before. I don't know what my father did to me, but whatever it was, it made me *think* I loved you." A smile tugs at the corner of his mouth. "Sorry if this sounds creepy."

"It is, a little."

"Yeah, well, I don't feel that anymore. In fact, I don't know what my father did to me to make me such a puppet, but I certainly don't want to follow his commands blindly anymore."

"Oh." I swallow. "That's good, right?"

He shrugs, his eyes sad. My heart sinks an inch.

Wait. Am I becoming friends with him?

I blink away the thought. It's way too heavy of a thing to care for such an enemy, on any level.

I lean forward, grab a berry, and pop it in my mouth. "So what have you done so far?"

"Done?"

I shove another berry in my mouth. "While I was asleep. Did you go to the wishing well?"

"No."

"What did you do?"

"Nothing."

I pause, swallow. "You did nothing?"

"We've been waiting for you to wake."

My head buzzes in confusion. "Whoa. You've been waiting for me to wake up? So you've, like, done nothing? At all?"

This coaxes a devious smile from the boy. "What would you have us do? We don't need to sleep. And I need *you* to find the book."

"Wait. You need me?" I blink, my food forgotten.

He pushes away from the table, leans back in his chair. "I don't trust them."

I glance at the door. "Them?"

"Yeah, them. Who else would I be talking about?"

I pout, but he goes on.

"Look, they hate me. They clearly don't trust me and probably never will. I owe them nothing and expect they feel the same about me."

"But they're going to help me get home. They said they'd help me save my dad."

He crosses his arms. "Will they, though?"

"Catherine sent Aibell to help me."

My shoulders droop as I consider the friend who kept so much from me. But she must've had good reason to hide the truth, right? She's still one of my closest friends.

I clear my throat. "I would trust Cat with my life. Therefore I trust Aibell. So yeah, I believe she'll get me home."

"Fine."

"Fine?" My nose itches, but I refuse to scratch it.

"You can trust them, but that doesn't mean I have to. Therefore I waited for you to wake up. So we can find the book. Together."

I bite my lip. "Why me?"

"Because I trust you."

"I thought you said to trust no one."

"I did."

The door bangs open, and I jump in my seat. Eric doesn't even flinch. His faerie hearing probably warned him of the intrusion, which just makes me all the more jealous I didn't inherit that trait.

"You're up," Aibell says.

I nod, standing and abandoning the remainder of my breakfast. Or supper. *Sigh*.

"Great. Let's get this over with." Her glare settles on Eric before she exits the room.

She obviously wasn't happy they had to wait until I woke to move forward with the plan. Did Eric wait just to annoy her or because he truly trusts me?

I follow her to the front of the cottage. The house is made of obsidian stone, tendrils of purple vines growing along the walls. It's small and square and sits on top of a tall hill. A winding stone path leads down and connects with a gravel road. Patches of brightly colored, glowing flowers the size of basketballs dot the grass.

The sky overhead is deep plum, tiny white stars clustered in patterns across the expanse. In the far horizon I spot not one, but two delicate moons holding hands as they rise for the night.

I gasp. I've slept the whole day away?

A crisp scent of cassia and never-ending night tickles my

nose. The chill doesn't bother me tonight. Not even a little. I rub my arms. Is it possible my fae side will take over until I'm no longer human?

Thwap!

I turn to find Gar a dozen feet away, practicing with a bow and arrow, Killian murmuring commands about his stance.

Aibell strides toward them, throwing words over one shoulder. "We'll be here." Her voice is clipped, stretched tight like a rubber band.

Eric bristles. I'm guessing I missed a conversation while asleep and am downright gleeful to have been absent for that fighting match.

"Come on," he mumbles. His brow is bunched together, hands shoved in his pockets.

I follow without a word, careful to step over piles of snow as we traverse the pink grass that grows only in Faerie during the eternal season of death.

He leads me behind the structure. A sharp noise that sounds like an engine turning over bites at my ankles, and I spin around as I walk. Nothing moves in the grass.

I walk a little faster to stay close by Eric's side.

Eric stops, and I practically stumble into the stone well I didn't see seconds before.

"How did—?"

"Hidden by magic." He cuts me off without even glancing at me. "My . . . *friend* hid it. Only a few know of its location."

"Will he be okay that we're using it? Without him here, I mean?"

He nods, looking into the darkness below.

I lean forward. Moss and dampness invade my nose. Murky water sits at the bottom, still. Waiting. I place a hand on the stone and jolt when heat radiates up my arm.

I pull away. "What was—?"

Eric looks at me. "Like I said, magic."

"I'm confused. How is this thing going to help us find the Book of Judgment?"

He grins. "It's a wishing well. We *wish* to see its location."

Of course. "So what do we do? Just ask it to show us what we want?"

"It's not quite that easy. A vision requires a sacrifice."

"A sacrifice? Like the well wants blood or something?"

He chuckles. "Not exactly. To grant a wish, the well requires something of great value. If you can prove you're worthy of a vision, it'll reward you with your heart's greatest desire."

I frown. Then reach into my pocket. Aubree's rabbit's foot rests in my hand. Eric raises a brow.

"Think we could get any information from Aubree? I mean, her mom is the reason we're even trying to find this stupid book."

He shrugs. "It's worth a try, I suppose. Go ahead. Toss it in and see what happens."

I twist my lips. I hate to lose this gift. I've kept it near ever since Aubree gave it to me, even if it is unlucky.

I nod, squeeze the rabbit's foot, toss it in. The water bubbles and churns, a slight mist rolling from the top.

But Aubree's face doesn't appear. Instead I see Oliver.

I gasp, my heart racing like an Olympic runner.

"Oliver?" Eric's question reflects my thoughts.

But I stay quiet, focused on the scene before me.

Oliver is with Aubree. Maybe that's why I'm seeing this? But the image focuses on him.

He's smiling, that front tooth of his turned slightly out of place. Tingles spill along my spine and down my belly. He's talking, but I can't hear his words.

"Why can't I hear him?" But I don't listen for a reply from Eric.

My gaze is intent on the image. Oliver runs a hand across his cropped hair, laughs at something Aubree says. Then he grows serious, hesitates. Reaches into his jeans and pulls out a small box. He lifts the lid.

My jaw drops.

Inside the box is a ring. A diamond one. Like ones used for engagements and adulty stuff.

Eric whistles.

I remain mute.

Could that be for me? Why would Oliver have a ring like that for me?

Oliver's face turns sorrowful. Aubree pats his shoulder, her smile empathetic.

Then Oliver says something, and I don't need to hear it to read his lips. *Come back to me, Caoine.*

The wind is knocked from me as the image disappears. I fight to breathe, my hands grasping the well like a lifeline.

"Why . . . why did it show him?" I blink away spots. "I mean, I thought I'd see something about Aubree."

Eric shrugs. "The well shows your heart's true desire."

Of course. I nod.

"Which means it's up to me to figure this thing out."

His fingers fumble with something around his neck, a necklace tucked deep inside his shirt. He holds a silver chain with a small lump in the palm of his hand, the edges of his mouth turning down.

"A thimble?" I ask.

"It was my mother's." He pulls the chain free and shoves it in his jeans. "It's the only thing I have left of her."

"Is she . . . I mean, did she pass away?"

He shakes his head. "I don't know. I haven't seen her in years. We parted on—" His breath catches in his throat. "Difficult terms." His eyes glisten.

I pull in a ragged breath. "You're giving up the only thing you have of your mother?"

He nods, wraps his fingers around the thimble in a way that says he would never let it go if he had a choice.

Wow. I only gave a trinket from a friend I'll definitely see again. What must it be like to give up something from a parent who's gone?

Sorrow is my closest companion as I watch him, the way he opens his hand, looks at the thimble as if it holds a thousand memories.

"Eric, I'm — I'm so sorry."

His eyes lock with mine. "It's what needs to happen."

I swallow. "To get me home?"

"To stop my father."

Right.

He slowly turns toward the well, and I swear I see a tear glimmer on his cheek. I'm still as he holds his hand over the well, holds his breath.

Then he lets go of his mother's memory.

THE ABYSS IS OPAQUE. Blacker than a moonless night or the ink of a pen or the heart of one who commits murder.

A splash, then ripples of endless water. And nothing.

Eric is frozen beside me. So still. I dare to breathe, my lungs demanding I do, even though my brain begs me not to ruin the moment with such a mundane act.

I refuse to tear my gaze from the sight that echoes below. Seconds tick. Eric could be a statue. A chill breeze tosses a strand of my hair, ruffles my shirt. Still, sweat blossoms beneath my arms, along my lower back.

Please work.

Whether I want this magic spell to work just so I can get my dad back or for Eric's humanity, I do not know.

Then, a ripple—

He gasps as a single bubble drifts to the surface of the water. Then another. A blink later and it's boiling like the blood inside my veins.

Eric's shoulders relax, tension still present, just in a different way. I glance at him. There's a tear along one cheek, but it doesn't remain alone for long. In seconds, his face is streaked and beautiful.

My heart squeezes, an invisible fist yanking it from my chest.

A picture erupts across the water as it suddenly goes placid. Eric hunches closer, his knuckles white as he grips the sides of the stone well.

The Book of Judgment rests on a table. Nothing ornate or special, just a regular table made of wood. Beside it, a chair. This with a high back, a fancy type of wood with carvings and paint embellishes along the edges.

The armrests and seat boast plush velvet, and my back longs to settle into something so comfortable.

The table may be ordinary, but this chair is anything but. This chair is fit for a king.

Eric's neck bulges as his face turns three shades of red. One of the stones beneath his hand cracks down the middle. Fury simmers below his skin.

I can't blame the boy. I would be livid, too, if the man I trusted with my life—the person I'd committed murder for— had betrayed me in such a way.

The man sitting in the chair *is* a king.

"Your father's had the book this entire time?" My voice is a squeak. No sooner do I say the words than I fumble to take them back.

Eric pushes back from the well, his hands still in place so his arms are straight, his head bowed low, as if he's stretching, preparing to run a race.

My heart hammers away at my ribcage as my throat shrinks two sizes. *Time.* He needs time. Time to process. To cool. But time is a luxury we don't have.

I twist a loose piece of string from my shirt around a finger. "Eric?"

No answer. Just heavy breathing, another crack of stone as it bursts to shards.

"Eric." This time my voice is commanding. He must listen to reason. We can't have the one person who has access to the book fall apart. "Eric, he—"

"He's had it this entire time."

I barely make out his words, they're so quiet.

Fear races along my limbs, and I involuntarily step back, images of Eric on Halloween flashing through my mind.

"He sent me on a mission to find the book, but he had it all along."

Eric straightens, his chest heaving, nostrils flaring.

"My father deceived me. He had the book. All. Along. The only thing he cared about was bringing you and the other book to him so he could complete his plan."

Anger seethes from each word, and his eyes appear red for a second.

"He used me just like he used me before."

"Maybe he—"

Eric rushes toward me, his face inches from mine. I'm so shocked I don't even bother to retreat. My breathing comes out in little puffs that makes me feel weak. Vulnerable.

"You don't understand, Caoine. I was told—"

He presses his lips together, his words said through gritted teeth. "I was told the truth, but I refused to believe it. I thought they were trying to deceive me.

"None of my brothers wanted to go along with father's plan, because they believed him to be mad. But I didn't believe them. My only goal was to gain a father I never had.

"But they would know, wouldn't they? The king's sons? Having grown up with a madman, they would know. Now I understand why they all left the castle long ago."

He looks at my arm, his gaze crashing with mine. "Please? Please, Caoine."

I suck in a breath, pushing up my sleeve. He wraps a hand around my wrist. His anger pulses into my skin, but it doesn't hurt me. I tremble at his touch, at the sheer force of malice and hatred that echoes from his muscles.

He closes his eyes, shudders, his shoulders falling. The

anger slips away like a light switch has been flipped. I breathe, relax. Focus on the boy before me.

It's like watching a druggie take a hit. Like he's been avoiding this for so long but can't stop himself for another second.

He settles, releases me. His hazel gaze finds mine. "He used me, Caoine."

You used me. But I don't say this.

Eric looks like a broken man, shattered fragments of a once-great faerie who has lost his way. Had he ever known who he was, before his father came along to destroy him?

I bite my cheek, stand taller. "So we use him."

He doesn't respond.

I take one step closer, his scent of wood and fire and soap and aftershave enveloping me.

"We break into the castle and steal that book. We save my father."

My gaze turns to flint.

"We give the things he most wants to his enemy. We hand the books to Queen Faílenn."

TIME DOES funny things in Faerie. I don't understand the way it works, and I'm not sure I ever will.

Maybe it's getting used to being awake at night, when the land of the fae comes to life. Or maybe it's the unknown of what happens during the day when the fae don't sleep.

No matter. The walk back to the hideout goes by faster than lightning in the fiercest storm. Similar to the storm within my heart. And it rages for truth, questioning if I should trust Eric, wondering if I will ever be able to truly forgive him.

Laoise greets us with a smile as the five of us stumble through the door. "Was the trip a success?"

Gar grunts in reply. Killian absently finds his way to a nearby chair. Aibell ignores her.

"It was," I say, because faerie or not, no one deserves to be ignored.

Her gaze rests on me like the heat of a summer day.

The smile she wears would be pleasant to the casual observer, but it doesn't fool me. Not by a long shot. Her eyes are empty, shamed. What's it like to be tormented by other faeries?

Flashes of memory clog my mind. Years spent in changing

schools with teens who cared only for themselves and nothing for the abnormal white-haired girl who only wanted to be left alone.

A mixture of pine and patchouli swirl around my head, and I close my eyes at its intensity.

Eric moves beside me, and it hits me that he hasn't moved into the house like the others.

"We need to get into the castle." He draws Laoise's attention, his jaw set.

This is the first time I've seen any of Aibell's associates not treat him as if he were a leper. Laoise simply nods and gestures for us to follow. As if she knew.

The air along my skin raises ten degrees, and I have a private discussion with my heart to *slow down*. We walk to the table, and I sit.

Eric places the Book of Discernment on its surface and settles across from me.

Laoise continues to stand but doesn't even bring up the fact that we now have a major item in the puzzle at our disposal. Only Killian is brave enough to sit close, Aibell and Gar remaining within earshot, in the far corner.

A fellowship of the ring we are *not*.

For a full minute we stare at one another. I fiddle with the edge of my shirtsleeve. I am far too human to think this could even be remotely comfortable. But none of them appears the least bit distressed.

I fight the urge to swallow. "So . . . ideas?"

The wooden walls suck away the intensity of my voice, leaving it vulnerable and afraid.

"I would think our prince can get in. No problem, right?"

The sneer on Aibell's face makes her look a lot less like Catherine. In fact, I'm not sure why I ever saw a resemblance in the first place.

Eric bristles. "I didn't grow up in that castle. I've barely lived there for more than a few years, all broken up by trips to the Mortal Realm." He ducks his head. "I'm not sure I'll be much help."

"You've got to know more than the rest of us, though." My statement is meant to reassure, but he glances at me as if I've slapped him.

"What do you expect me to do? It's not like I can break the enchantments that surround it. The place is guarded. It's impossible for anyone to get in, let alone get out."

"Enchantments?" I ask.

Eric nods. "My father made sure every square inch inside those walls remain untouched by faerie magic. No one can do any sort of magic within his castle, unless he allows it. Remember how I said we need the book to save your dad? Magic beats magic?"

I worry my lip. "But how will we do that if we don't have both books?"

He shrugs. "It will be considerably more challenging. We'll need to get creative."

"All right, so we go old school." Aibell fingers the sword at her side with her lame hand as she thinks out loud. "What are our strengths? What can we do collectively that they can't?"

Gar brightens. "You mean hand-to-hand combat? Without magic?"

Aibell nods.

He grins. "Now we're talking!"

I fight a smile.

Killian dips his chin. "This, we can do. I assume we'll assist Caoine and Eric to enter the castle? Create a distraction?"

"A distraction, yes, but hold up there." Aibell squints at the prince. "I'm not so sure it's wise to send him in."

Eric gives her a pointed stare. "How could it possibly be unwise? How will Caoine know where to find the book unless I guide her?"

Aibell flinches, narrows her gaze at him. She waits a beat.

I look between her and Eric. She's not saying something.

"Draw her a map," she deadpans. "Tell her how to get past the enchantments."

I blink. It's unclear whose side I should take. That of a deceiver who will surely make the trip successful, or the sister of my best friend who—although rough around the edges—has a valid point about sending our enemy into his lair.

"Maybe there's another use for you, Eric," I say. His gaze weighs on me, and I look away before I can see the disappointment in his eyes. "Let's hear what Aibell has to say."

Everyone turns to look at her except Eric, who looks in the opposite direction.

Aibell lifts her chin. "I don't trust sending the prince in with Caoine. If the king gets his hands on her, this whole thing will be over."

"Agreed." Gar's bass voice rumbles across the smooth wood floor.

"I second that," Killian adds.

Heat creeps along my cheeks, and guilt pricks my nerves. I had no intention of throwing Eric under the bus, but that's exactly what I've done.

"I will accompany Caoine inside the castle," Aibell says as if it's gospel.

I begin to nod. But then I glance around the group. "No . . . you can't."

Her face flushes as she turns toward me. "What?"

"You can't. Come with me, I mean."

She freezes, so I try to smooth over the awkward.

"There are only five of you. We'll need every one of you to distract the king's men. I'm a big girl. I can take care of myself. I can certainly sneak around a castle by myself. I used to spy on my dad every night when I was little." I frown. "Not sure what I thought I'd find out."

The others stare blankly at me.

"I'll be fine," I assure them. "Especially if Eric draws that map for me."

Aibell's eyes flash. "You may be a *big girl*, Caoine, but you're still human."

"Half-human. Which makes me half-*faerie*. Don't you all have crazy Spidey senses? Maybe I've got that too."

Killian blinks. "Pardon me, but what is a spy-dee scent?"

Aibell ignores him. "So you're half-fae. Which also happens to be a race you know nothing about, don't understand, and can in no way predict."

"Exactly. Which means I might think differently than the rest of you. I just might be successful at stealing that book."

Aibell's right eye twitches, but otherwise, she doesn't move. She stares at me.

I'm not looking directly at Eric, but I swear he smiles.

"The girl is right," Killian says, the voice of reason. "We cannot spare even one of us if we're to be successful. We must trust the human to do her part."

"Half-human," I mumble.

"I still say I should tag along with Caoine." Eric crosses his arms. "I don't like the idea of her going in alone."

Aibell's eyes flash. "In case you haven't noticed, that conversation is over, prince."

He sits straighter. "And I'm saying I'm not done—"

Aibell starts to jump down his throat, but I stop them. "Eric, please. It's for the best. For everyone. They need you outside the castle. I can do this."

Silence impregnates the room. Eric's eyes don't leave mine.

His face softens, his shoulders sinking. "Are you sure? I can't—" He licks his lips. "We can't lose you, Caoine. You're too important."

"I know." I pause. "But we're forgetting one thing."

"Yes?" Laoise's eyes shimmer silver as she looks at me.

"Well, if we're already in the castle, wouldn't it make sense just to spring my dad while we're at it?"

Aibell shakes her head. "Not necessarily. This is risky enough."

My jaw drops. "What? No way. If we're breaking into the castle, we're saving my dad. End of story."

"It's too risky," she insists.

"But we've got the element of surprise. We might not have a chance like this again."

Her gaze is hard. "Let's get this part done, then we can focus on freeing your father. One quest at a time, mortal."

I scowl at the way she belittles me. There's zero chance I'll convince them when their leader is against the plan.

But she's wrong. We won't get another chance to save him if we don't do it now. King Raghnall will probably chain my dad to his side once he discovers the book is gone.

"It's settled, then," Killian says.

No, it isn't. But they don't need to know that. I'm not leaving that castle without my dad.

For the first time since we've been back, Laoise actually looks alive. "Perfect. And I do believe Killian is correct, which gives me an idea. If my calculations are right, we cannot fail."

30

I BANG my hands together to get some feeling back into them. I'm squatting below a tree overlooking King Raghnall's castle, too far away for any guards to see.

The castle is as massive and boring as any other I've seen in picture books, aside from the statue I assume must be of King Raghnall's liking, the size of a small mountain and towering over the entrance.

The trees around me look like any other trees from home, brown bark and green leaves. Except for the one next to me. It *talks*. In fact, it's been talking to me for the last half hour.

My nerves buzz along my fingers and toes. *Stop talking.*

But it won't. I already asked.

The early morning brings a bit of warmth, like when I was a kid and my midnight banshee walk took longer than usual.

As soon as I shed my frozen outer clothes, my dad would have a blanket ready to wrap me in like a moth in a cocoon. Then he'd bring me hot cocoa and would put on my favorite cartoon, even though it was way past bedtime. As if being that cold made it impossible to sleep.

I close my eyes, try to grab hold of that smell of how much

my dad loved me, hoping for a whiff of hot chocolate. All I get is fresh leather and lilacs.

My eyes fly open, and my heart skitters. The way my dad *loves* me. He's still alive. I need to believe this.

Hold on a little while longer, Dad. I'm coming for you.

"Under the reign of the Fifth Kingdom, our king second in succession declared . . ."

That tree behind me still won't shut up. It's like he's a living encyclopedia, monologuing the entire fae history every minute of the day.

I shove my fingers through my scraggly hair. How can I enter that castle and *not* attempt to rescue my dad? I pull in a shaky breath, hold it for four seconds, push it back out. But my fellow faerie friends assure me now is not the time to save him. They will get him free as soon as we get both books.

Well, they're wrong. I'm in control now. And I plan on finding my dad the minute I have the book in my hands.

"Then came the Great Wars . . ." The tree's soft cadence disappears on the slight breeze.

I pull a folded piece of paper from my pocket. The paper is stiff, stubborn to the touch. I unfold it, memorizing the lines and the curves for the millionth time.

Eric drew this map. In another few dozen heartbeats I'll be inside the castle, traversing the hallways and grandiose rooms of a place only found in fairy tales. Until just a few short months ago.

A gust of wind flutters the edge of the page, and I straighten. What was that? I flip it over, my eyes landing on the bottom right corner. Familiar, box-like words scrawl in glittery ink. How had I missed this before?

Caoine,

 Keep this safe. Not only will it be your lifeline once you're inside the castle, but I've placed a protection spell on the bearer of this map. I don't know how far my father's magic extends beyond the walls. It's possible you will set off an alarm the minute you touch the stone.

I was able to secure a cloaking spell that will last ten minutes from the time you begin. Be safe but know you have limited time. I'll do whatever I can to ensure your success. Good luck.

~Eric.

I blow out a slow breath. Glad I found this now. Not that I intend on taking my time getting in the joint.

My fingers smart as I fold the paper and shove it back in my pocket, my dry skin aching for warmth.

Movement to my right catches my eye. I whip my head around. Was that a—?

I blink. I swear an orange tabby cat just slunk around the tree. A chill falls down my spine. Or was it merely another fantastical creature of the Faerie Realm?

I shake my head, my gaze landing on a plant at my feet.

Its azure petals sag, the honey-colored leaves shriveled and dry. I frown. Despite this being the Winter Realm, I haven't seen many plants that are actually dead.

My fingers shake as I gently cup the dead flower in my hand. Heat flares in my chest. The flower quivers and perks up, color deepening in the leaves and petals.

I gasp and pull my hand back.

It was never dead. The plant is alive.

I grumble under my breath. Even the plant life are tricksters in the Unseelie Realm.

"King Oísin and Queen Faílenn enacted the Laws of Necessity . . ."

I freeze. Turn to the tree behind me. "What did you say?"

". . . full control over the Veils . . ." The tree stops, his leaves twittering for half a second. "Did you speak, young human?"

"I heard you say the name Queen Faílenn. What were you saying?"

My pulse echoes in my ears, and I strain to concentrate on his words. The name of Aubree's mom is the first familiar thing I've run across in this foreign land.

"I was simply relaying the Great Wars."

"Which were . . . ?"

How has this tree been talking nonstop, and now that I want information, he's suddenly gone cryptic?

"Yes, yes. That would be nigh two hundred fifty years ago. The Faerie Realms grew weary of watching the Mortal Realm destroy itself with endless wars. The human race did not appear to cherish the land or the life they were given.

"King Raghnall and Queen Mairéad of the Unseelie proposed a plan to wipe out every living thing in the Mortal Realm so that the fae race could have unlimited access beyond their borders for merriment and enjoyment. To build a new realm for the fae to occupy."

Heat flares within my core. "King Raghnall wanted to use Earth as a freaking vacation spot for his people?"

"Not to worry. King Oísin and Queen Faílenn of the Seelie stopped the magic and put an end to King Raghnall's plans. The seven plagues were never released on Earth, and the Laws of Necessity were put in place—"

"Wait, what?" I lick my lips.

"The Laws of Necessity are—"

"Yeah, I know what they are. Go back. What—?"

"Good morning, pretty girl." Nym suddenly pops up beside me, and it takes all my effort not to squeal like a toddler.

Crud. The time has come to storm the castle.

I shake my head. "Just one more question—"

"No time, friend." Nym gives me a childlike grin. "My prince is about to reveal himself. We must make haste."

"But—" I look to the tree as if it can possibly give me aid.

Its stupid leaves stay perfectly still. It doesn't even mutter a word.

Traitor. "Fine."

I stand, my knees protesting. A quick glance to the castle confirms our hopes: the walls are manned with a limited number of guards. The sleepy castle has all but settled for the day, giving us an advantage to sneak in without detection.

A horn blares, and I jump. Nym watches, as if this happens every day.

Far below, the minuscule guards run along the wall's edge, gathering in two different spots. One will have Eric and Aibell, the other Killian, Gar, and Laoise. The idea is to pull as many guards to the two points of distraction as possible.

I count two minutes. The tree stays silent. A breeze picks up, and a sweet scent of honeysuckle tickles my nose.

Nym turns his large eyes in my direction, holds out a hand. "Ready?"

Adrenaline smacks into my chest. "Ready."

I take his hand. We disappear.

31

WE LAND in a section of soft blue moss, my head continuing to spin and twist and scream as I stumble into the cold stone of the castle wall. Open fields surround us on all sides other than the massive royal wall behind me.

My heart constricts. We're too exposed.

I turn toward Nym. "You'll be here when I get back?"

"Of course, pretty girl. Where else would I be?" The small man looks genuinely confused, his brow crunched like a paper sack.

Hiding from certain death. But I don't say it. Instead I take another look around.

Vast fields of rainbow-colored grass and a castle wall as far as the eye can see.

Awesome. Time to get to work. My gaze skitters across the plain, gray rocks before me. Identical. Unimpressive. My blood vessels squeeze right along with my throat. How does Eric ever expect me to accomplish such a daunting task?

Then I see it, a distinctive section of rock that's been punctured, hollowed out just enough for a handhold.

I reach forward, wiggle the tips of my fingers into the crevice of fae stone. They fit perfectly. A few rocks below is another hollowed-out section just big enough for a foot. I place the toes of my sneaker inside. Again, a snug fit.

I take a deep breath, glance at Nym, his orb eyes watching me with interest.

Then I climb.

Each section of rock is just wide and tall enough for fingers or toes to scale the grandiose boulders. My body scrapes against the rough surface, the chill of the minerals seeping through my shirt and pants. It's still early, but the day is already warming. I pant, grip the stones tighter. Close my eyes.

Plummeting to my death isn't part of the plan.

Don't look down. Don't look down. Don't look down.

I look down. My arms and legs shake.

Not a good idea, Caoine.

I'm already so high. I look up. The top of the castle wall isn't visible yet.

Why? Why did Eric think I could even do this? And how many times has he done this exact climb to escape from his father?

I ignore the spike in my blood pressure and climb some more. A pungent odor of mildew and musk weeps along the walls, making me dizzy.

The plan is simple. No magic is allowed inside the castle walls, so Nym teleporting me inside is a no-go. With Aibell and the rest of the gang by the front gates, causing as big a distraction as possible, Eric is strangely confident I can climb my way in before the guards return to their posts.

The question is, just how long will those guards be distracted by said distraction?

My heart climbs another inch toward my throat with each foothold. What if I face the wrath of a faerie with a pointy sword once I pop my head over the top of this thing?

I bite my lip. *Focus, Caoine.*

I'll worry about that when—no, *if*—the time comes. For now, I need *not* to fall to my death.

A sudden breeze tosses the hair that's come loose from my ponytail and whips it across my eyes. I blow at my eyebrows, turn my head to catch the breeze just right. Nope, that hair stays in place. I blink. Hair goes inside my eyes. Literally.

Ouch!

I shake my head, blink rapidly, squeeze my fingers as if my life depends on it. Because it totally does.

Ugh. I blow again. Half the hair releases, and I can open one eye. My eye still stings.

I need to get this climb over with, quick.

Another glance up and I can see the edge of the wall, like a lighthouse beckoning me to safety.

Step. Reach. Pull. Step. Reach. Pull.

My legs begin to quiver from the strain of something I haven't done in a while. Maybe not since gym class? I swallow.

The world around me goes completely silent. I pause. Listen. Where has all the sound gone? I blink at that stubborn piece of hair that won't leave me alone and command my heart to stop thumping like it's in an Olympic relay race.

Why did everything go silent all at once? Flags as red as blood flash through my mind.

I move.

My toes scramble to find footing, and my fingers split and bleed each time I cram them into ragged stone holds. Muscles I didn't know I possessed complain, whisper that they might not be able to hold on.

The top ledge of the wall floats across my vision. I push against the pain that threads my limbs, creeping toward my heart, threatening to attack. To stop it altogether.

The silence pounds against my ears, echoes inside my head, and vibrates like the beat of a drum.

Something is wrong.

Step. Reach. Pull.

Something is very wrong.

Step. Reach. Pull.

Don't look down to see what it is. And for the love of all the realms, please don't let an arrow sink into my back!

I reach to grab the top of the edge of the wall, my fingers wrapping neatly around the top rock, blood slick on their tips. *Pull.* I seek one last foothold—

I slip.

The scream doesn't even have time to leave my lips.

The right side of my body swings down, my left fingers the only thing anchoring me to the wall. My left foot lingers between the rocks, but I can feel it loosen, betraying me to the death my song so easily calls to others.

Every banshee song I've ever sung flashes through my mind.

I see my dad—not as he is now, a prisoner to an unfeeling king—but as my dad. Every moment we've spent together. Hiding my secret. Missing my mom.

I see Oliver, regretful I didn't get to say goodbye, that I might never feel his lips against mine again.

That I'll never get the chance to sit with Aubree one last time as she drinks the coffee I so despise.

My eyes have time to blink once as all these things flit through my mind. Then my fingers weaken. Release.

I fall.

32

M Y B O D Y C O M E S to an abrupt halt, my shoulder practically yanking out of its socket.

Fire crashes through my shoulder, slices across my back. I stifle a cry. My elbows and knees scrape against the stones, freezing ice coating my skin, and I hang mid-air, a puppet on strings. I glance up.

Eric hangs over the side of the castle wall, his legs wedged between crenellations. His hands wrap around my left wrist, his face as red as blood. A vein pops on his forehead, and his jaw flexes from the strain of holding my entire body weight.

"A little help?" he mouths.

Instinct kicks in, both my feet fighting to attach themselves to the rocks, my right hand already extended to grab the edge.

He pulls just as a new surge of adrenaline slams into my muscles. I'm up and over the ledge in a second, the two of us tumbling onto our backs.

Pain races along my elbows, knees, fingers, toes. Every part of my skin feels the effect of what I've just done. My left shoulder pounds as pain grows by the second. I cradle my arm to my chest.

I freaking climbed a super high wall without any restraints.

Oh my gosh, I just went rock climbing without any gear! What was I thinking?

My chest heaves with each breath. Scents invade my lungs: dirt, winter air, jealousy, death.

I'm alive. How am I alive?

I look at Eric. He's in the same position I am, flat on his back, breathing like he's just played the hardest soccer game of his life.

"You're here?" I blubber between my ragged breathing.

This wasn't part of the plan. I have a map. I was supposed to traverse these castle halls alone.

He shakes his head. "Plans have changed."

"How so?"

"They were ready for us. I don't know how, but they were. The others put up a good fight, but we got separated. By the grace of the realms I slipped through the gate undetected. My father had too many men focused in one area."

I sit up, brush dirt from my clothes, wince as I tenderly hold my bloody fingers and bruised elbows. "That was dumb, Eric. You should've stuck to the plan. What if one of the others gets hurt or captured because you left?"

I don't mean for my words to be so heavily laced with anger, but they are.

He frowns and sits up. "They'll be fine."

"How do you know? What if—?"

"Caoine, relax. They'll be fine. I promise."

"Aibell's going to have your head."

Eric scowls. "She doesn't scare me. And she'll get over it. Can you just accept I'm here to help?"

"But I've got the map—"

He shuts me up with his narrowed look. "And it'll go much faster now that I'm here. Now stop complaining and shut it."

I begin a retort, but he shoves a finger against my lips. He then points toward the ledge we've just crossed, climbing to a crouch and crawling to the wall. I follow in the same fashion.

We both peep over the frosty stone.

In the fear of almost falling to my death, I'd forgotten the silence. It still smothers like a wool curtain. I glance below.

At first there's nothing. Those vast, open fields remain untouched. My eyes wander straight down. Nym is gone.

Where is he? He promised he'd stay right there to help me. He said he wouldn't leave unless—

Then I see them. A mass of small creatures. Human-like, but with distinct animal features. Faeries.

It's hard to see from this vantage point, but I swear they have furry, tufted ears and goat-shaped legs beneath their pants. They walk upright with purpose in their steps. A group of fifty or so gather together, focused on an unknown point in the distance.

I release the breath I've been holding. At least they're not looking in our direction.

"The silence," Eric whispers. "A relative of the satyr. They bring silence wherever they go, hence the name."

He shrugs as if to say he wasn't the one who came up with such a stupid name.

"But we can hear each other."

"Only because we're right beside one other. I couldn't yell to you when you were on the ground."

I raise my brows but look back at them. Sound slowly fills the spaces behind them as they retreat. My insides quiver, and air puffs in front of my mouth. "Where are they going?"

He shakes his head. "Who knows? Most fae avoid them because of how uncomfortable their unnatural presence is."

I look at him, at his brown skin and that mole right next to his eye, at the way his chestnut hair tumbles down his neck, hiding his shoulders. "You don't know much about them."

"None of the fae do. They've always been a bit of a mystery. Keep to themselves. I honestly don't even know if they're dangerous or if they would've turned on you if they saw you."

His hazel gaze meets mine, and my heart trips over cold, cold stones within, like the ones I just climbed.

"Come on," I whisper. "We should move."

Eric dips his chin in quick affirmation and backs away from the edge, standing to full height. I'm ready to walk into the unknown, but he stops me, grabs my hands.

"Wait," he whispers.

His gaze holds mine as heat pulses through my fingertips, flows along my arms and into my shoulder.

He's healing me. Which makes me want to ask how he can do this kind of magic within the walls when other magic can't be done. But now is not the time for questions.

A minute later my hands feel like new. I nod in thanks, heat racing along my cheeks.

He nods in return before he turns and ducks into the darkness of the closest blackened doorway.

I blow out a quick breath, the intensity of that short moment making me dizzy. Will I ever grow used to that boy? He's like a pendulum, swinging back and forth between kindness and temper. Completely unpredictable.

His footsteps echo away, and I race to catch up.

Adrenaline slices in my legs, my entire body in stealth mode. I fight to keep my heartbeat steady. Quiet.

Down one hall, then another. Descend a staircase, a hall, two corners. Another staircase. I attempt to keep track of where we are, but all too quickly I'm winded. Like, really winded. Why does this stuff look so easy in the movies? I've literally walked two flights of steps and need a rest!

The place is so quiet, void of any life. I should be thankful, but it just freaks me out. Is everyone out front taking care of our friends?

We silently sprint for what must be five minutes, and my back pours sweat. Not just from physical exertion, but because we're deep in the bowels of the castle. Like, so deep. Which makes sense.

Where else would the king keep a magical book that can either save or end the world? Still . . .

I suck in the stagnant air and force a swallow. Something about this doesn't feel right.

Eric stops smack dab in front of me. I walk right into his body and slam my nose against his ridiculously well-toned back. Ouch.

He's totally still. Staring.

I pop my head around his shoulder to peek.

A room—large . . . no, massive—looms before us.

Cathedral ceilings, tapestried walls, sweet incense mingling with the shadows. A throne made of ornately carved wood sits at the far end, light from vertical stained glass windows casting colorful shapes of unease across it.

Eric takes off toward it, his footfalls softer than a cat's.

I stumble along, proud of the way my feet make so little noise, even though I sound like an elephant compared to my fellow faerie.

I see it, the Book of Judgment. It sits on a table exactly like in the vision at the well.

Memories of Aubree flood my chest, and I need to swallow them down before they consume me. The last time I was in the same space as this hunk of paper was when I had my best friend by my side. And now I've gone and lost her rabbit's foot.

I close my eyes. I will see her again. Soon.

"This is it." Eric says this as if I don't know, which is silly, since he was with me when we looked through its sister-companion book in the janitor's closet of our high school.

Well, *my* high school. Eric was never there for the education.

He picks it up, his fingers white knuckled as his gaze grazes the rough hardback cover, the symbol that sits dead center. The symbol of enslavement of the Unseelie fae. His eyes flash with something familiar and alarming. Then he huffs, exhales, grips the book tighter.

It's thick. Thicker than the biggest dictionary at home, the old-school one my dad insists on using despite the fact he could just look it up on his phone.

And then Eric does something unexpected. He shoves the book into my arms, his look determined.

"You carry it. If we get split up, the others will be focused on getting you out of here, not me. We have a better chance of getting this thing out of here if you have it."

My jaw wobbles open. "Okay."

How is this boy so different from the Eric I encountered on Halloween night? I can see it in him. He's . . . sincere.

"And now we get my dad."

Eric hesitates, nods. "I know where they're keeping him."

The book is in my arms, against my chest, and we're running toward that door, the one that leads to our freedom. One step after the other, we close in on our destination.

My blood zips through my veins, and I'm amazed we might actually pull this thing off.

We reach the doorway, Eric steps through first, I follow close behind, and—an alarm sounds.

A gag lodges in my throat. Eric gapes at me.

"What did you do?" His voice is accusatory.

"Nothing!" I strain to keep my voice quiet, but panic takes residence in every inch of my body. I brace the book tightly to my chest.

He licks his lips, his eyes darting to the throne. His jaw flexes, and an angry grumble swims in his chest. "My father spelled it. To set off an alarm if it left the room."

I glance around. "But how? I thought you said no magic could be used inside the castle?"

Eric shakes his head. "No magic from others. My father can use all the magic he wants." He grinds his teeth again. "Come on. We need to get out of here. Now. No doubt we're being tracked already."

Eric takes a step, but I grab his arm. A vice squeezes my heart. "But my dad!"

"There's no time—"

"No! I'm not leaving without my dad!"

He tugs against my hold. "How can you save him if you're sitting in a jail cell right beside him?"

I grind my teeth. He's right. I hate it, but we run.

Down those halls, up these steps, around every single corner we took on our journey in. This isn't a trap—on his part, anyway. For minutes we run, no noise or indication that anyone is on to us. And then . . .

Behind us. Voices. Steps.

Terror spikes, and I stifle a cry as I gasp for breath.

Eric grabs my hand as we run. My other arm cradles the book to my body like it's a precious baby. My feet slap the hard stone ridiculously loudly, and I wish away every ounce of my humanity.

We *will* be caught, and it *will* be my fault.

Finally we're in the last hallway. I remember the broken bit of stone at eye level, feel the familiar scent of crisp air and dead things that coat the walls. The exit is just around the corner. Eric's fingers leave mine as he pushes me forward. As if he knows.

I'm around the corner when I hear the yell. *Eric.* His voice is coarse and chilling. In agony.

I slam my back against the cold stone, my breaths nowhere near quiet as I gasp and struggle and beg my lungs to breathe.

Eric was beside me a second ago and now he's not and I'm freaking out. I'm freaking out. I'm. Freaking. Out!

The sound of something hard slamming into something soft. A grunt from Eric. They're beating him.

No! I dig my nails into my palms and glance around the corner. Two guards have him against a wall, taking turns as they punch and kick and beat the boy who just saved my life.

"Thought you could come back and our king wouldn't know about it?" the taller of the guards taunts.

Ice forms in my belly. What can I do? How do I help?

Go.

I hear it plain as day inside my head, but I don't believe it.

Go now.

This can't be right.

Run, Caoine. I didn't sacrifice myself for you to get caught.

That's all I need. I don't know how he's doing it, but Eric is communicating with me. In my head.

His sacrifice won't be in vain.

In three quick strides I'm out the door, back into the bright light of the lavender day. I squint against the light but keep going. Prop one leg on the edge of that stone wall, my feet suddenly under me as I stand, teetering in the wedge between the raised stones.

I squeeze my fingers around the book, the nails of my other hand digging into the stone wall. My heart pounds inside my chest so hard I think it might leave my body. I *know* it might leave my body.

I glance behind me, toward the screams from Eric, the way he's being tortured for me. He took on this pain to save *me*.

I look down the wall, to the death that awaits me if I fall.

Where's Nym? How do I escape?

Jump.

I gasp.

Jump.

No.

Jump.

I squeeze my eyes shut, tears falling down my cheeks, blood oozing from the cuts along my fingernails. Eric screams once more. My heart shatters into a million pieces.

I jump.

33

I CLOSE my eyes and accept my fate. Prepare to die.

Air rushes past me so fast I can't tell which way is up and which is down. I don't even have time to take a breath, the ground racing toward me faster than a bolt of lightning.

I open my mouth—

And spindly arms suddenly wrap around my torso. A *pop* explodes against my ears. The world around me disappears and reappears in a blink.

My feet slam into hard ground, a jolt rocking through my bones. The arms release me. I roll onto my back. The book falls from my arms. Prickly grass stabs my shoulder blades, and a strong earthy scent climbs up my nose.

I open my eyes. Purple expanse unfolds above me.

I'm alive.

I inspect my limbs. Nothing broken.

"Pretty girl all right?" Nym asks.

A few stray rocks dig into my skin as I push up on my elbows, then my hands, and come to a sitting position.

Ow. I wince and yank a large rock from under my rear end. "Pretty girl is just fine."

Mostly. I look around me. I'm on the ground. Nym must've

caught me mid-air and done his little teleporting trick. Nifty. And wonderful. I literally owe him my life.

I sigh, lift my hands to my face and inspect my fingers. Each one is still intact, not broken. Every part of me is fine.

Except not.

All is fine except for the fact I just abandoned Eric to torture. To save my own butt. There's no convincing myself he deserves being left to the wolves anymore. He doesn't.

For whatever reason, he's changed since he was on Earth with me, in the Mortal Realm. I still don't know why his motives are different or why he suddenly cares so much about . . . *everything*. But he does.

He cares for me. He cares about bringing his father down.

Guilt gnaws in my belly, sends heat up my neck, spilling onto my cheeks.

But at least I'm alive and we retrieved the book. Now we can work on saving my dad. I'll convince Aibell to spring Eric from jail while we're at it.

"Need help?" Nym looks down at me, which is odd since he's so much shorter than I am.

I wave him away and groan as I pick up the book, struggle to my feet. "Where are we?"

I look around. We're back in the forest, but it's not where we started. We're definitely farther away from the castle. There are rocks and at least one cave entrance. And water is trickling from somewhere.

"Meeting spot," is all he mumbles.

I nod. Not because I understand what he means, but because I'm growing used to him, I think. I'll find out about all the things before too long, I have no doubt.

A bird calls to another in the distance, its answer coming seconds later. Otherwise, I hear no other animals nearby.

Then again, it's daytime. From what I've seen, the animals are happier roaming at night, just like the fae.

I stretch, rub my bottom where the rock stabbed it hard

enough to leave a bruise. My palms are shredded. Small cuts lace my flesh, and dried blood is caked between my fingers.

Yuck.

Instinct tells me to wander a bit, take note of my surroundings, but lack of sleep suddenly catches up with me. I collapse on a nearby rock, gingerly setting the book beside me. Nym stands at attention, as if awaiting a command.

I pick at a section of rock beneath me. "How did you know? To catch me mid-air like that. To bring me here?"

"Meeting place." He bounces on his toes as if this answers everything.

"Yes, I got that. Eric told you to bring me here because it's the meeting place. But what about while we were inside the castle? How could you possibly know to catch me *as I was falling*?"

"My prince told me."

"Eric told you to catch me as I jumped from the top? When?"

"When you jumped."

I frown. "That doesn't make sense. How did he tell you when he was inside being—um, detained?"

No need to worry the poor creature with details.

Nym points to his head. "The way he always speaks to me. In here."

Wait, what? I sit up straighter. "He's done it before?"

The little man shrugs. "Always."

So Eric can read Nym's thoughts too?

"How?" I ask again.

Nym's orb-like eyes wander to the forest, and I sense the conversation is over. Not sure why I expected any solid answers from him anyway.

Seconds later, twigs snap and footfalls alert us to an approaching faerie.

I jump to my feet, brace myself for a fight.

Aibell crashes through the trees, out of breath, her shoulders heaving as her gaze falls on me. She visibly relaxes as she walks toward me. "You made it."

I blink. *Barely.* If you count jumping to your death as making it. "I made it."

"Good." She pauses, glances around. "Where's the traitor?"

Anger immediately takes root in my chest. Why does she insist on calling him that? "The *traitor* gave himself up, chose to save me so I could get away." *That's what friends do.*

I gasp at the words that almost fall out of my mouth.

She snorts. "How noble. Guess he was good for something."

I open my mouth to retort, but she's already moved on, her focus on the entrance to the cave. She strides past me with purpose, almost swiping my shoulder with hers.

"Come on." She disappears inside the cave.

I grind my teeth and turn to vent my frustration to Nym. But he's gone. Again. Seriously annoying.

I grab the book and follow her inside the cavern.

As soon as I'm inside, I locate the sound of the running water. The cave is nowhere near as dark as it should be, a luminescence coming from the small pool and waterfall in the back. The walls and floor are damp.

Crude drawings of the symbol of enslavement cover one section of wall to my left, but there are no other markings. I walk to the pool only to discover a small opening above the cave, allowing ample light to shine down.

"Hey," I say. "I'm serious that Eric saved me by giving himself up. Think it's possible to free him when we save my dad?"

"First things first. Let me see the book." Aibell's voice comes from a corner, her face shadowed. She's seated on a rock, her feet propped up as she reclines against the wall.

I glance toward the cave opening. I wish Eric were here. With a sigh, I cross the short distance and hand her the book.

She immediately begins flipping through.

I say, "It was a trap. King Raghnall spelled the book so when it left the room, it set off an alarm. There was zero chance of ever getting out of the castle without getting caught."

She gestures to me. "But you obviously didn't."

I blink. "We almost made it out, but a few of the king's men caught up to us. I was already around the corner. They never even saw me. But they got Eric. They were beating him pretty good when I left."

She laughs. Literally laughs.

I suck in a breath but force my face to remain stoic.

She smirks. "Can't imagine the king allowing the princeling to get too banged up."

"You don't understand. Eric doesn't work for the king anymore. Those men were hurting him. His father could kill him if we don't go back and—"

"We're not going back." Aibell rolls her eyes. "He'll be just fine."

"No. He. Won't." I spit out each word. "I know you don't believe it, but he's changed. He isn't working for his father anymore. His life is in danger—"

"Relax, Caoine. The king won't kill his son without trying to use him as leverage. Believe me."

I want to growl but hold my attitude in check. "Why do you hate him so much? What do you know that I don't?"

Her smile fades, and her eyes go glassy as she looks toward the pool of water. Like she's weighing every thought. She licks her lips and shifts in her seat.

I wait, intent on forcing her hand this time.

Her gaze meets mine. "You want to hear this?"

I nod.

She sets the book aside, motions to the rock beside her. "Have a seat, sweetheart. You're about to find out why I hate that boy so much."

34

THE GENTLE RUSH of the waterfall echoes against the narrow cave walls as I settle onto a rock closer to the entrance.

I don't take the space offered by Aibell. Not because it looks less comfy, but because I grow weary of the way she orders me around.

Her words don't control me the way my dad has been forced to for so many years, to keep me and my song safe from the rest of the world. And they're not even controlling in the way my banshee song has always controlled me, leaving me no say whether I sing each night or not.

But why should I follow her every command? For eighteen years I've done what others have told me. I need to start making my own decisions.

"Princeling didn't notice who I was at first, but I'm sure he has figured it out by now."

Aibell pulls a dagger from her boot, a metal so shiny it's certainly not of Earth. She cups a small stone in the palm of her left hand, the deformed one, her fingers tight around it, as she sharpens her blade.

"Our rivalry caused quite a stink in the castle. I'm sure he hates me just as much as I hate him."

A brown curl falls loose from her hair tie, casting a shadow over her eyes.

"You worked in the castle?" I narrow my gaze at her.

Since when did I come to trust Eric—the boy who tried to murder my boyfriend and my dad—more than the girl sent to save me?

She doesn't look up as her blade *scrapes, scrapes, scrapes* against the heavy minerals in the stone. Like the steady tick-tock of a clock, or the cadence with which my pencil coasts across a sheet of paper as I write my poems.

My heart sinks. It's been too many days since I've written something. No wonder my anxiety is growing like an invisible monster.

"Eric didn't discover the king was his father until several years ago. As soon as they connected, he left his mother in the woods and came to live at the castle. A complete change of scenery for him, I guess." She snorts. "He was eager to please the king. Too eager. That boy is like a puppy, ready to bow to anyone who would give him attention."

"So you met him at the castle?"

"I grew up within those walls." Aibell's lips purse. "Worked my way up through the ranks of soldiers. When princeling arrived, I was being trained for a brand-new position, a special place by the king's side. An assassin."

I frown, glance at her left hand. "But how could you be a soldier when your hand—"

I falter, heat flooding my cheeks.

Her brow slants with wicked speed. She lifts her hand. "You think this little thing could stop me from being the best swordsman in the realm? That I couldn't keep up with the boys?" She leans forward. "Because I have a few things to tell you if you believe someone lame, or a *girl*, might be less than."

I fumble for words. "I'm sorry. I—I wasn't thinking. I didn't mean anything by it."

Aibell settles back in her spot, sharpening her blade once

more. "No one tells me what I can or cannot be. I would've been the best assassin the king had, if he'd let me."

What would the king need one of those for?

"What happened?" My voice is smaller now that I've stuck my big, fat foot in my mouth.

"I was to be *the* assassin. The king's marfóir. I've trained with the blade my entire life and was mastering the bow and arrow. My hand-to-hand combat was better than most of his private guard."

Her upper lip curls, and she saws her blade a little too hard against stone.

"Then Eric walks in one day, full of spirit. Full of promise." She rolls her eyes. "The king was clearly enamored. Raghnall immediately threw the boy at me, ordered me and a handful of guards to train him for the position I was supposed to have."

My eyes go wide. Yeah, I'd be pretty mad if Jessica walked into the school paper as a new student and demanded to have my job.

She shoves the dagger into her boot and pockets the sharpening stone. "At first I humored the king, assuming he would find something else for the boy to do once he discovered the kid was an idiot."

Aibell shakes her head. "I mean, he had no training, no skills. He literally threw an ax around to cut wood his entire life. He wasn't even good at social stuff. You know, being all sequestered in the woods with his mother."

Actually, I didn't know. This is all news to me. But I remain silent to keep her talking.

"For months I trained the pathetic kid, thinking the king would toss him on guard duty at the front gate or some nonsense. But no. After only a few months, the boy is hailed as the king's new protégé. Like the king did any work himself."

Her nose flares. "He acquires the position of the king's marfóir, and not a word is said about me. I assume the king thought I would melt into his guard."

Finally, she goes quiet.

"But you didn't," I say.

"But I didn't," she confirms.

We sit in silence as the story washes over me. I feel bad for the girl, I really do. She lost her dream job to the child of the company's owner. Familiar story to many on Earth.

Her animosity still feels out of place, though.

I lick my lips. "So Eric knew you were supposed to have his job?"

"Not at that time, no. He assumed I was one of his trainers —among many. He worked hard, had far too much enthusiasm." She barks a laugh, looks toward the water. "It wasn't until I demanded King Raghnall give me my rightful position that Eric took notice of me."

Now I do react. My jaw drops open. "You demanded it?"

She nods, her poker face still in place. "I fought hard for my job, but in the end, there was no room for me. Eric took the only thing that has ever meant something to me. Ever."

Her jaw flexes, and her body goes rigid.

"But couldn't you have had another guard position, one super high in authority? If you just talked to the king —"

She pushes off the rock, takes two long strides toward me. "You don't understand. That position was *mine*. I was always supposed to be the king's marfóir! Some idiotic, illegitimate child never deserved such prestige."

Oh.

"You . . . you just don't understand." She spins on her heel and walks toward the pool, hands on her hips.

She's right. I still don't understand. But why won't she help me understand?

Instinct tells me to run, to get some fresh air outside the cave. But I've been that girl for far too long. If I'm going to call this fae my friend, I need to know what makes her tick.

I step alongside her, my gaze on the swirl of water beneath

the waterfall. "Why was it so important you hold that specific position? There must've been a reason."

She releases a breath, her shoulders slumping. "It—it was because without it I had . . . *nothing.*" Pause. "I'm what you call a . . . neamini."

Okay. I wait, nibble on the inside of my cheek.

"It means *less than.*" She slowly raises her deformed left hand. "This means I'm less than."

It's as if she plunges that sharpened dagger of hers right into my heart.

Of course. Of course this would have everything to do with her disability. With the fact she trained so hard for an impossible position, to become so much better than any male faerie—just to have it taken away by a spoiled brat.

"The fae are near-perfect creatures, Caoine. It's why Raghnall thinks we should command all the realms, not just the fae ones. Faeries are not born this way." She turns her withered hand back and forth, her gaze sad. "It takes deep magic . . . or a tragic mistake, I guess, to make this happen."

I state the obvious. "Cat isn't like this."

She huffs. "No. My twin didn't get the brunt of . . . whatever made me like this. Clíodhna is a normal faerie. No deformities. Born for a purpose." Aibell swallows. "The image of perfection."

Cat is everything Aibell always wanted to be, just like being a normal teenager is all I've ever wanted.

"A neamini doesn't have any special powers." Her voice is so quiet, I almost don't hear this last part.

"Powers?" I shiver.

She finally looks at me. "You know, how Eric can do that soak-up-your-emotions thing and Laoise can disappear? They're called gifts, actually."

She goes on even though I've heard some of this before. I lean forward slightly.

"The Gift of Empathy—that's Eric's—and Laoise has the

Gift of Evanescence. Killian has the Gift of Faithfulness and Gar the Gift of Intention."

I shake my head. I don't follow.

She sighs. "Killian has the ability to have more faith than anyone else, even against all odds, and Gar always hits his mark when using his spear."

"Oh. Wow." Yeah, her anger makes so much more sense.

In fact, she's probably handling it better than I would, if I were in her position. I open my mouth to tell her this—to comfort her—but don't.

Instead I say, "Is there a way to know what a faerie's gift is? Like, before it shows itself?"

She narrows her gaze at me. "Not that I'm aware of."

"Huh." I look away, avoid the dead weight of her eyes on mine. Will I ever get my gift? I clear my throat. "Can I ask you something?"

She nods.

"Erm, about my banshee song. You said not to let any other fae know who—uh, *what* I am. Why not?"

She looks directly at me. "If any faeries find out you're a banshee, it would be bad."

"Bad how?"

She scowls. "Just bad, Caoine. Take my word for it."

I prepare for a fight. I want answers. I need to find out why I'm not allowed to be myself in a place that's partly my home. But I don't get to ask her.

Before I can say another word, Eric walks into the cave.

35

HE STANDS at the mouth of the cave, his lower lip cut, blood as blue as cotton candy. His hair and clothes are mussed, but otherwise, he looks the same.

Before I can think, I bound across the few feet that separate us and fling myself into his arms.

He stiffens, groans.

I freeze. What am I even doing? How is it possible I'm happy to see him?

He's still frozen beneath my embrace, his body all angles and sharp curves and discomfort. I'm just about to let go when I remember—

I slide a single hand from his shoulder to his wrist.

Immediately he relaxes. Warmth from his skin seeps into mine, stealing the shiver from moments ago. I can smell sweat and torture on him, and my heart shrinks.

Am I doing this right? I'm the worst at comforting others. My heart aches with how much I wish Oliver were here right now. Especially just to hold me.

I sigh, slowly pull back. He winces and pulls a hand to his belly, his uneasy gaze on Aibell.

I state the obvious. "You're here."

He coughs, cringes. "I was able to—"

"Surprise, surprise. The prince escaped the castle." Aibell remains in her spot near the water.

The peace he pulled from me seconds before is gone, his body tense as he steps toward her. "You think I planned that? Escaping wasn't easy. Do you know how many guards I had on my tail?"

"Too many." Her voice is sharp as ice. "And if you led them here, I'll kill you myself, boy."

He squints daggers at her but remains rooted where he stands. "No one followed me." He spits each word.

I tilt my head. "How did you get away? They had you pretty good when we, uh, parted."

I avoid looking at Aibell. If she knew I'd abandoned him, she'd never stop torturing him with that knowledge.

Eric pulls in a shaky breath and finds a rock to collapse on, one hand still across his belly. I can only imagine the bruises he has.

"The two guards who had me were imbeciles." He finds a quick laugh, that dimple in his left cheek appearing. "They should've known how well I know the castle. And the hidden passageways." He gives me a wink.

I jolt to life. "Hidden passageways? Why didn't we just sneak in that way from the beginning?"

He shakes his head. "Enchantments, Caoine. The passageways can be found to sneak out of, in case the royal family needs to escape, but they're hidden otherwise. We couldn't have used them on the way *in*."

"And once we were inside? Why make me jump to my death?" Heat builds in my core, and I reconsider that peaceful hug I so willingly gave the boy two minutes ago.

He shakes his head. "What was I supposed to do? Stop running and explain how to find one of the secret passageways? We were being chased."

His voice is raised, probably in response to the fact my

hands are now on my hips.

"Besides, we were nowhere near them."

"Oh stop it, you two." Aibell rolls her eyes. "Now you see what a trickster he can be. Boo-hoo."

"It's not a trick." Eric pounds a fist against his thigh and sends a murderous look in her direction.

I cross my arms. "Fine. You slipped away from the dumb guards and sneaked out of the castle. Glad you're back."

His face falls as if he's hurt by my words.

"What about the other — ?"

I stop. I never told Aibell about the telepathic thing between Eric and me. Well, Eric and Nym too, I guess. My eyes skitter in her direction and back again.

He shakes his head minutely.

Right. So the talking-in-the-head thing is a secret. I say instead, "Are you hurt badly?"

He sighs, touches his lip where it's busted. "I'll be fine. Just don't ask me to scale any walls anytime soon."

I chuckle, but it fades.

Aibell's voice cuts the air like a knife. "Laoise?"

Eric and I whip around to find the other faeries at the mouth of the cave, including Nym.

Aibell's on her feet, and I'm hugging each of our friends in turn. Eric tends to his wounds.

"How are you feeling?" I ask Laoise as I step back from our embrace.

Her smile is genuine. "Much better now."

Nym toddles over to have a private conversation with Eric, but no one appears to care.

"You made it out, daughter of Earth." Killian's demeanor is father-like. "Where's the book?"

I motion to it on the rock as Aibell strolls over and picks it up to show them.

"It was a trap," Aibell says as she throws Eric a distrusting look. "They knew we were coming and spelled the book so it couldn't leave the castle."

Eric's face twists in rage. "Just because my father put a spell on the book doesn't mean he was expecting us to attack. Only that he was on alert for *something* to happen. Any good soldier knows to always be on alert."

She huffs. "I don't buy it. I think they were tipped off."

Eric scowls. "They were surprised. Otherwise the number of guards out front would've been double." His brow furrows. "You of all fae should know that."

She bites back a retort.

"Enough." Killian stands regal. "We now possess both books. What is our next move?"

We save my dad. I swallow, look at my blood-stained hands. "We go back in."

Aibell shakes her head. "Not possible. They've just been attacked. They'll be expecting it."

"No, they won't," I argue. "They might be jittery, but they won't be expecting another attack so soon. We need to save my dad."

She doesn't look happy that I'm challenging her. That's Eric's domain. No one looks convinced, so I go on.

"Look, I get that we're all running on adrenaline and need to rest, but that's exactly what they're expecting." I tuck a strand of loose hair behind my ear. "Why not go back in, right now, before they can debrief and figure out the details? They're blind, still getting stories of who did what. There's zero chance they'll suspect anyone would be crazy enough to break in immediately."

Each of them look at me like I've got two heads.

"Please. We must go now."

Images of my dad being tortured by Unseelie guards flit through my mind, and I suck in a breath like I've been gut-punched.

"Won't you help me?" My shaky voice threatens to tattle on the fact I'm about to cry.

Eric's jaw is clenched, his gaze drifting to my bloodied hands. "Yeah, but it's insane." He frowns.

"It is, you're right, but . . ." Gar narrows his gaze. "It just might work." He looks to Killian. "Thoughts?"

The faerie shifts, looks from Gar to Laoise and back again. "Statistically, there is truth in her words. It could work in our favor if we attempt to retrieve her father immediately."

The Gift of Faithfulness. Killian believes we can do this.

Sometimes believing is all it takes.

36

THE GENTLE LILT of tumbling water is the only sound in the cave as all eyes turn to Aibell.

Her lips pucker as she nibbles her cheek. "Give us a moment to discuss this."

Her gaze catches each of her companions, except Eric and me. My insides crawl like they've been invaded with worms. Heat tumbles off Eric.

Make it more obvious we're not invited, why don't you?

Aibell leads the way to the far side of the cave, followed by Killian and Laoise, who don't appear the least bit concerned we've been banned from a discussion about my own dad.

Fire boils in my veins, but I stay quiet. Whatever it takes for them to save him. I guess.

Gar gives us one final glance, then harrumphs and stomps over to a nearby rock. Whispers begin as the four debate.

Eric looks at me, his gaze as heavy as a May downpour, soaking and bleeding into my skin. We stand in silence for ten seconds. He frowns again, taking me by the wrists and pulling me gently toward the pool. He sits us on a damp rock.

The chatter of the others fades until it's just Eric's heat

195

beside me and the unending barrage of liquid as it splashes and plays in the waterfall.

He pulls me closer, my skin searing from his touch.

Eric pushes my hands under the water, rubs the dried blood from my palms. The cuts from my nails sting, and I grind my teeth but don't whine. Not when the man who was just beaten is helping me heal.

He tugs my hands deeper under the water. "Are you going to tell me what happened?"

My knee begins to bounce, and I stare at my lap. "No."

He chuckles but doesn't stop flecking away blood. "So your hands spontaneously started bleeding?"

"I—we—" I lick my lips. "You made me jump!"

He raises his brows. "I made you jump to a spot where Nym could transport you to safety."

I glare right into his eyes. "You made me *jump*."

He sighs, shakes the water from my hands, and gives them back to me so I can wipe them on my pants. "It was a split-second decision, Caoine. I didn't know what else to do."

"So you make me jump off the side of a castle?" I flare my nostrils.

He scrubs his hands over his face. "I did what I could in a bad situation. I promise I wouldn't have told you to jump if I wasn't 100% sure Nym would be there to save you."

I continue to glare.

"Really."

I huff. "Well . . . thank you. I guess. I mean, it did save me from getting caught and all. But still . . . when were you going to tell me you're a telepath? And why is this just coming out now?"

"Actually, all fae are telepaths."

"What?"

"It's true. I mean, not in the Mortal Realm, no. I couldn't do it then. Only in the Faerie Realms. And the fae can't just talk to anyone. We only have the ability with those we trust.

Like, a lot. Usually with family members, but not always. As soon as I betrayed my father, I lost my connection with him."

I play with a loose string on my shirt. "So it can come and go?"

He nods. "According to the relationships we have with others. Those we are closest to, whom we have a deep spiritual connection with, we can speak to inside our heads. Only those we are most loyal to."

"Wow." Pause. "You have a deep connection with me?" I try not to twist my lips but fail.

He wipes his palms on his jeans, rests his elbows on his knees. "Looks that way." He won't look me in the eyes.

"Huh." Another pause. "You have this connection with Nym too?"

He nods.

"Which is why you know we can trust him."

He nods again.

"Which Aibell wouldn't understand because you haven't told her."

"Bingo."

I frown. "But if all faeries can do it, why not just tell her? Why make her doubt?"

He scowls. "Why should I? I don't owe her a thing."

My earlier conversation with her comes back, and I bite my lip. *I beg to differ.*

But I don't say it.

"So we have a strong connection—for reasons unknown—and you can read my mind and place thoughts in my head?"

"Sounds about right."

"When did you discover this?"

"Actually, it was when we were outside Tumblecreek, during our discussion over breakfast." A boyish smile spreads across his face. "I wanted to know what you were thinking, and suddenly I did."

My eyes go wide, and I smack his shoulder.

"Ouch!" He rubs it like it hurt, even though it absolutely didn't. Not compared to the beating he took inside the castle.

"You've been reading my thoughts all this time and haven't told me?"

He rolls his eyes. "It doesn't work that way. I need to concentrate. Hard. I haven't been eavesdropping, if that's what you're afraid of."

"Good." I lift my chin. "But does this mean I can speak to you too?"

His lips curl into a smile. "You're fae, aren't you? Of course you can. You just need to try."

"Oh." I squint my eyes as tight as I can.

"What are you doing?"

"Trying."

Eric laughs. "It's not a magic trick, Caoine. Just think about it, and it'll happen."

I open my mouth . . . shut it. I can do this, right?

The waterfall's echo rushes against my ears, drowns out all other thoughts, sounds, smells. I look into Eric's eyes. Focus. On him. On the humming deep inside my mind . . .

Marco.

I jump. "What?"

He laughs again. "You say *Polo.* It's a game. From the Mortal Realm. Remember? Or have you been stuck inside the Unseelie too long?" He winks.

I hold back the desire to smack him once more. *Turkey.*

"But you heard me, didn't you?" He raises his brows. "You heard my thought?"

I nod.

"Good. Try to say something back."

I blow out a harsh breath. Think, focus. *Polo.*

A smile spreads across his face. "Nicely done."

I glance at my hands. "Hey, how come you could heal me at the castle? I thought you said no magic inside the walls?"

He runs a hand through his hair. "Healing isn't magic. It's just . . . a part of being fae."

Huh.

"Hey, Princeling," Aibell interrupts. "Where's that friend of yours?"

Eric looks at her, our conversation forgotten. "He should be back soon. He comes and goes every few minutes."

He stands and walks over to the others, so I follow.

Nym pops up right beside Eric. I gasp. Did Eric just tell him to come through that telepathic thing?

Without missing a beat, Eric takes the Book of Discernment from Nym and starts flipping pages. The little guy must've gone back to the hideout to retrieve it.

Aibell picks up the other book and grips it to her side like a vice. Her wary eyes don't leave Eric. *Don't trust anybody.* Clearly she's still got problems with the Unseelie prince.

I refrain from rolling my eyes. This whole battle between the two feels like drama from high school.

I clear my throat. "So, uh, what's the deal? When are we going back for my dad?"

Laoise's gaze connects with mine, her face stoic. Gar looks my way too, his expression hard, like always. Killian is the only one of the three who falters, his eyes dropping to the floor.

Aibell steps forward. "We aren't."

37

THE CAVE WALLS tilt around me, the sweet air fading quickly.

I squeeze my eyes shut, wish away tears. This can't be right. I didn't hear her right.

At Eric's voice, my eyes pop back open.

"What's that supposed to mean?" Eric moves closer, his brows pulled down in a V.

Aibell shrugs. "It means what it means. The most important thing right now is getting these books to Queen Faílenn."

"Wait, what?" My voice wobbles.

"Relax." Her face shows no sympathy. "I didn't say we'd never get him out. We're simply delaying the process. Once you've crossed into the Mortal Realm and delivered the books to the queen's daughter, you'll return and we'll free your dad."

"No." The word spills from me like an explosion. "I'm not coming back here. Not ever. We get my dad out now, or I'm not taking the books to Aubree. Besides, Eric said we need both books to save my dad."

Eric avoids my gaze.

I glare at Aibell. "Why don't *you* take them to the queen? Why does it have to be me?"

Aibell scowls. "Only a human can bring the books across

the Veil without detection. The king will immediately know they are no longer in the Unseelie Realm."

It must be a human?

Killian frowns. "I don't understand why this vexes you, human." He stands straight and regal. "We are in no way backing out of our agreement to assist you in recovering your father. We simply ask that you follow through with your end of the bargain first."

"Bargain?" My eyes shoot to the cave ceiling. "Is this a faerie deal we're making here?" I look between them. "I thought you agreed to help me of your own free will."

Laoise tips her head slightly. "There's nothing free when it involves the fae, daughter of Saoirse."

"You snakes!" Eric shoves the book into Nym's arms and steps up to Aibell, their noses practically touching. "You promised! There was no faerie bargain involved."

Aibell places a finger against Eric's chest and pushes. He takes a step back. "I never make promises, traitor. You of all fae should know this."

Eric's hands ball into fists, and his shoulders raise a few inches. His eyes are cold. A growl rumbles inside his chest.

I try to hide the way my hands shake, the quaking of my body as I fight to remain standing.

A single tear spills down my cheek. "I can't leave my dad."

Why does it come out a whisper when all I want to do is yell?

"Fear not." Laoise appears beside me, a hand on my shoulder. "All will be well in the end."

"Do you believe this?" Killian asks.

I blink free a few more tears. "I—I don't know." Another gasp pulls at my chest. "Will it?"

"Don't believe them, Caoine." Eric's stance remains rigid. "There's a trick in this. I can feel it."

I frown. "But Killian said it will work out. If his gift displays true faith, then wouldn't he know?"

Killian startles, clearly surprised I know of his talent.

Eric shakes his head. "That's exactly what they want you to think, Caoine. The human part of you is falling right into their plan."

"I assure you there is no plan," Laoise says. "We have every intention of fulfilling the queen's request and of helping Caoine free her father."

Gar grunts in agreement.

I swallow. Look between Aibell, Killian, Laoise, Gar. Turn to Eric, Nym bouncing on his toes by his side. Who do I believe?

"I—I—" I want to believe they're telling the truth. But what if they aren't? What if I can't return to the Unseelie Realm? Or what if they trap me here forever?

My head pounds a drumbeat faster and louder than my thoughts can match. My breath catches in my throat. I squeeze my eyes shut. If only Oliver were here to help me decide. He would know what to do.

I need you, Oliver. I need help.

Aibell places a hand on her hip, clearly done with this conversation. "Caoine, listen—"

"No," Eric interrupts. "You listen. We stick with the original plan. End of story."

Before anyone can respond, he glances out of the corner of his eye, Nym turning slightly to look up at his friend. In a flash, Eric grabs me around the waist, hoists me over his shoulder.

Nym grabs Eric's arm and closes his eyes just as a blast of bright light envelopes us.

Someone screams as we disappear. But it's not just the three of us who leave the cave.

Nym has the Book of Discernment in his arms.

38

WE APPEAR INSIDE THE HIDEOUT, a scent of lavender greeting us. I breathe heavily, disoriented from our jump. Frantic.

"Go back! What are you doing?"

Eric literally just kidnapped me. Again.

I'm still flung over Eric's shoulder, so I beat his back. What I'd like to do is split that lip of his again, make him bleed the sorrow that invades my soul.

Eric winces and ducks as he struggles to set me free, effectively dumping me on the wooden floor. Hard.

"Ouch!" I rub my bottom and glare the sharpest daggers I can manage.

He crosses his arms, not amused. "If you quit fighting, maybe I would've been more gentle."

I scramble to my feet and slam my hands into his chest and push him back, only a foot from his face. His injuries from earlier are almost completely healed.

When will I learn to do that healing thing? Or do I already have the ability without knowing it?

"My prince?" Nym nervously rubs his hands over the book he still holds as he looks between Eric and me.

Eric glances at him, gives a nod.

I roll my eyes. He just spoke inside his head. What is this, kindergarten? Are we no longer using our words?

Nym places the book on the table. Once the little man disappears, Eric faces me and steps back.

I fling an arm in what I think is the direction of the cave, but let's be honest, I have no clue where I am right now.

"What. Was. That?" I grind my molars. "Why did you just steal me away from the only friends I've got in this realm?"

His brows pull together. "Hey. What am I?"

I huff.

He points a finger directly at my nose. "Are you honestly telling me you want to go along with their plan? That you want to go home *without* your dad?"

I press my lips together.

He takes a step closer. "Listen, Caoine. You may not be familiar with the fae or the way things work here, but I can guarantee you they have no intention of honoring their words."

I pout. "But Killian. He believes things will work out just fine if we do it their way."

Another step closer, his hands on my upper arms. "Maybe he does believe that, but I have no doubt Aibell will deceive every one us. You. Me. Them. You come back here for your dad, and you won't be leaving again."

I open my mouth but stop. This was exactly what I was afraid of. "So you stole the book? What good will that do?"

He swipes a hand down his face, looks weary. Like we're back in high school and it's final exam week.

I temper my emotions.

Eric grabs the book off the table, his expression worried, laced with hues of blues and grays. "We hide this. Until your dad is free and safe. Then you can take the books back to Aubree without needing to return here. Ever."

Eric's voice is soft and rough.

I sigh. "I like this plan a little better."

He grins. "I thought you'd say that." He licks his lips.

"Sorry about . . ." He scratches the back of his neck. "Well, for taking you against your will."

I nod. "At least it was to *help* me this time."

He chuckles. "Come on."

We exit the hideout into chilly winter air. Eric leads us in and out of trees, weaving and wandering in what appears to be a random direction. Except I'm sure it's totally not.

His internal woodsprite GPS is leading us to the perfect place to hide the book until the time is right.

I'm out of breath by the time we've gotten it hidden and return to the treehouse. Not soon enough, either. We've only been settled for a few minutes when World War III arrives at the front door.

Bang! It flies open, and we rise to our feet in unison. My muscles tense.

Aibell and Laoise lead the way with Killian and Gar close behind. They all wear grim expressions.

Aibell charges us like a bull. "What do you think you're doing ?"

I instinctively step behind Eric.

He sucks in a quick breath, his chest puffing out. "I did what needed to be done. For Caoine's sake."

"For Caoine's sake?" Aibell's voice rises an octave. "What about what's best for the realms, prince? Tell me, are you on the queen's side or do you remain loyal to your father? Because right now it appears you're the traitor I always took you for."

Instead of answering her taunts, Eric takes the high ground. "Here's the plan: You help Caoine free her dad. Only then will I reveal the location of the Book of Discernment. Then the two of them can cross to the Mortal Realm with both books. This plan is non-negotiable. You will keep Caoine and her dad safe and return them home, or I will personally end you."

Aibell snorts. "I would like to see you try, *boy*."

The two narrow their gazes, seconds passing in their staring match.

Finally, Aibell exhales. "Agreed." She steps toward Eric. "But if I see one bit of deceit on your part—if I feel you will jeopardize this mission in any way—I'll do worse to you than whatever your puny little head could think up."

Eric crosses his arms. "Oh yeah?"

"Count on it."

Another thirty seconds pass in silence as we wait for someone to speak next.

Which, it turns out, is me. "Great. So how do we get into the castle to get my dad?"

My heart flutters a million beats per minute that I just said those words. My tears from earlier are long gone. I'll actually get to see my dad again. After six months.

A wave of emotion slams into my core, and a laugh bubbles inside my chest, although I refuse to let it spill free.

Focus, Caoine.

Aibell breaks from her challenging stance and turns to me. "The spell we need to break your father out of prison is in the Book of Judgment. We have everything we need."

I look at Eric. Didn't he say we needed both books?

He shifts on his feet and looks at the wall.

The boy tricked me. *He* needed both books. But *I* only needed one to save my dad.

His eyes meet mine. I glare at him.

Eric clears his throat and looks at Aibell. "Which spells will you use?"

She curls her upper lip. "We use the counter spell the king used to prevent magic from being used inside the castle." Aibell looks at me. "Along with a smaller spell that will unlock Brent's cell. Once we get the barrier down, we go in the old-fashioned way. We break her father free using everything we've got."

I smile. Finally, a plan I can get behind.

39

Aibell grabs an apple from the table and bites into it as she carries the Book of Judgment to a chair and plops down. She opens the cover and sifts through pages.

While she reviews the spell, Killian and Gar head to the opposite corner to clean their weapons. Gar laughs at something Killian says, but I calm my frantic heart from wanting to know what they're discussing.

The fae can have all the secrets they want. As long as I get my dad back.

"I'm going to go—" But I never finish the sentence. I don't know where I'm going. The only thing that fills my head is I'm one step closer to going home. *So close.*

Eric lopes off to dig through the cabinet for sustenance as I slump into one of the armchairs in exhaustion.

Laoise glides near. "May I?" She gestures toward the other armchair.

"Sure." Although, truth be told, I'd much rather be alone right now.

"You appear melancholy. Is there something wrong other than the safety of your father?"

I sigh. "Just missing . . . someone."

"A loved one?"

My cheeks warm. "Maybe." I pick at a hole in my jeans. "His name's Oliver. He's my boyfriend."

She purses her lips. "Boyfriend. This is a term of endearment?"

I hide my smile. "Yes. It means we are committed to one another . . . romantically."

Warmth blossoms in my belly, and I find it hard to swallow. Why am I sitting in a faerie treehouse discussing my love life with a wisp I barely know?

Laoise nods. "I understand what it's like to miss loved ones. Do not fear, Caoine. You will be reunited soon."

My feeble smile doesn't reflect how grateful I am for her words.

She tilts her head. "I heard you did a valiant job on your mission."

Her voice is soothing, and I relax. "Right. It's almost as if I had no idea what was going on." My sarcasm isn't hidden.

She giggles. "It's thrilling, is it not? Working alongside them?" Her gaze is on Killian and Gar. "I'm never much good, other than my Gift of Evanescence."

"Yeah." This was her idea of fun? I'll take high school, thanks.

"I am impressed Eric was able to follow through with the mission so well. His past with the king was a concern for Aibell."

"His past?" I frown. "You mean, the fact that he betrayed his father and no longer works for him?"

She tilts her head again. "Well, that. And all the other things, too."

"Other things?" I sit up, my curiosity on high alert.

"Well, the way the king tricked Eric into leaving his mother and living at the castle. I mean, everyone believed Eric had left of his own free will. But now—" She glances at Eric. "Even the most skeptical are questioning just how much of it was a choice. It's not the first time those closest to the king have behaved contrary to their nature."

"Really?" This is some juicy gossip.

"There's also the way the queen died."

My mind wanders to the conversation with the tree just outside the castle. I lean forward, my eyes wide. "Queen Mairéad's death?"

The conversation with Eric from days before comes back to me. The queen is not his mother. Then who is?

Laoise nods. "Mm-hmm. The Unseelie queen passed away almost ten years ago of mysterious causes." She shrugs. "It didn't bother many of us, since she was just as nasty as he is. Still . . ."

The tree did mention it was her and the king's idea to wipe out every living thing on Earth. She does sound nasty.

"Still?" I dip my chin, asking for more.

She bites her lip, sits on the edge of her seat so our words can't be heard. "I don't know if Eric would appreciate us talking about this, but—" She looks to Eric, then back at me. "It's said the king still has her body in the castle."

I do a double take. "He has her body? Like, he didn't bury it after she died?"

Laoise shakes her head. "No, he didn't. But that's not the strange part." She purses her lips. "A select few inside the castle claim to have seen her dead body preserved in a case in a room off his bedchamber. They say it looks like she's sleeping, that the case prevents her decay."

I pucker my lips. "Wait. I thought faeries turned to dust when they died? That they became one with nature?"

She nods. "Most do, yes. But it depends on the lineage. Those of royal blood most often remain in bodily state for the burial ceremony attended by the kingdom. It's an ancient spell connected to their bloodline for thousands of years."

"Huh. Interesting."

My thoughts flit to Seamus, and pain stabs my heart. His loss will forever be a part of who I am.

"So this queen, she's dead but inside the castle? And no one knows why? Like, why the king is keeping her around?"

"Yes."

"Did he have a burial ceremony for her?"

"Yes, he did. Which is confusing. Why would he have a fake burial and then keep her body? It doesn't add up."

"No, it doesn't." I glance at Eric, suddenly curious—why all the secrecy whenever we bring up his father?

Could he have secrets about Queen Mairéad, too?

I sit back in my chair and watch him as he munches on a hunk of bread, his thoughts clearly elsewhere.

Maybe there's more to Eric than he's told me. I plan to find out exactly what.

40

I AWAKE AT MIDNIGHT, when the sky is deepest eggplant and the faerie creatures come out to play and seek revenge.

The others insisted I sleep. My eyelids didn't disagree. I needed rest, but so did the faeries.

Aibell was antsy before I laid down. *It's a complicated spell,* she said. One that involves me, apparently.

This particular spell requires a banshee to enact it. Not too big of a deal. Aubree has walked me through plenty of spells over the last few months.

But still, Aibell is worried. Worried that we won't be able to complete the spell if I'm not at full *power,* whatever that means.

So . . . *complicated.*

Faint scents of bread and sugar linger, and I suspect someone did some baking. My belly rumbles. I run my fingers through my hair and scratch my scalp to fully wake. My heart races. We're so close to ending this thing. To freeing my dad.

Food can wait.

I sit up in my little makeshift bed in the corner, run a hand over my face, rub my eyes until all the sleepies have been cleared. I scrub my fingers through my hair.

My hand hits something pointy.

I gasp, run my fingers back to the spot. My ear.

The top of my ear is pointed. Just like a faerie!

I jump to my feet and grab both ears at once. Yep. Not imagining it. I have faerie ears.

My heart pounds. I spin in a circle as I continue to touch them. Look for a mirror. Why don't fae have mirrors? Ugh!

I spy the five faeries huddled in chairs and run to show them my discovery. Then I stop.

A heated discussion is ongoing, and I'm aware I'm not meant to overhear. They don't notice me.

". . . sure she can handle that? She's never done this before." This from Killian.

"We don't have a choice," insists Aibell. "She's the only one we've got."

Eric's voice cuts like a blade. "Don't talk about her like she's an object."

Thank you. At least someone stands up for me. Although I have no idea for what.

Laoise says, "We'll assist her. She will be safe."

Gar next. "I don't see why we care so much. Would not the sacrifice of one mortal be worth saving the Faerie Realms?"

My jaw drops. *Enough.* I make myself known.

Eric and Laoise are the only two who don't squirm like they've just been caught saying bad things about me when I stand next to their group.

"Good morning, daughter of Saoirse," Laoise greets.

I frown. She never explained how she knows my mother.

Eric stands. "Did you sleep well?"

My heart stammers in response. I shouldn't trust the boy. He's got too many secrets. He's too willing to deceive me. And he's got a past to be reckoned with.

I swallow. Yet he's the closest thing I've got to a friend within this realm. And the way he looks at me now, as if he's standing on a precipice—the world on one side, a never-ending void on the other.

His skin begins to sparkle, and his eyes turn a plum color.

I step back. "Yes. Fine."

His brow pulls together, but he returns to his seat. I sit on the sofa, between Laoise and Aibell.

"What's the plan?" I ask as I glance at the ancient book on the small table.

Aibell turns to me. "I have good news." She doesn't flinch at the look Eric tosses her. "I have secured a way to get you across the Veil. As soon as this is over, you're going home."

My jaw falls open. "I hadn't realized that was ever a problem."

Aibell's lips flatten. "All things take planning. I never doubted we'd get you across. But now I have everything in place."

"Let's go get my dad."

She frowns. "We were just working on that part."

Eric's jaw clenches.

She goes on. "The minute we recover Brent from the castle, we'll get you to the Veil to go back to the Mortal Realm."

I huff a breath and take a beat to just *breathe*.

"But there's a complication."

My heart sinks. "Is it something we can work through?" *Please say it's something we can work through.*

She licks her lips. "Regardless how things go, the spell should work just fine. We're committed to freeing your father. Either both of you, or at the least your father, will be able to return to the Mortal Realm with the books."

"Excuse me?" I flinch. Had I heard her correctly? "Where will I be?"

I glance at the open book on the table. The pages are familiar from when I saw it back at Halloween—the margins, fancy script, colors. Even many of the words appear the same, although I wouldn't know, considering it's written in the language of the fae.

Aibell avoids my gaze and the question. "We think we have everything ready." Aibell runs a finger along the old book as she checks the words. "We're going to do the spell tomorrow night, at midnight."

I glance from her to Eric. Why isn't she answering my question? "Is there a significance for that? I mean, why can't we just do it now?"

She shakes her head. "It's too late. We've missed the window for tonight. The spell will be the most powerful in the moment when the days are one. When it is no longer yesterday but it is also not tomorrow."

"Huh." I nod as if it makes sense, but it totally doesn't. "So what's the problem?"

Visions of Eric with a knife at Oliver's neck flash in my mind, and heat fills my chest. I try not to look at him, but I can sense he's watching me. Is he remembering that night too?

My throat constricts, and I fight to breathe. "What do *I* do?"

Now Eric does move. He shifts so swiftly in his seat, it draws all our attention.

He sits forward, elbows on his knees, one of which is bouncing uncontrollably. "Go ahead, Aibell. Tell her."

Aibell glares the blackest of hate at him. She turns to me, her normally rugged demeanor softening. "You'll be singing."

I blink. Try not to laugh. "Singing?" I glance at the members of the group. "You do realize I can't carry a tune? Like, at all. I'm the worst of the worst of singers."

Aibell shakes her head. "No, not like that."

Eric pulls in a sharp breath, his jaw flexing.

Sweat breaks out on my back and under my arms. "How can I be singing if I'm not singing?" I freeze.

My banshee song.

I look to Aibell. "But I can't. You said my song wouldn't

work here. And you said I shouldn't tell anyone. That a banshee inside Faerie was a bad thing. If I sing my banshee lament, won't that put us in danger?"

Aibell glances at the book. "You need to understand . . . it's the only way."

Fire ignites inside my core. "What does that mean?" I look to Eric. "What does she mean, *it's the only way*? Is something going to happen to me?"

"Singing a banshee lament inside Faerie can come with a great cost." His voice is steady even though chaos is in his eyes.

"Great cost? What kind of great cost? How can I sing my banshee song when no one has died?" I look to Aibell, fury melting up my neck and onto my face.

She licks her lips. "Someone is going to die, Caoine. That's the only way your song can come out."

I jump to my feet. "Are you kidding me?" I step away from the sofa, putting distance between the faeries and myself.

Eric is on his feet too, but he stays in his spot.

My nails dig into my fists where my skin scabbed over, pain shooting through my hands. "My *song* is what I use to *save* lives. Not to *murder* someone for some stupid spell!"

Now Aibell's standing. "Hold on, Caoine. I don't think you understand—"

"I understand perfectly, Aibell. Someone must die for me to sing my banshee song, yes?"

She reluctantly nods.

I suck in a breath. "And when I sing my song, what will happen? You said it was dangerous for anyone in Faerie to know I'm a banshee. Why?"

Pause. "Banshees are not looked kindly upon by our race." Another pause. "In fact, if any of the fae were to find out—" She clears her throat. Sighs. "If they find out . . . any faeries within earshot will try to . . . silence you."

I raise my eyebrows. "To silence me? What's that supposed to mean?"

Killian steps forward. "It means you're the harbinger of death, daughter of Earth. The fae don't look kindly on those who bring death with them. So they'll do whatever they can to put a stop to it. This is why banshees do not remain within the fae realms. They live in the Mortal Realm because there's no other place for them."

"Great." I throw my hands up and roll my eyes.

Aibell looks directly at me. "They will also rip you to shreds once they get their hands on you."

At least she's giving me the full truth now. I think.

"Awesome. So as soon as I begin to sing, it'll draw every foul creature within a mile who will then literally peel the flesh from my bones. Is that what you're trying to tell me?"

"It will put you in a precarious situation, yes."

I put both hands over my face, close my eyes. I can't believe this is happening. "You've been using me this whole time, haven't you?" No response. "Haven't you? You just needed a human—any human—to take the books from the Unseelie Realm!" I don't mean to shout.

Oh wait, I *do*.

"Caoine—" Eric's voice is gentle.

"Don't!" I hold up a finger as I step back. "Don't you dare. You knew about this. The entire time we've been together, you *knew* what would need to happen to save my dad. You knew what it would mean for me to sing, that I might not come out of this alive."

His eyes cloud, lines cut deep between his brows.

I stifle a cry. "And I was beginning to believe you actually *cared* about me."

His throat bobs as he swallows, but he stays silent.

"I get it now." I try to calm myself, but it absolutely doesn't work. "I thought you needed me because the king targeted me in the last spell. Because he has my dad and you could use that as a bargaining chip to get me to help you."

He shifts uncomfortably.

I look at Aibell. "I thought you wanted to help me get back home. Because Cat wanted me home." I blink tears onto my cheeks. "But I was wrong. This is why you wanted me to take the books right away. You always knew both of us wouldn't make it out of here alive."

Aibell frowns. "Caoine, it isn't—"

I throw my hands in the air. "Why can't you people just be honest? The entire time I've been in this stupid realm, you've only given me half-truths. But what good has that done anyone? You never counted me as fae, never looked at me as one of you. I'm just a silly little human."

The tears flow freely now, warm salty liquid dripping from my chin, soaking my shirt.

"You have no idea what it was like being trapped on Earth with nothing, *no one* who understood me. For eighteen years! I had so many questions. My dad practically killed himself trying to find answers . . . and not one faerie cared to visit. Not one. To explain what being half-fae means. To *help* me."

I'm shaking now, flecks of red and black dotting my vision.

"I don't care about you or your stupid faerie friends who trap each other in bottles just to play nasty tricks on each other. I mean, who *does* that?" I'm going to be sick. "Not me. *Not* my friends."

Aubree and Oliver and Seamus appear in my mind. My heart crumbles to dust.

"And I don't care what happens to Faerie. As far as I'm concerned, I'm ready to burn those stupid books."

Eric flinches.

My voice is guttural. "None of you ever cared about me until I fell through that pathetic Veil and you realized you could use me." I turn and walk toward the door. "I'm done. I'm finding a way to get my dad that *won't* kill me, and we're going home. You can find another human to do your dirty work. Goodbye."

"Caoine!" Eric's voice is muffled as I step through the

magical door to the forest. I hear footsteps, and I know he's chasing me, but it doesn't matter.

He won't be able to find me.

Because as I step through that door, I'm not in the forest where I thought I'd be. I'm somewhere else.

And I don't know where that somewhere else is.

41

My world is dark. Not black. Not completely void of light. But shadowed.

Above me hangs an abyss of purple sky, stretched like a threadbare sweater to a sea of bubbling onyx.

The nothing that surrounds me swells to engulf me in a hug so tight I almost can't breathe. Except that I can, which confuses me. It's like I'm underwater, but I'm not. Floating but standing. Breathing and choking and wallowing in despair so thick I can dig my nails deep inside.

I blink. The illusion remains.

And then . . . then . . . I see *her*.

The most beautiful woman I've ever laid eyes on. Or maybe she's the most plain woman. With every second that passes her face wavers, changes, melts into a new vision.

It's as if I'm not seeing the real her but an image of someone she wishes me to see.

"Hello, Caoine." Her voice is instrumental music and apple pie and all the sweetness of summer honeysuckle.

I go to wipe my eyes but can't move my hands. I look down, but—

I'm looking up, my eyes only for her.

Every time I try to look away I *can't*. Her presence is blinding and unyielding, demanding my attention despite the fact she refuses to show her real self.

"My name is Queen Faílenn." She glides toward me as if on a rail, even though I can clearly see each step she takes, her feet bare and perfect.

Queen Faílenn? "Aubree's mother?"

The woman smiles.

Caramel-brown hair—no, wheat colored. Or is that a touch of strawberry blonde? I can't focus on her appearance. Only her eyes. Glowing and golden, with flecks of gray and bursts of every color in the spectrum as they fade in and out and in and out and—warmth bleeds across my skin and absorbs my every emotion.

I'm safe here. I never want to leave her.

"Aubree is one of many of my children. A special love tasked with a mission. One that involves you, Caoine Roberts."

Yes. I know. But—"Why am I here? Where did the Unseelie Realm go?"

"You are still there. I am but a dream to you. I remain in my own realm, unable to cross the Veil. King Raghnall made this so, long ago."

I frown, but her expression remains unchanged. At peace.

"I have come to encourage you, daughter of Earth."

"To encourage me?" My voice comes out a squeak.

"All is not lost, my child. No matter how hopeless the situation might feel."

I stay silent, content to listen to the melody of her words for a lifetime.

"You are at a precipice. Filled with so much fear you wish to turn from your path. To choose the easy road."

I nod. *Why do I nod?* Because it's true. My heart slams in my chest at this realization.

"You have a part to play, Caoine Roberts. No one else can do what you were meant to do."

"But I might die. I don't want to die." Like, really, really don't want to be ripped to shreds. "There must be another way to get my dad free."

She tilts her head. "What frightens you so?"

"I—I don't know. This spell . . . if I sing, I might die. I don't want my life to end that way."

"Life? What is life, my child?"

I furrow my brow. "Life is . . . *life*. It's a beating heart inside my chest. It's waking and breathing."

She leans closer, and a scent of a thousand lilies swirls around me. "Your spirit is what gives you life. It lives inside you now, as you see each day begin and end on Earth. When your heart stops beating, your spirit will continue to live, as it moves on to another place."

"The afterlife?"

She nods. "Nothing ever truly dies, my child. Your spirit will live forever. Just as the fae return to whence they came when they pass on, to the trees and dirt and all living things."

Aubree told me this the night Seamus died. That he wasn't truly dead but had gone back to a time that was *before*.

"Just as the fae go back to their creation, your spirit will live on with your Creator."

"But . . . but I don't know what to do." My voice is whiny compared to her ethereal words. Heat plumes across my cheeks in tendrils. "I've waited so long to see my dad. It will kill him if he finds out I died to save him. I can't do that to him. How do I save him?"

"You will sing, Caoine. Just as you always have."

"But the sacrifice. Someone is going to die—"

"And that is something you cannot change, my child." She pauses. "Do you not want to do what is best for all the realms? Including the Mortal one?"

My bottom lip trembles, yet I don't speak.

"You love Oliver, do you not?"

I nod.

"Why would you not want to save the one you love? To make the world whole for your father to continue living? Do not allow fear to hold you back, child."

"Am I strong enough? I've only just learned to control my banshee gift. What if I fail?"

"The threat of failure is what stops you from trying?" Her smile deepens. "You don't know the truth of your heritage, do you?"

My heritage?

"Would you like to hear the truth about the night you were born?"

A two-by-four slams into my chest, my breath halting in my chest. "Yes. Please." This is the only thing I've ever wanted.

She nods. "Saoirse was born a faerie."

I blink. My mother was fae? "No. That's not right. The only reason I'm half-fae is because a faerie cursed me to be part fae the night she made me a banshee. That's what my dad told me."

"No, lovely girl. Your banshee side doesn't make you fae. You are only part fae because of the one who gave you life. Your mother."

I gasp. Of course. How had I been so naïve to believe a simple spell had made me who I am?

The queen nods. "She chose to give up her true nature when she fell in love with your father. Not an easy thing to do, to give up fae powers."

I lick my lips and focus on her words.

"You were always destined to be half-fae and half-human. But being birthed in the Mortal Realm meant you would have more human characteristics than fae. And you would not be tasked with an occupation."

My chest swells. "But that changed the night I was born."

"It did. A faerie named Nia visited your parents that night, the same faerie who helped your mother escape the Unseelie Realm, to give up her faerie side. She came to warn Saoirse that you were meant to be the final sacrifice in a spell King Raghnall had enacted. That your death would unleash a horror kept under lock and key for centuries. Saoirse's banshee cry would release for the first time in years, that night, announcing your death and completing the spell."

"My dad. He said he didn't know faeries existed before that night. He never knew my mother's true nature?"

Queen Faílenn dips her chin. "All he heard was that you would die, and he had to make things right. He begged and pleaded with Nia to change things, to help him and Saoirse. Nia agreed, but at a great cost."

"I would become more faerie than human." I already know the answer in my heart. "I became a banshee that night."

"You did."

"And my banshee cry, it—"

"Did not kill your mother, Caoine."

I gasp.

"No one killed her. It had always been what would happen, despite what you or your father might believe. There was no saving your mother."

"But . . ." All the excuses I've carried for years, blaming myself, assuming it was my fault, die on my tongue.

"You were allowed to become banshee so your life would be spared and to stop the spell King Raghnall so desperately wanted to complete. Nothing more."

I exhale, my body reacting to the news as if I just sprinted a mile. That's it? All this time I thought I became part faerie as part of the sacrifice to save my life, but I never had any way to avoid that fate?

"So my mom was a banshee too? But she's no longer living, which means she became part of the Faerie Realm, right? What does that mean? Can I, like, visit a tree or something to talk to her?"

She hesitates. "Saoirse did not return to her natural state when she died."

An anvil slides toward my belly. "What do you mean?"

"We believe it was part of the magic Nia used to stop the spell. When your mother lost her life that night, she didn't return to the Faerie Realm, because her spirit was not at rest. It remains this way."

"Which means?" I grind my teeth at the riddles these faeries speak.

"She remains a banshee, Caoine. Saoirse never stopped her banshee lament."

"But—then, where is she? Why haven't I met her?"

"Saoirse isn't a banshee like you. She does not have the luxury of a cloak to bring out a calming song to usher the hearers to a pleasant afterlife. She has lost her mind."

My jaw drops open.

"She no longer knows who she is or the purpose for which she was created. She is wild, untamed."

"My mom turned into a mad banshee?" I can't even begin to wrap my brain around this.

"She is what we call a *bean-nighe*. A wild banshee, without intent or emotion. When she screams, humans can hear her for miles. It's a sound that shatters glass and hearts, can drive the most sane into insanity in seconds."

"A *bonny*?" The word is foreign to my ears. "So my mom became a monster?" I blink. "Like, she literally became a deranged person who now drives others crazy?"

Every part of my body is chilled to the bone.

"Saoirse is just as powerful as she ever was, but, yes, she is lost, my child. She wanders the Earth looking for that which she does not know."

"Can she be saved?"

"That is unknown, Caoine Roberts. Only you can decide that fate."

Blood begins to pound inside my veins again, as if I've just woken from a year-long slumber. "What must I do?"

"First, you must complete the task before you. Save your father and bring the books to me. Then all will be clear."

"What if I fail? What if the king gets the books?"

Her face echoes sadness. "This cannot happen, child. Obtaining both the Book of Judgment and the Book of Discernment will give King Raghnall more power than he has ever had before. It is imperative the books come to the Seelie Realm, to ensure the safety of all the realms."

"What do you mean?"

"That conversation isn't meant for this moment. I believe in you, Caoine."

"I won't let you down, Queen Faílenn. I promise."

She nods, her body drifting back toward the darkened sky. "I believe in you, daughter of Earth. Remember, life does not ever truly end. Do not hold so tightly to yours, and maybe you can save the lives of countless others."

She disappears on the horizon of purple just as my vision grows dark, my eyes heavy with the weight of responsibility.

I will succeed where my mother couldn't. I will give my life if it means saving others.

And if I happen to survive, I'm going to find a way to bring my mom back from the dead.

42

I'M IN A COCOON. My world is shadows and sadness. But something holds me, squeezes me like I matter in this universe.

I blink. Hazel eyes connect with mine. I relax into the embrace that cradles me, then I sit up.

Eric releases me, his gaze washing over every part of my body, inspecting me with a suspicious glance.

The earth beneath me is hard. Frozen. Foliage dangles from the trees above, clawing fingers around me as they fight to consume me.

Moss. Anger. Crisp winter air. These scents smother me.

"You all right?" Eric asks.

I sigh and slump where I sit. I just met the Seelie queen in a dream, and she told me I might die saving my dad, but it's all good as long as those books get across the Veil. And my mom is still alive but as a crazed mutant banshee.

Nope. Not all right.

"Caoine." His voice is low and urgent.

The boy lied to me. Well, sort of. In whatever way a faerie can lie. How can I trust him again?

A groan slips through my lips as my joints creak, knock,

scream as I stand. He moves with me, a mirror to my every action. Like he's inside my head.

Which he probably is. I scowl.

"Hey. I'm sorry. I didn't mean for you to find out this way."

I turn a weary head toward him. "How did you hope I'd find out? Is there a way that could possibly make my dying seem any better?"

He dips his head. "No one said you're going to die—"

"But it's a real possibility. Right?"

"You—I . . . I'll be there. To protect you."

I almost laugh. "To protect me? Like you did on Halloween night?"

He doubles back like I've just sucker-punched him. Which I sort of did.

Guilt floods my chest and belly. "That was out of line, I'm sorry."

He lifts his hands. "No. You're right. I haven't been the hero in this story. I deserved that."

"Yeah, but . . ." He saved me in the castle. He saved me from his father.

He shakes his head. "It's no big deal. Just . . . will you come back in? Please?" He glances around us. "We're not safe."

Chills ripple down my arms and legs even though my face is heated. I loosely pull my arms across my belly, holding on to my emotion like a thread, a torrent of pain and regret ready to spill into the invisible chasm at my feet.

I step inside the hidden house, taking small steps, embarrassment tying knots in my gut. What did I even look like, running from here in a tantrum?

But no one pays much attention when the two of us come back inside. Aibell, Killian, and Gar are still huddled in the chairs, too busy talking to bother looking up. Laoise is missing, but that doesn't mean much.

For all I know she's simply invisible, standing inches from my face. How much time has passed?

I halt, and Eric slips around me. Without a glance.

Knives stab my insides, and tears prick the backs of my eyes. I've alienated my only friend here.

I walk over to the bed that held such peace moments ago. The bed sinks as I settle on it, my gaze on my lap.

So much to take in, to believe. What I wouldn't give to go back in time, to my first day of school. Before my world was filled with Unseelie princes and my dad's death and the burden of sacrifice.

The tears come quickly. In abundance. Pulsing heat slides down my cheeks and neck, staining my shirt's collar with pain and grief.

I thought my dad was dead, but he's alive. He's alive and I can't get to him. He's locked in a cage, so, so far away.

My shoulders rock with each sob as I twist my hands, rub my skin raw.

The only boy I've ever loved is on the other side of a Veil I can't cross by myself. Separated from me for eternity until someone has mercy on me and reunites me with my world. The world I miss.

I curl into myself, holding my body with my arms, holding myself together so I don't fall into a million pieces.

Everything about my mom has been a lie. All I knew about my past, a farce. My banshee song isn't a gift to save others. It's my burden to unleash on the unsuspecting, to murder and to be killed.

A cry escapes my throat as I pull my feet up, wish myself into oblivion.

And then there are arms. And warmth. And words.

Eric envelops me, his comfort the only thing keeping my sanity hanging on by a frayed thread.

He pulls me close, my face against his chest. He whispers

and soothes and urges my tears to flow, to ebb away. Like I could actually be his friend. Are we friends?

How I miss my boyfriend, the one who should be holding me right now. Where is my closest companion when I need him? The tears flow freely.

I don't even know how long we sit there. Time becomes an enigma.

But the boy who caused me so much agony rocks me and holds me and melts away my fears.

In the silence of the night, Eric does what no one else is willing to do for me.

43

THE NIGHT AIR nibbles at my skin. We're gathered outside the hideout amid the forest and shadows.

A scent of fire and smoke wraps around my body, proof of a campfire nearby. The trees are silent, the animals alert to the imminence of what is about to take place.

I pull in a nervous breath, glance at my watch. 11:47 p.m. Thirteen minutes until midnight. Thirteen minutes left for me to live. Maybe.

Thirteen minutes until my dad is free.

"You ready?" Eric asks softly.

I nod.

He stands close, so much closer than I would've allowed just days ago. His stance is protective.

Killian, Gar, and Laoise gather around a circle drawn in the dirt, the one only I will be standing inside. They've got the Book of Judgment open, whispering fiercely over the placement of specific objects needed for the spell.

Aibell is off to the side, her posture tense, gaze darting over the trees.

Eric bumps me with his shoulder. "Caoine, I know you're expecting the worst, but . . . you won't die tonight." He strug-

230

gles for words. "I can *feel* it. You'll be fine." Pause. "No matter what happens tonight, I won't let anything happen to you. You'll be safe, I promise."

I frown. "You don't think I'll die, but you still think there might be trouble?"

He looks around. "Anything's possible. It takes a powerful spell to bring down magic put in place by my father. I think it'll attract . . . *something*. But you won't die. I'll make sure of that."

I try to smile but know it looks more like a cringe. I may not have the same confidence, but I appreciate his optimism.

My watch shows 11:51pm. I smack my hands against my legs to wake them up, hop on my toes a few times. This is going to work. It has to.

I glance around. No one is present other than the six of us. Where's the sacrifice? The one who'll die by my banshee song?

A breeze chills me, and I shiver. In the circle are objects I don't recognize. Things of Faerie, crafted with care, made of wood and leaves and fabric. A clay cup. Something shiny but definitely not metal. Piles of herbs.

All we need is that sacrifice. I look around again. Pull in a shaky breath.

Once the spell is done and the enchantment around the castle is gone, we'll spring my dad from faerie jail and get back to the Mortal Realm.

I almost laugh out loud. The Mortal Realm. I'm even thinking like a faerie now.

Minutes crawl by, Eric an all-consuming presence by my side. He shifts, his gaze on the trees. "You never told me what happened when you left the treehouse? What made you faint?"

I nibble my lip. "I . . . saw Queen Faílenn."

Eric's eyes widen. "How?"

"It was sort of a . . . dream. But it was her. She told me to take a chance on the plan." I give him a weak smile. "And that my mom is alive. Sort of."

"Whoa. She is?"

"She's a *bean-nighe*."

His eyebrows rise to his hairline.

I go on. "The queen alluded to the idea I might be able to save her. To bring her back to sanity. But only if I can save my dad and get the books to her first."

Eric's gaze softens. "Caoine, you don't need to do this. You can't save everyone in your life."

I don't know if he's talking about following through with this spell or if he means saving my mom. Either way . . . "If you had a way to save your mom, wouldn't you?"

He blinks like he's just woken from a dream. Then he nods, swallows. "Yeah. Yeah, I would."

We stand in silence another thirty seconds, the weight of the conversation replaying in my mind.

"It's time." Aibell's command springs the others to life.

"But where's the sacrifice—?" I stumble over a rock before I can finish, and Aibell doesn't even hear me.

Sweat pours down my back and sides. Where's the one fated to die? And how can I possibly be okay with this? I shiver again.

All the faeries take position around the circle, ushering me dead center. My throat closes. Maybe they'll appear once I've screamed?

Killian holds the book toward me, already turned to the appropriate page. I take it, cradle it against my body, its worn cover rough against my fingers.

My gaze lands on Eric's. A chill washes through my body, and my lips go numb. Spots float across my vision, each of my fingers and toes going to sleep. In all my life I've never experienced such fear. He nods, a tick along his jaw.

I breathe in, glance at the moonless night. Then back down to the words before me.

I take my position, await for Aibell's command.

Something rustles in the bushes beside me. The sacrifice?

That scent of smoky darkness grows stronger.

Another chill falls down my spine.

Eric shifts on his feet.

A howl far in the distance tumbles across the expanse of the woods.

My gut tightens.

Aibell looks to me. "Begin."

I begin to chant.

Simple words. In the language of the fae. Eric taught me how to pronounce them. They roll off my tongue as if it's my native language. As if I've been speaking it my entire life.

Back and forth my eyes roam as I speak one line after another. The objects in the circle begin to glow, making a buzzing sound.

My voice grows louder, heat rising from my core. The words fly faster and faster from my mouth, coming out in a flood.

My heart pounds inside my chest. The language makes no sense, yet I understand every word I say.

Word. After word. After word.

The spell goes on. I'm almost to the end, anticipation building in my arms and shoulders. Pressure builds inside me, a song that must be released. To be set free.

My banshee song has awakened, something I haven't sung in days. Weeks? I've lost track.

Except I don't have my cloak. This won't be a song anyone wants to hear.

A familiar tingle sparks across my entire body. I relax into the sensation, welcoming it. Finding rest within the comfort of my purpose.

I open my mouth and scream.

It's earsplitting and tragic. Vibrations bounce off trees and shatter eardrums. Pleasure and pain spilling from my soul.

And then it's over.

I collapse on the ground, warm hands suddenly on me.

I look up to see Eric's gaze on mine. He's speaking, but it sounds like he's underwater.

I don't understand. Can't understand.

Nothing around me is different. Everything looks exactly the same. Where's the sacrifice? When will the spell work?

Terror floods my veins. The sacrifice.

My banshee song has come out. All creatures know where I am. I'm in danger.

I choke on the realization.

My time has come. I'm the sacrifice. I've always been the sacrifice.

Eric leaves me, yells something at Aibell, runs to a space ten, fifteen feet away, bends toward the ground. Digging for something. What's he doing?

Tears fill my eyes as I look to Aibell. She turns toward me. Walks to me. I'm frozen in place. What's happening?

Eric looks up, a crease between his brows.

Aibell reaches me, her eyes wild. What's she doing? She has my left hand, the glint of a blade in hers. A dagger! She brings it down where my pinky finger meets my hand.

Agony flares up my arm, and my scream shatters the night.

I can't catch my breath.

There's blood. So much blood.

Eric scrambles to his feet and runs toward me, but he stumbles and falls. He shakes his head.

I cradle my hand against my shirt, an endless flood of crimson bleeding into the fabric. It blooms and spreads like a summer flower, its petals opening to the warmth of the sun.

Warmth. Fire. So much pain.

Fire rages across my hand. I can feel the pain in my neck, my head.

Aibell tosses my finger into the circle.

I gag at the shock that the finger is *mine. That's my finger!*

And then a scream. A shout.

I'm weak, can barely lift my head. But I glance to the others.

Killian pulls an arrow from his quiver. Gar has his spear in hand. Laoise disappears.

Aibell stops what she's doing, her eyes no longer crazed. She whips around, her sword out in half a second.

Eric yells something at me, tries to get to me, only a few feet away. But he stumbles, falls again.

Figures emerge from the trees. Eric yells at me once more.

I squeeze my hand inside my shirt, unable to move. The world is fading.

Guards. The king's guards appear in the trees. Surround us. Enclose us.

Gar never looses his spear. A sword protrudes from the middle of his chest, blue blood oozing, flowing to the ground where he falls.

No. I gasp.

Killian's face is smeared with blood, his eyes panicked as he reaches for another arrow in his quiver. But it's empty. He disappears into the trees.

I cry out. Look for Aibell.

She's gone.

My belly lurches, and I turn to the side, empty its contents into the useless circle.

Where's Eric?

My heart is shattering into fragments smaller than I can ever put back together. My friends are dying. For me. And I can't stop it.

Just before my world goes black, Eric appears at my side.

But then there are guards. They descend on us.

Then I'm gone.

44

IT'S PITCH BLACK. And frigid. Wintry.

I push up from the icy floor and groan, whimper in pain. Shackles cut into my wrists, burn my skin like nothing I've ever experienced before. A bandage is wrapped around my left hand, the spot where my pinky used to be. Empty.

An expletive falls from my mouth. Pain pulses through my hand. I squeeze my eyes shut and stifle a wail. Jagged bits of rock and dirt dig into my palms as I wobble to my feet, immediately thankful for the relief from the frozen earth.

Earth. That's all I smell. Earth and mold. And dead things.

I sway right into the wall, which catches my fall.

Nothing. I can see nothing. How can I possibly be this dizzy?

The fingers of my good hand grip the uneven stone wall. Something drip, drip, drips nearby, and I sense a dampness in the air. Probably why it smells like mold.

"Hello?" My voice both echoes and is swallowed by the void. *Breathe. Think, Caoine. Figure out your surroundings, then come up with a plan.*

I reach into nothing, feeling, grasping with both hands.

236

I work along the wall, the wrappings on my left hand snagging on sharp rock.

The circle I make is miniscule. I'm crammed into a space that can't be more than five feet across. I reach up. Nothing. There's no telling how high the ceiling goes.

I rest both hands against the cold, wet stone, close my eyes. *Relax. You'll get out of this.*

I'm somewhere inside the king's castle. And I've been here a while, considering they've had time to bandage my hand.

I've been captured. The question is, who got away?

Where are Aibell and Laoise? And Killian? The sight of Gar dropping from his wounds springs to mind, and I spin to the side to wretch, but my stomach is empty.

Where am I? Where is—

Eric.

I squeeze my eyes shut, even though it does no good.

"Hello?" My voice is louder this time. And goes just as far. Which is nowhere.

A creaking noise jolts me to life, and light floods my tiny room. My eyes scream.

One wall has swung open, a hidden door I never felt as I worked my way around the room. I cower against the wall, closer to the light than I'm comfortable with.

There's only one kind of person who would open that door. A guard. Not a friend.

But a friend stumbles toward me.

Through my rapid blinking, I barely make out Eric, shoulders slumped, face ashen.

A guard behind him gives him a hard shove, and Eric falls into me. He's warm, his strong arms careful as he fumbles against the wall. His breathing is heavy and ragged.

As soon as he sees our surroundings, he backtracks. His gaze is wide, wild. Frantic. "Wait! No!"

He pushes off the wall to grab the door, but it closes in his face.

A sound, guttural and desperate, spills from his throat. "Wait. I changed my mind!"

He slaps the cold stone, but it does no good. The guards are gone. At least he isn't shackled like I am.

"Eric," I say.

"Wait!" he begs to no one on the other side.

"Eric." This time louder.

A slice of light is left this time, along the edge of the door I suppose hasn't closed exactly right. But right enough to keep us inside.

Eric embraces the door, caresses it as if it might open. His shoulders shake. Is he crying?

No. His whole body shakes. He's trembling. Falling apart. Cracks forming in his soul.

His fear of closed spaces.

I lean toward him, my hands resting on his back. "Breathe."

He's shaking and moving like a tidal wave is crashing inside his mind.

I pull him away from the wall, force him to face me. "Eric, look at me."

Light and dark shadow his face, illuminate his agony. His eyes are squeezed closed, his face twisted in torment.

"Eric!" I pound his chest with my good hand.

His eyes fly open, and he's panting. I trail my right hand along his wrist, my left hand hanging loosely by the handcuffs. My palm touches his skin, and he shudders.

He exhales, relaxes, shoulders falling.

His eyes connect with mine. His breathing slows. "Thank you."

I swallow and remove my hand, take one step back. "Are you okay?"

Eric sucks in a breath. "I was supposed to—" He frowns.

"Supposed to what?"

He struggles.

"Supposed to do what, Eric? What were you going to do?"

"They told me—"

"Who told you? When? Did they say something to you? After they captured you?"

Sweat drips along the sides of his face. A notch forms between his brows, and he blinks. "Yes."

Hope rises in my core. If they said something, maybe we can use it, leverage to get out of here.

"What did they tell you? Can you remember?"

"I'm supposed to find out—" He grimaces, glances around our little cave. Panic tugs at his face again.

"Concentrate, Eric. Think about what they said."

His gaze finds mine again, his look melancholy.

A sharp stab of pain shoots through my wrists, and I recoil with a hiss. His eyes travel to my cuffed wrists, and he immediately takes my hands in his.

"Why . . . why is this happening?" I can barely whisper through the pain.

The heat from Eric's body warms me. He hasn't left me. Hasn't betrayed me like I feared. This is the real Eric, the one I've come to know only in the Realm of Faerie.

A loyal friend.

"Your faerie side—" He coughs. "The longer you spend in Faerie, the more fae you become."

I gasp. He's right. My incredible balance, tolerance to extreme cold . . . even my pointed ears.

My fae side is becoming stronger.

"The iron . . . it hurts you now. In the Mortal Realm it never bothered you because you'd always been more human. But here—"

Another cough. When he speaks again, his voice is more strained than before.

"Here you can't help but becoming what you were meant to be. So iron hurts you, just as it hurts me, or any other faerie." He forces a chuckle. "Genius, really. What better way to keep you under control than to use a substance poisonous to you?"

"Poisonous?"

"That's right. The longer you're exposed to iron, the more sick you'll become. Eventually your body won't be able to handle the poison any longer and you'll—" He sucks in a quick breath.

"I'll what?" I hate myself for asking the obvious.

"You'll pass into the afterlife, Caoine. You'll disappear from Faerie for good."

Just like Seamus. I swallow.

Eric glances at my left hand. "How does it feel?"

"The fact that I've literally lost an appendage?" I immediately regret my sarcasm. The boy is in pain too. "It hurts."

He nods. "I'm sorry I can't bring some healing. I'm too weak to fix it right now." He licks his lips. "And I hate to bring this up, but growing back body parts doesn't fall within the abilities of the fae. The most I can do is heal the skin and ease the pain."

"Figures."

He winces once more, leans closer, and whispers, "It'll be all right, Caoine. The king wants us alive. They won't keep you in these much longer."

My heart slams against my ribcage, and I order my hands to stop shaking. Maybe. Maybe the king wants me alive. But Eric? My core turns to ice as I consider what the king might do to him.

I bite my lip until I taste copper as a tear slips down my cheek. I reach out, place my right palm against his chest. He's shaking, trembling like a leaf.

"Eric." I say this more as a command, giving him a shake.

"It's no use." His voice sounds like a child's.

"What's no use?"

His teeth chatter. "This place." Something wet drips onto

my hands, and I reach up to feel his cheeks covered in tears. "It's a tomb, Caoine. They've put us in a tomb."

"What have they done to you?" I whisper.

"Caoine." His voice is pained. "Caoine, I'm sorry. Just know I'm sorry. I never meant for any of this to happen. Not to you."

I blink, focus on his words. "It's all right, Eric. I know you never meant for us to get caught. It's a chance we took."

"You don't understand." His voice is laced with agony. His eyes find mine. "I'm so, so sorry."

The door beside us scrapes open. Light floods our space again, this time not as shocking.

I grip Eric tighter, my hand digging into his shirt. His hands hang limp at his sides.

A man stands outside the door. A giant man.

He's at least seven feet tall with honey-brown skin and dark hair and eyes, just like Eric.

Is this his true form? Or a glamour?

King Raghnall has several warts along the right side of his jaw, and pockmarks lace his skin. The effects of a spell gone wrong? His gait is off, and he favors his left leg.

More questions flit through my mind.

Even beneath his layers of royal clothing I can see his trim build and beefy muscles.

Standing with a menacing gaze and hands on his hips, he reminds me of The Rock. No wonder Eric is so afraid of him.

He holds out a hand, his voice even deeper than I imagined. "Bring her out, son. The time has come."

45

I STARE at the king's hand as if it holds a viper, confusion my only friend. I glance from his hand to Eric. To Eric who stands straight and sure, his face resigned.

His gaze is locked on his father's.

Eric steps from the tomb, turns on his heel and stands by the king. A tick pulses along his jaw like the beat of a drum.

Ba-dum. Ba-dum. Ba-dum.

It echos in my head.

Ba-dum. Ba-dum. Ba-dum.

My throat closes, and tears slam into my eyes. This can't be happening. "Eric?" I whisper as my hands shake, my body weak from betrayal.

But he won't look at me.

King Raghnall coughs, and I swear I see the shadow of a smile. "Were you not told never to trust anyone in the Unseelie Realm, girl?"

My head spins and spins. Round and round. The ground tilts toward me, and I grasp the edge of the doorway to stay on my feet. "Eric—" I choke.

The king turns to Eric. "Were you able to get any information out of her?

Eric shakes his head, his gaze still on the floor. "I . . . the space. It was too small—"

"Don't give me that claustrophobia excuse again. Pathetic."

Eric's hands clench.

The king nods to his guards, two of whom grip my arms with no amount of gentleness. They yank me down the hall like a rag doll, my wrists screaming against the iron restraints that burn like fire.

I strain to catch Eric's eyes, but he's fallen in step beside his father, who walks in front of me.

Their backs speak to me. They say I've been a fool. That I've been played. They confirm my worst suspicions of Eric.

Were you not told never to trust anyone in the Unseelie Realm, girl?

Tears well in my eyes, and I can't catch my breath. Of course someone told me not to trust anyone.

Eric. Eric told me. So many times.

How was I so naïve?

I don't bother to fight the guards as they drag me, prod me like a wild animal. I'm taken up stairs and around corners. Too many turns to remember. But what does it matter?

Eric marches in front of me, proud son to a king who couldn't care less. How hadn't I seen this coming? No one ever truly changes. Not that much, right?

So Eric convinced me his father tricked him, brainwashed him into helping him the first time. But he still wants to be by the king's side. Can that kind of selfishness ever go away? Is it possible for someone so evil to truly turn good?

I squeeze my eyes shut, and hot tears slip down my cheeks. Drip off my chin. Sink into the frozen floor at my feet. Remind me I'm human. So very human. I'm not like these people. I'm not fae and never will be.

We arrive at the top of a set of stairs, and I'm paraded down a familiar hallway. Into a familiar room. The throne room.

King Raghnall marches to his seat, plops in his rightful

spot. Eric walks up the dais, stands beside his father, stiff and unbending. His gaze is on the back wall, hands clasped behind his back. Like a good soldier.

Aibell was right. She warned me of this.

How did I believe a long-lost son—one so openly welcomed into his father's castle, put in such a high position—could possibly leave fortune and power?

So he failed the spell in the Mortal Realm? No king who put that amount of time and energy into a child would give up on him that quickly. And I'd fallen for it. Like an idiot.

Raging fire snakes up my neck, across my face. Embarrassment. Anger.

The guards roughly remove the iron shackles, the relief only momentary before pain from my missing finger shoots through my left hand. They fling me to the floor. I stumble onto my hands and knees. Eric flinches but doesn't look at me.

"Hello, Caoine." The king's voice is deep and gravelly. He grasps the scepter that leans against the throne. "You have been a thorn in my side."

I don't look at him. I've got zero energy left and remain on the floor.

He chuckles, leans forward. "You're quite the stubborn one, aren't you? There's a fire inside you." A pause. "I see why you like her."

He must've said that to Eric.

I look at Eric.

He tenses but never breaks from staring at that single spot on the opposite side of the room.

The king sits back. "Your spell didn't work." He says this as if he's announcing the menu for supper. "It failed miserably, in fact. You can't defeat the magic that resides in this castle."

Great.

He must see the way I attempt to hide my scowl. "Don't be too hard on yourself. You did nothing wrong. Your performance of the spell was perfect. Eloquent, I would say."

I roll my eyes. Now he wants to compliment me?

"The spell would have worked flawlessly . . . if you had all the ingredients."

Heat flares in my chest. "We did." My voice is ragged. I sound like a prisoner of war in need of water.

He raises his eyebrows. "You believe you did, true." He tilts his head toward Eric. "Save for one key piece. An important one."

A growl grows deep in the back of my throat. "Let me guess. A key ingredient that your *traitor* son knew about but conveniently forgot to tell us."

Eric recoils minutely, his gaze finally finding mine.

Why does he look sad? Doesn't matter. I hate him.

The king nods. "I knew you were smart, Caoine. Just not smart enough."

Sourness curdles my belly. What did we forget? There wasn't anything else listed in the book. We had everything.

The king looks at me, waiting for me to ask what I forgot.

But I won't. I will never ask anything of this beast.

Two minutes go by. Three. He sniffs. I stare at him.

I can last all day.

He finally nods to the guards. Footsteps sound behind me, the slam of a door.

"What have you learned since you've been here, Caoine?" the king asks kindly. As if we're having a civil conversation over a cup of coffee.

I blink. I want to snort. This guy wants me to tell him what I've learned? What *haven't* I learned? I knew nothing of either Faerie Realm before arriving. There's no way to relay all that knowledge. Not that I would to *him*.

"You know of the Gifts. You have certainly learned this from your time with Eric." He looks to his son, a wide smile in place. "Especially your time together just a few moments ago."

Eric freezes, his jaw the only thing moving. Flexing. Tight.

My anger subsides for a split second, and I feel sorrow.

Sadness for this boy tortured by his father. The king knows of his son's problem with claustrophobia, yet he forced him into a space that size? The cruelty is too much.

I pull in a sharp breath. "You. Are. A. Monster."

King Raghnall shrugs. "I never claimed to be otherwise."

Yuck. How can he be this slimy? "What do you want, Raghnall?"

He laughs. "What do I want?"

"Other than to gloat, of course," I snarl.

He taps Eric's arm, but Eric doesn't budge. "She thinks I brought her here to gloat. She has no clue, does she?"

Eric inhales, holds his breath. Stares straight ahead.

The king leans back into his chair. "You'll find out soon enough, human."

And that's all he says. We wait in silence, the king watching me. Me watching Eric. Eric watching the wall.

Until a door opens. Something soft scrapes the floor. Footsteps as the guards bring whatever the king has demanded.

Something falls to the floor beside me, but I refuse to look, refuse to take my eyes from the front of the room. Refuse to do what King Raghnall wants. Because this is all I have. The only freedom left in my world is this small act of defiance.

But then there's a scent, a sound. A familiarity I've come to know over the last eighteen years of my life.

I whip my head to the pile of rags on the floor. The heap tells me this is a mound of laundry and nothing more. Because nothing could be under the sharp edges that poke from beneath.

Or nothing living *should* be.

But there is. Something living. Barely.

In a single breath I'm beside him, a man hanging on to life by a thread. Beaten and bruised and covered in dirt.

The king has brought me my dad.

46

I'M BROKEN BUT COMPLETE. A shell of a corpse but filled with the opposite of death.

Every breath I take, each pulse of my heart can't get my arms around him fast enough.

My dad is alive. *My dad is alive.*

I can't believe my dad is here with me. Right now.

I'm beside him, my hands everywhere at once, my voice a soothing blanket of love, compassion, healing. My eyes rove over his flesh, the way his bones protrude at such awkward angles, as if he's a carcass on the side of the road.

My belly lurches. Every inch of my skin is vibrating, buzzing with questions.

"Dad?" This, more a sob than a question.

He shifts, and a scent of puke and filth tumble over me. When did he last wash?

Probably never. Not since he's been here.

"Dad." My voice is gentle.

"Caoine?" His throat is so parched, it sounds like sandpaper scraping on wood.

My face is hot. Hot with tears and disbelief and anger at

the creature just a few feet away who forced my dad into this place. The creature sitting on the throne.

I attempt to say his name again but choke.

A bony hand reaches for me, and I grab it like it's my lifeline. Because it is. My entire life is within that too thin palm.

"What a happy reunion." The king's voice is out of tune and dissonant. "Do I not get any thanks? I am the one who has willingly given your father back, after all."

"You snake!" I snarl, lunging to my knees. The only reason I stay put is because I don't want to let go of my dad's hand.

The king flinches, just a flicker, but I notice.

I spew the poison invading my blood. "He's barely alive. Why would I *ever forgive you?*"

I'm breathing so heavily my chest hurts.

My gaze betrays me, flutters over Eric, even though I'd love nothing more than to slice him open like a stuffed pig. My blood boils, and pain shoots through my head.

King Raghnall sits back as if he's watching a leisurely sporting event. "What is your gift, Caoine?"

My eye twitches. I begin to shake.

He blinks. Waits.

I will not answer the scum.

He tilts his head. "We can wait here all night. But sooner or later, we *will* have this discussion." Finally, he leans forward. "Your gift, Caoine. What is it?"

I flare my nostrils and spit at his feet. "You know what I can do."

He chuckles. "Not your banshee song. Your *other* gift."

"My song is my gift." I sit a little straighter, proud to finally claim my song for what it is, even though I couldn't see it for eighteen years.

The king raises his brows, glances at Eric, who still doesn't budge. "So naïve." He looks back to me. "Oh, Caoine. You cannot be this thick." He gestures to my dad. "I've given you what you want. You have your father back. You can be honest with me. This whole thing will be far easier if you are."

My dad groans, and I press even closer in a heartbeat. I run my good fingers through the little hair he has left, the rest having fallen out from malnutrition, I assume.

I whisper comforting words to him before pulling back to address the traitor king. "You know what I can do."

He laughs. Short and soft, at first, then growing and building and pounding against the walls.

He laughs and laughs as if I've told the funniest joke he's ever heard. He laughs and jabs Eric and slaps his knee like it's some sort of demented sitcom.

"Caoine, you're fae. I'm not talking about the job you were created to do. I'm talking about your gifting. The thing you've been blessed with. The special nature that sets you apart from other faeries."

I shake my head, frown. "I—I don't have that. I'm only *half*-fae. I don't have a gift—"

"All fae have gifts."

"That's not true." I clench my fists. "I know one who doesn't. You can't fool me. They're called neamini. Faeries who have no gift at all."

Again, the king laughs. "And they're the rarest of the fae. The average faerie most definitely has a gift, and you are most definitely *more* than average, Caoine. There's no doubt you have one." He drops his smile. "Now think. Have you experienced anything out of the ordinary while in my realm? Is there nothing you've questioned, something that might be a clue to the power you possess?"

I roll my eyes at him. "Are you kidding me? *Everything* has been out of the ordinary since I've gotten here. I've never been to either Faerie Realm."

King Raghnall doesn't appreciate my sarcasm. In a second he's on his feet, his face hard, sharp angles, one hand still on that ridiculous staff. He points a beefy finger at me. "I need your gift. Now tell me!"

I stand, frown. "What are you talking about?"

In a blink his towering figure envelopes the space around me. "I'm fully aware that humans can lie, child. Now tell me!"

His colossal hand wraps all the way around my throat and squeezes. My air supply is immediately cut off, my hands instinctively grasping, scratching, fighting to be released. He presses tighter, and all I see is black.

"Father!" Eric's voice cuts through the void.

The pressure on my neck decreases a little, and I can see again.

Eric's eyes are wild, his face red. "Your plan, father. You need her, remember?"

The king lets go. I crumble to the ground beside my dad, coughing, my hands soothing my neck.

Eric sucks in a quick breath, and I glance up. His gaze is on mine. Is that relief I see?

The king growls. "If you won't cooperate, then maybe it's time I gave you incentive."

My jaw hangs open. I glance to Eric and back again. What does he mean? Nothing about his words can be anything but bad.

King Raghnall stares at my dad. Something behind his irises change, and I swear his pupils shift to gold. "Brent, your reunion is over. It's time for you to go."

My dad begins to gasp for air, his eyes wide as the moon that's missing from the sky tonight.

"Dad?" I scream. "Dad!"

I shake him and pull him, but he only gasps and gasps and gasps.

"That's it," the king purrs. "Time to go. Don't fight it."

"Dad!" I pound on his chest as if that will do any good. Then I whip around to look at the king. "Stop it! Stop whatever you're doing!"

"I'm not doing anything." His lips curl into a wicked smile. "I'm simply suggesting he follow the path he was on when he first arrived in Faerie."

Suggesting. The king is suggesting that my dad die?

The Power of Suggestion.

That's his gift. The king can persuade people to do whatever he wants. I glance at Eric. He wasn't lying when he said he didn't understand why he'd done those things for his father, how it felt like he was coming out of a fog.

So why is he joining forces with the man now? His eyes look bright, clear. As if he's all there.

Eric's not under his father's influence. He has no intention of stopping what Raghnall is doing to my dad.

"Stop it!" I scream again.

The king laughs. My dad gasps. Tears flood my cheeks, soak my neck.

"Please." My voice is small now. Just like the child I am.

The king tilts his head. "I'm sorry, Caoine. It has to be this way."

Eric's gaze finally slides to the king. "Father?" His jaw clenches repeatedly, his hands in fists.

My throat itches. Aches. I cry in anguish.

"Father!" Eric's eyes land on mine.

But it's too late.

A tingle spills across the back of my neck, and a headache the size of Texas slams into my head. I go dizzy, my vision fading in and out.

Power pulses up from my core, clawing its way into the world. My mouth wants to open. My body wants to sing.

No. Sing. *No.* Sing. *No.*

The king looks into my eyes. "Sing for me."

Eric takes a single step toward me but stops.

My jaw drops open, and a scream shatters the air.

My head splits in two as the sound rips from inside me for

the second time tonight, attacks the walls and the faeries and the edges of the realm.

I collapse against my dad as my banshee song is released. I'm weak, can barely move.

"No." The word is almost inaudible as it escapes my lips, my eyes settling on my dad.

Eric's eyes are wide.

The king doesn't stop his torture, and my dad doesn't stop begging for air.

He begs and begs and begs.

Until there is none left. Until he goes still, his chest no longer rising and falling.

And then my dad is dead.

47

My world stops. Things move in slow motion, like I'm stuck in mud and can't move fast enough no matter how hard I try.

All sound is muffled. The king is speaking to me, but all I hear is an echo. My heart pounds. My pulse races. My soul fragments into a billion different pieces.

"Dad!" I scream, pressed so close to his warmth, a sign that life should still be inside him.

But it isn't. He isn't.

Hot tears claw my cheeks, tear into my skin.

"Why? Why would you do this?" My voice no longer sounds like itself.

King Raghnall's gaze softens.

I look to Eric, who stands stunned. He's no longer stiff and rigid like a robot. He takes another step forward, both hands shaking at his sides. His lips are parted, words left unspoken. Eyes in shock as they dart from his father to me.

"Why didn't you stop him?" I growl.

He blinks. Looks to the king. "Father, this wasn't what we agreed—"

"Enough, Eric." King Raghnall looks at me as if expecting something. Anything.

My fingers dig into the threadbare shirt my dad wears, his glassy gaze locked on the ceiling.

"But you promised." Eric flinches. "You said—"

The king whips his head around. "I said this would all be over soon, and it will be. Now shut up and wait."

Wait? For what? For more death? For me to dissolve into the nothingness I so long to be a part of?

Eric's gaze finds mine. Sadness. Confusion.

Fire threads its way up my neck, grasping the base of my neck, my ears. My tears flow freely, and I begin to shake.

"How could you do this to me? After all you said?"

He huffs as if I've punched him in the gut. "Caoine, I—"

"How could you?" Over and over I repeat the accusation.

As I hunch over my dad's dead body, I lament the loss of the one man in my life who always had my back. No matter what. The man I already lost once.

"Dad, I'm so sorry. I'm so, so sorry," I whisper against his ear, against his cheek. "I'm so sorry." My tears mix on his skin, melt into the little warmth left in his body.

I cry. My hands rub his hair back from his forehead until finally I lay beside him, press close in a hug, one side of my face flat against his chest. My tears roll along his collar, settle into the dips and valleys of his skin. Tingles of electricity niggle my fingertips. Heat flares in my chest.

I lament. This is so different than Halloween night. When I watched him get stabbed and fall through the Veil. I didn't actually see him die. Although he was gone and I knew he was gone, a part of me still believed he could be alive and well in the Unseelie Realm.

Because I didn't see him take his last breath, I could convince myself the knife missed every vital organ.

But this? This is real. My dad just died in my arms.

My dad is dead.

Every muscle in my body quivers. This is an agony I never expected to face once we were reunited.

I don't know how long we lay there. The king makes no move, Eric obediently by his side.

Everything disappears, and suddenly it's just my dad and me. Just like it's been from the beginning.

I place one hand on his cheek as my tears sink into his corpse. And then . . .

Then.

A breath.

He takes a breath, and I gasp. I pull back. His eyes are still glassy, staring straight ahead.

No. It's my imagination. I've heard of dead bodies doing extraordinary things like this soon after death.

Except it's not just one breath. There's another. Another. *Another*. Until those staring eyes, the ones that announced to the world that his spirit was no longer inside, blink.

Then land on me. "Caoine?" My dad winces as if he's in excruciating pain.

I can't believe it. "Dad?"

"Caoine!" He's stronger now, struggling to sit up.

But I don't let him. I'm pushing him down, hugging him, collapsing against his body. *Laughing*.

I'm laughing in the court of the Unseelie king who took us prisoner. Who used his persuasion to kill my dad just moments ago. I'm laughing with delight.

My dad is alive. Again. And in much better health, from the looks of things. His frame is filled out, his hair full, his skin glossy like he hasn't missed a meal.

I pull back. "How did you—what happened?"

My dad shrugs. "Your guess is as good as mine."

He turns his hands over and looks at them as if they aren't attached to his body, then looks at me.

"Your ears." He gently touches one of my pointed ears, disbelief in his gaze.

"I'll tell you what happened." The king is seated again, that smug grin in place. One hand still rests on his scepter as he lounges, as if bodies raise from the dead all the time here. "You found your gift, Caoine."

"M-my gift?" I frown.

"The thing that makes you uniquely fae?" He points to Eric. "My son has the Gift of Empathy. I have the Gift of Suggestion."

"Brainwashing is more like it," I mumble.

He points to my dad. "And now you've found yours."

I glance between the two men, horror growing like a seedling from deep in my core. "I can . . . bring people back from the dead?"

King Raghnall leans forward. "You have the Gift of Life, Caoine. A rare gift, indeed. The ability to heal even beyond death, one I long suspected you possessed. One I need to use."

Eric shakes his head. "But that's impossi—"

"Do you deny what you just saw, son?" The king's voice is as sharp as the edge of a sword.

Eric opens and shuts his mouth, looks to me. "No, but—"

"Whoa, whoa." I hold up a hand, fight to a standing position. "You want me to believe I just brought my dad back to life? That I . . . *healed* him?"

The king smiles. "You saw what I did. I told him to die, so he did. *You* brought him back to life."

"I—I don't understand. That's impossible. How could I—"

"On the contrary, human, it would appear it's quite possible." He points to my dad again, who is now standing beside me, fully restored, no longer weak.

I glance at Eric. His gaze is heavy. Filled with awe and . . . fear? I look at my hands. I healed my dad with these?

But where's the pain? I gasp. The pain in my pinky is gone.

I rip the bandage from my hand. The skin around my finger is smooth, not a red patch in sight. It appears as if the scar tissue is years old.

"I'm healed," I breathe.

Now that I get a good look, I see the finger was disconnected at the joint, leaving a small hump where it used to be.

Without pain. Like a miracle.

My dad gawks at my hand in shock. This is going to take a lot of explaining.

I look at the king. "What will you do with us?"

The king laughs. Loud and obnoxious. He laughs for seconds that feel like minutes, that feel like hours.

"I'll tell you what I'm going to do. First of all, I have a queen who needs to be awoken from quite a long slumber. And you're just the fae to do it."

"A queen?" Does he mean Queen Mairéad? His dead wife?

I never get an answer.

The doors at the back of the room slam open. My dad and I jump, a sinking stone in my belly as I turn.

A guard looks at the king. He's trembling. "Your Majesty— King Raghnall—I . . ."

The king's gaze goes dark. "Spit it out. Explain why I shouldn't behead you on the spot for entering my throne room without permission."

The guard's eyes shift between the king and me. Without another word, he sprints to the dais, whispered words only for the prince's ear. Eric starts and steps off the dais. In a split second they're both out the back door.

King Raghnall's nostrils flare, no doubt in fury that he wasn't included in the conversation.

What could possibly be so urgent Eric would risk not telling his father?

The king chooses to take his anger out on me. His fingers wrap tightly around that stupid scepter. "Caoine Roberts of the Mortal Realm." The scepter begins to glow. His gaze shifts to my dad. "Brent Roberts of the Mortal Realm. You are hereby indebted to the Court of the Unseelie for all eternity, or until I deem it fit to revoke the law."

With each word the scepter glows a little brighter.

My jaw drops. "What?" My voice is shrill. Childlike. "Y-you can't do that. That's not fair —"

Tingling encircles my wrists, a sudden weight pulling each arm. The shimmer of golden manacles appears, a solid gold chain connecting both. A quick glance at my father's wrists shows his are burdened with the same glittery shackles.

In a split second they've disappeared, although the heaviness remains.

Raghnall is on his feet, in my face, his hot breath coating my skin. "Would you rather rot in prison? Do you want that for your father? I'm offering you freedom. But I must ensure you will aid me in my quest to restore my kingdom."

I bite my lip until it bleeds. "Freedom? But you just said we were indebted. Doesn't that mean — ?"

"It means you will remain in the Unseelie Realm. Both of you."

I open my mouth, but he continues.

"You may leave my castle, but I have full dominion over your every move. Whenever I need you, you will come. You will never be able to raise a hand against me, not without my knowing."

A sour taste curdles in my mouth. "That's not freedom. We're still prisoners."

"You call the gift I offer a prison?" his voice booms. "I'm giving you more freedom than I've ever offered any in your position."

"And why is that?" My dad's voice is soft but cuts through our challenge with precision. "Why do you suddenly offer such a gift when moments ago you were happy to allow me to die? After all these weeks you've kept me trapped in darkness?"

The king prepares to answer. Stops. Looks around at a noise far too timid for my ears to decipher. He turns his body toward the solid stone wall to my left.

Before I can say anything, the world around me explodes.

48

AGONY SHOOTS ACROSS MY BACK, my arm trapped at an odd angle beneath me. My left calf stings, and I sense something wet dripping down my ankle.

I open my eyes and immediately regret it.

Dust and dirt invades them both. I cry out in pain. I blink away the foreign substance as fast as I can. My dad is a few feet away from me, struggling to his feet.

Every inch of the throne room is littered with broken pieces of rock, stone shards everywhere I look. The room has a hazy white edge to it, bits of wall floating all around.

I cough, double over from the effort. My dad helps me up. My legs shake uncontrollably as I fight to my feet, my dad's arm tight around my shoulders.

"Ouch!" I complain when his hand pushes against my upper arm.

"Can you walk?" he whispers, his gaze somewhere to our right.

I strain to look. King Raghnall is waking up as well, his voice a grumble, deep with curses.

My dad motions toward the nearest exit, and I nod. Agony

shoots across my back and shoulders. I attempt to breathe. Force my feet toward freedom. If such a thing exists.

Step, drag. Step, drag. What's wrong with me?

I spot a deep gash in my leg. My dad limps beside me.

We traverse the debris, my dad pushes against the large wooden door, and we practically fall into the hallway.

And breathe. Blessed, clean, untainted air fills my lungs and makes them sing hallelujah. I almost sigh. Except for the fact we're running for our lives. My elation is short lived.

Two guards step out of nowhere, blocking our path.

"Check on the king!" one yells to the other as he thrusts a sword at us.

The other guard races into the throne room. My dad and I sag against each other as we stand, trapped. We were so close!

The guard sneers. "Prince Eric thought you might try something like this. Lucky for him, he sent us back as soon as the first explosion went off."

The first? What is even going on?

"Awesome. So glad the traitor is loyal to someone." I wince at the way I refer to Eric, at the word Aibell so often used to describe him.

How was I so stupid? How did I believe he was actually a friend?

I squeeze my dad tight and cough on a blast of dust that tumbles from the throne room. Smoke and dirt attempt to claw into my lungs.

"Where are they?" the king yells from behind us.

A chunk of loose rock in the wall behind the guard falls to the floor. We duck around the guard while he's distracted and sprint down the hall. Only to face a dead end.

The king stumbles from the room, leaning heavily on the other guard. "Think you're smart?" He stands on his own. "Your feeble attempt to escape is useless. Even if you leave the castle, you cannot withstand—"

A shout comes from down the hall. Three figures race

toward us. Their faces are shadowed, but the way they're being chased by more guards confirms they aren't with the king.

Which means they must be with us.

"Caoine!" Aibell shouts.

My pulse takes off like a rocket. Steel on steel echoes down the hall as Killian and Aibell swing their swords. Just as my friends must use their physical weapons without the use of magic, so must the guards.

Laoise disappears in a blink. A miniscule ball of light zips through the air. The guard closest to her immediately begins swatting at the air, as if being bombarded by bees. Which he sort of is.

I almost laugh, but the pain shooting through my body won't allow it.

My dad and I attempt to sneak behind the mess of fighting.

"What's going on?" The king's voice booms as loud as the explosions. "Guards!"

The two guards protecting him run toward the fight. In a matter of seconds, Aibell and Killian have taken care of them all.

"Caoine!" Aibell yells again.

Finally we can run. My dad grabs one of the fallen guard's swords along the way.

"You know how to use that?" I ask.

He shakes his head. "No clue."

My heart tumbles, and I can't help my grin. I've got my dad back!

We don't make it two steps before something pulls on my shirt.

"Have you forgotten?" the king says in my ear. "You belong to me. You will not leave this castle until my queen is awake."

Except his grip falls from me before he's done talking, and the king bats at something in the air.

Thank you, Laoise!

My dad and I are moving again. Aibell and Killian flank us as we run down the hall in the direction they came.

"This way!" A shout comes from around the corner.

Aibell shakes her head. We spin and run in the opposite direction. We pass the king as he continues to fight Laoise.

Right back to the dead end.

"You know another way out?" Aibell asks. "Any secret passageways?"

My heart sinks. "You don't?"

"I only had time to memorize the one way in."

"Fantastic."

Killian glances at me in confusion, sarcasm still lost on him.

"This way," my dad says through gritted teeth. He leads us toward a corner door.

"Why are you in pain?" Aibell asks, her eyes traveling over our bodies.

I do a double take. "You don't see our injuries?" I look down. There's no blood on my leg. Every bruise on my dad is gone. "What—?"

"It's an illusion."

"Huh?" I falter.

Aibell motions to keep going. "I'll explain later. Just run!"

We go through the door. And slam into another group of guards. We fall back into the hallway.

"Behind me!" Aibell yells at the same time she and Killian engage the fae soldiers.

I flinch with every clash of metal. My dad stands between me and the fight, his sword raised. As if he's grown used to this sort of interaction.

My chest aches. He shouldn't be used to this.

Killian yelps as a sword slices through his tunic, cobalt blue blooming on his upper arm.

"I'm fine," he says calmly to Aibell.

Clang! I jump as another few guards come into view,

surrounding us. My dad holds me tight, my head balanced in the crook of his neck.

"Aibell!" Laoise's voice comes from nowhere.

Literally. She's invisible.

And in seconds, Aibell and Killian are invisible, too.

"What—?" My dad looks around in amazement.

But I know exactly what's happening.

Laoise has used her Gift of Evanescence and extended it to the other fae.

One by one, each of the guards falls from injuries out of thin air. None of the guards even see them coming. Two minutes later, we're free.

"Let's go," Killian says, heading in the direction we ran before.

"To the right." My dad directs us at each intersection.

We twist through the halls. Left. Right. Right. Right. Left.

And we come to a dead end. Again.

"Wait." My dad stops. "This can't be right." He looks behind us, then forward again. "I think we made a wrong turn."

"Yes, I believe you did."

A feeling of spiders crawling along my spine accompanies the king's voice. I turn with a cry. King Raghnall looms behind us. My dad and I both backpedal, gasping.

The king stands at the end of the hall, blocking our exit.

Aibell and Killian lift their swords and step in front of my dad and me. Where is Laoise?

"Did I not tell you, *girl*, that you are indebted to me? There's no escaping my control. I will use your gift."

"Run, Caoine. I'll distract him," my dad whispers. He lifts his sword.

But when I try to move, I can't budge an inch. My feet won't move. Neither will my gaze, connected with the king's.

He laughs. "You're not going anywhere." Footsteps come from behind him, and the king smiles. His guards are coming.

Eric appears over his shoulder. His face falls when he sees our group. "Father . . ." His voice gives out.

The king continues to watch me. "Have you taken care of the problem beyond the castle walls, son?"

Eric shifts. "It—it's not quite that simple."

King Raghnall turns to him. "What's so hard to understand? Enemy forces stand against us, therefore you kill them. Kill them all."

"Yes, but—"

Red splotches appear on the king's cheeks. "But nothing! Did I make the wrong decision when I chose you, son? When I preferred you to that girl?"

The king nods to Aibell. She bristles but remains silent. Eric flinches, his face neutral.

The king looks at me. "Caoine and I were just having a discussion, were we not?"

Eric's jaw and hands flex.

He gives me a smile dripping with sarcasm before turning back to his son. "You see, your mortal friend and her father are now indebted to me. We won't have a problem keeping them under control again."

"What?" Eric's face spirals into panic. "Tell me you didn't."

King Raghnall crosses his arms. "I knew it. You never rid yourself of that ridiculous obsession with her."

Eric turns red, leans closer to his father. "That's not true—"

"It's time you cut ties with this girl. Become the prince I trained you to be."

"But to create a law, father? You have no idea what you've done!"

The king's face turns a putrid shade of scarlet, and I swear he's going to explode. But in the next instant, his eyes roll back in his head, his face turns pale, and he collapses.

Eric's eyes go wide. He drops to his knees, working to revive the king. "Father!"

Laoise appears out of thin air standing over the king and

Eric, a large chunk of stone wall in her hands. She drops it unceremoniously.

Eric blinks, then jumps to his feet. "Go, now."

He looks right at me. Breath catches in my throat. He leans in and whispers to Laoise, pointing somewhere behind us. Then he drops to his knees to care for the king once more.

Laoise floats over to us. "Come. We haven't much time."

She races to a nearby tapestry. I glance between her and Eric, pressure on my elbow as my dad urges me toward Laoise. She flips up the tapestry and pushes a rock jutting out at an angle. A doorway drops open. A secret passageway.

Just like Eric told us about back in the cave.

Did Eric just help us?

Aibell and Killian keep their swords pointed at the Unseelie prince as they pass him.

"Caoine," Laoise is out of breath. "Come. We don't have much time." She holds out a hand to me, my dad pushing me into her arms.

But I can't take my eyes off Eric. The way he huddles over his father, checking for signs of life, terror lacing his every move. My chest aches with grief I can't place. *You were supposed to be my friend.*

"Caoine!" Urgency fills Aibell's voice.

"We've got to go, sweetheart," my dad says.

I bend to enter the shadows just as Eric looks at me.

Our gazes lock, his eyes pleading.

Caoine . . .

I open my mouth but am shoved through before I can speak.

Caoine, please.

No. He betrayed me. Again. There's no way he can be trusted. I squelch the voice in my head, push it far away so I'll never have to hear it again.

So why does my heart feel as if I'm the betrayer?

49

My legs shake from exhaustion. The sky is turning a deep shade of purple, ushering in the night in all its glory. I shift the Book of Judgment from one hand to the other.

We've been running forever. Twenty minutes. Maybe thirty. So much longer than I believed I could handle.

Or my dad, for that matter.

I glance at him as he traverses a fallen tree trunk. He looks strong and healthy. So much better than in the king's throne room. His brown hair is thicker, longer, spilling over his collar. His skin is no longer that sickly, pasty shade. He practically glows with life. How did I heal him?

Lavender drifts past as we push our way through foliage, Laoise in the lead, Aibell taking the rear. We're headed to the Veil, the one that will take my dad and me back home. Home.

Killian is to meet us there with the Book of Discernment. I gave him specific instructions on how to find it. He ran off as if he hadn't just fought three dozen of the king's guards and survived an attack during the casting of the spell.

It would've been much easier if Nym were with us. I'd love if we could just disappear in one spot and reappear right next to the Veil. But that friendship is lost. Along with Eric's.

My gut squeezes tight, and I swallow back bile. How could I have trusted him? Why did he help us escape?

My dad puts a reassuring hand on my arm. Seamus used to say my face was an open book, that he could tell my every emotion from my expression.

I throw my dad a faint smile. Maybe he'll buy it.

Aibell speeds up to walk beside me, her look sheepish. "Hey, about what happened at the circle . . ."

Her gaze drifts to my left hand. An apology is so out of character for her, even if it's not a proper one. Faeries have an aversion to saying sorry.

I nod, glance at my missing finger. "Why did you do it? Cut off my finger?"

She huffs. "It had to be done. It was part of the spell to bring down the castle's magic. But with the way you reacted when you found out you needed to release your banshee song . . . well, I thought it best to leave that part out."

"My finger was part of the dumb spell?"

"The banshee needed to make a sacrifice of her own. It was required."

I frown. "Couldn't it have been a lock of hair or something?"

"It had to be a real sacrifice. It had to mean something to you. Not something that would heal easily and not something that could grow back." She pauses as we continue walking. "If I told you a physical piece of the spell bearer was required, would you have gone through with the spell?"

I shrug. "I guess we'll never know." Because I'm not sure I would've been on board with the spell if I knew I'd lose a finger. Or any other body part. "Maybe things happened the way they were meant to happen."

My gut squeezes tight at the words. Was Eric meant to betray me again?

We round a tree, and the Veil comes into view. Along with three faeries who make me stop in my tracks.

Eithne, Elan, and Einin all stand proudly by the Veil. Killian stands awkwardly beside them.

My dad stands beside me. "Caoine?"

"What are they doing here?" I ask, even though I know they can hear every word I say.

Eithne smiles broadly.

"They're your ticket home." Aibell tilts her chin toward the lot, not bothering to hide her sneer.

Clearly she's as excited about this prospect as I am. "How did this come about?"

My question is for Aibell, but Eithne gladly answers. "Did Aibell not tell you?" She gloats like she just won a beauty pageant. "She has learned some . . . *sensitive* information about us." She purses her lips at Aibell, but it's obvious she's teasing more than she's concerned. "She promised to stay quiet as long as we helped you into the Mortal Realm."

I glance at my dad. Then clear my throat. "Oh. Cool." I think.

"What secret?" My dad still holds the sword he took from the castle.

I cringe when rage flashes in Eithne's eyes.

"Oh relax, Eithne." Aibell rolls her shoulders and looks around, still in guard mode. "Does it matter if the mortals learn you've been selling Unseelie secrets to the Seelie queen?"

Elan and Einin leap toward Aibell, curses on their lips. But Eithne puts a single arm out to stop them. "That was uncalled for, Aibell. I can take back my offer to help them cross."

Aibell puffs out her chest. "And I can take back my vow not to inform the king of your betrayal. You do wish to remain in your realm, do you not?"

Eithne growls.

"That's what I thought." Aibell laughs. "Besides, what does it matter if a few mortals know the secret? Who will they tell?"

I frown. *I'm half-fae, thank you very much.*

Eithne eyes my dad and me for a minute too long. Finally

she relaxes. "It matters not. Let us be done with this, Aibell. I have better things to do."

She looks away as if she doesn't care we're even here.

I turn to Aibell. "Wait. Before we go, I need to know . . . what happened outside the castle? Before we escaped?"

"The silence, the fae who carry silence with them? We got them to work with us."

"You did?" I can't keep the astonishment from my face.

"They don't only void all sound. They can also enact their own magic. In this case, it was creating chaos through illusion. They conjured an imaginary army of thousands to surround the castle. The king's men were literally fighting ghosts."

"Whoa." I pause. "The explosion . . . was that a vision too?"

"It was."

"So the castle wall isn't torn to shreds?"

"No. The castle is fully intact. Those inside only believe they saw it explode."

I nibble my lip. "Illusion. Which is why I saw injuries—even felt them—but they weren't real? Because the illusion wasn't real?"

"Exactly."

A smile breaks across my face. Working with the silence? Genius. As cold as Aibell is, she truly is a warrior.

But—I clench my hands, melancholy squeezing my chest. "I don't suppose my vision of Gar was illusion?"

Aibell's face falls. "That was real, I'm afraid."

Pain slides along my spine, nudges at the backs of my eyes. "Oh." My banshee song did require a sacrifice.

"You couldn't have known, Caoine." It's odd that Aibell's trying to comfort me.

I nod and clear my throat. "So, uh, is this it, then? We're leaving the Unseelie Realm?"

She nods. "You have your wish."

Yeah, I did get my wish. But how do I save my mom without help?

Tears prick the backs of my eyes. "And you kept your word. Thank you." Emotion trickles over my skin, goose pimples spreading like wildfire.

"Thank *you*. For being willing to take the books across the Veil."

I turn to Laoise, who immediately leans in for a hug.

"Goodbye, Caoine," she says. "Thank you for your sacrifice. For all you have done for us."

A single tear slips down my cheek. "I don't feel like I did anything."

"You have done more than you can possibly know."

I give her one more hug, then walk toward Killian. He hands me the book but doesn't give me a hug.

The other three faeries begin their thing. They spread out in a half-circle around the Veil, hands raised. A faint glow appears in the air, identical to the one I fell through.

"Be quick, mortal," is the only thing Eithne bothers to say to me.

But I have one more question before I'm done here. "You're a Seer."

She nods, her eyes still on the Veil.

"You knew Eric would betray us, didn't you?"

A smile forms on her face, but she stays quiet.

"You agreed to help me and my dad cross the Veil, believing it would never happen."

Her eyes find mine. "It was a good deception, was it not? Allowing Aibell to think I was a team player?"

I glance at Aibell. "Yeah. It was."

I motion to my dad to step through the Veil, turn to Aibell one last time. "I'll tell Cat you said hi."

She smiles, a gesture that surprises even me.

I step through the Veil and back to my life.

<h1 style="text-align:center">50</h1>

I STAND IN THE SHOWER, hot water streaming down my body, swirls of dirt circling into the drain. I've been here for at least thirty minutes, but I'm not ready to give this up. Not yet.

Days or possibly weeks spent in the Unseelie Realm. I haven't figured out just how many passed. And my dad? I still can't believe he's alive and *home*. We're both home.

I suck in a breath, blow it out. Memories flit through my mind. Thoughts of new friendships and schemes and climbing walls and traitors.

Traitors.

I fist my hands against the wall as Eric's face dances across my vision. Why did I ever trust him?

A knock makes me jump.

"Caoine! You've got some visitors downstairs." My dad's voice is the most beautiful music I've ever heard.

How many times was I angry with him for rushing me while getting ready in the morning? Never again. I will never take for granted the time we have together.

My heart goes into overdrive, and I jump out of the shower, towel dry as quickly as possible.

I glance at my hand and stare at the unusual shape of four

fingers on one hand. This new me might take a little getting used to.

A noise in the hallway distracts my thoughts, and my heart runs away with the knowledge that my boyfriend is a matter of feet from me.

I slide into a clean pair of jeans and a long-sleeved tee, hand-knitted socks from Aubree on my feet. A new hobby she's taken up since having so much time without Seamus.

I run my fingers through my hair but let it go. Oliver won't care a bit if it's all tangles. At least it's finally clean.

The minute my dad and I walked through the door, I called him. Aubree, too.

Oliver didn't care that it was four in the morning, and he didn't seem shocked that my dad was alive. He was just happy to hear my voice.

I assume it took some time for his parents to let him leave the house, or I wouldn't have gotten such a long shower. But my heart pounds like a soccer ball in the middle of a game.

Oliver is here.

He's here and I'm safe and my dad is safe and —

I pause at the top of the stairs, breathe. Take a moment to be grateful for all I have in this life, for as long as I have it.

It takes only seconds to leap down the steps and run into my boyfriend's arms.

"Hey, you," he whispers, his breath warm against my face.

My only response is to kiss him. More fiercely than I've ever kissed him in all the months we've dated. With more passion and love than I even knew I had.

"Ahem."

The voice invades our happy reunion.

A laugh bubbles up from my belly, along with a fair amount of heat that our kiss wasn't exactly private.

Without another word I attack Aubree in a bear hug the size of Montana.

"Hey, girl." She squeezes me in return. "It's good to have you back."

I sigh and pull away. "It's good to be home." Untamed tears run down my face.

Oliver's gaze lands on my left hand. He frowns, taking me into his arms, special attention on my hand. "What happened—?"

I shake my head. "Another time."

No need to ruin our perfect reunion.

His eyes roam my face and hair, going wide. One hand cups my ear. "And this?"

My pointy ears! My cheeks warm.

"By the way, I'm fae?" I flash my cutest smile, despite my tears.

He sighs. "That might take some getting used to."

I shrug. "Miss me?" I reach up and pluck an eyelash from his cheek.

His gaze swallows mine. "Longest two days of my life."

I frown. "Two days?"

He blinks. "Yeah. We had no idea where you were for two days. I still can't believe what happened." He pauses at my confused look. "Why?"

"Whoa." I shake my head. "They told me time in Faerie is kooky."

Aubree nods. "How long was it for you?"

"Weeks?"

Oliver's eyes bug out, but I just shrug.

"Hey, let's be happy I didn't lose more time in the Mortal Realm."

"The Mortal—"

I bite my lip. "Oops. I mean Earth. It's just how they talk in Faerie, I—I guess I'm more fae than I thought."

Aubree snorts at this. Then she comes from behind me and envelopes me in another hug. "It is *so* good to see you again, sister."

Oliver laughs, takes my hands in his. "No way, Caoine Roberts. You're as human as they come. And you're mine." My boyfriend kisses me.

My belly lights on fire, and I delight in every sensation.

"All right, you two," Aubree interrupts. "We've got business to discuss. And unfortunately it can't wait."

I blink. "We do? It can't?"

Oliver's shoulders fall, worry in his eyes.

Aubree looks from him to me. "I need to talk to you about what I was trying to figure out the night you disappeared."

The night Eric kidnapped me.

My throat closes, but I push past my swirling emotions to listen to Aubree.

She gives Oliver a wary look. He simply squeezes me in another hug from behind.

My heart races. What is she about to tell me?

"Okay, I'm just going to spill it." She licks her lips. "My mom borrowed magic from a spell she put in places ages ago. On Halloween night, the night Eric tried to enact the original spell, I placed Seven Seals in the ground to create a circle to trap him. What I didn't tell you is they were connected to a deeper magic. Magic my mom embedded into them." She pauses. Takes a deep breath. "When Eric banished my spell, he broke the Seven Seals."

"And breaking them is a bad thing?" I hate to ask the question, considering I already know the answer.

She nods. My heart sinks.

"By breaking the Seven Seals, Eric released"—she swallows—"*I* released seven plagues on the Earth. The first of which is the Blood Moon."

"You did what?" I don't mean to scream, but I can't keep my voice under control.

Aubree trembles, and guilt floods my core like a tidal wave.

"I didn't mean to do it." Her cheeks pink. "I didn't know what would happen. I—"

Oliver steps forward, places a gentle hand on her arm. "You didn't cause this, Aubree. Eric did. None of this is your fault. You were simply trying to stop a madman."

I come to my senses, shame heating my cheeks. "He's right, Aub. This has nothing to do with you. Your mom will see that. We already got the books for her. I mean, your mom can make this right, yeah?"

She shakes her head. "I don't know. Not until I talk to her. I knew if the Seals changed in any way, it would be confirmed. And they have."

She laughs at herself, even though there's no mirth behind it.

"I mean, I knew what was happening when that stupid moon turned colors, but . . ." She sighs. "I just thought maybe, *maybe* I was wrong, ya know?"

I loop my arms around her neck, pull her close. "I know, Aubree."

And I do. Sometimes denial is the only way to face another day.

"Wait." I pull back. "Why is this just happening now? The seals were broken almost five months ago, right?"

Aubree shrugs. "It's got something to do with the spring equinox. With the days finally being balanced or something."

Oliver takes me back into his arms. "Hey. Can we talk about this later? Right now I'd like to spend time with my girlfriend." He kisses the top of my head. "And maybe never let her go again."

Aubree laughs. "Okay, okay! I can take a hint." She heads toward the front door. "You two *reconnect*. I'll go grab us some donuts for breakfast." She clears her throat. "But we need to talk once I get back."

"Thanks." I give her a quick wave before she's gone.

Then I willingly turn back to my boyfriend, who's already pulling me in for another kiss. He holds me and I hold him. Perfectly content to regain the days we've lost.

The news of the Seals will weigh on my mind another time.

In this single moment in time, I hold on to this man I love with all the strength I have in my physical body. I will never let him go. Will never leave his side again.

I've been over how things went down with the king again and again. Nothing makes sense, and I don't know if it ever will. But we're here. My dad and me. And Aubree.

And Oliver.

He pulls back to look in my eyes. And I promptly snuggle in for one more peck of his lips. I will not take another moment for granted when it comes to my loved ones.

I once was lost but now am found.

This is where I'm meant to be.

THE END

Do not miss

Silence

Book Three of the Banshee Song Series.

Coming Soon from L2L2 Publishing.

CAOINE'S SONG

Music has always been a big part of my life, so when it came time to write Caoine's story, it felt natural to put a strong focus on her song and how it would feel to hear such beauty. Thankfully, I'm surrounded by talented friends who can bring my crazy dreams to life! Special thanks to Delany Callahan-Bird for capturing Caoine's heart and soul in song!

Scan the QR Code to hear Caoine's song. ("'Caoine's Fan Song" written and performed by Delany Callahan-Bird.)

ACKNOWLEDGMENTS

Reader. When you feel you've lost your way, know that you are never alone. The Creator is always beside you. May this story be an encouragement to you.

Tim. My perfect partner. Thank you for listening to my crazy ideas and for always being there to pick me up when I doubt myself.

My beautiful girls, Gabby, Gracie, and Scar. I am so proud of each of you. Thank you for being my biggest cheerleaders.

Mom and Wayne, Dad and Judy, Paige and Rich. Thank you for your unending support and love in everything I do.

My agent, Tessa Emily Hall. Thank you for your patience and wise direction. You are such an inspiration to me!

Michele and the whole L2L2 team. Thank you, thank you, thank you for sticking with me! With each of my revisions and my horrible editing abilities. I swear you live inside my head, Michele! These characters are just as much you as they are me.

My beta readers. Jill, Kelly, Rachel, Hannah, and Brandy. Thank you for your honesty and your red pens. This story would be boring without you!

Jordon. What can I say? This book wouldn't exist without

our brainstorming session. Thank you for Saturday writing sessions and for being awesome.

Writer's Block. Jordon, Becki, Hannah, Rachel, Ainsleigh, Sarah, Kaitlyn, Sarah, Scott, Avery, and Jenn. You guys are my lifeline to sanity. For real. Getting to hang with you each week encourages me more than you will ever know. Editions Bookstore, thank you for closing the shop so we can be loud and for putting up with us every Friday.

The Armorers. Your input is invaluable! Thank you for being there when I need help "by tomorrow."

My Street Team, the Caffeinated Readers. My faithful support group. You guys are so much fun! Thank you for playing along with my silly Facebook posts.

Jesus. The ultimate storyteller. I am forever grateful that you trust me with your words to share with others. Proverbs 3:5-6.

No one else can do what you were meant to do, Reader. Believe.

~Laura

ABOUT THE AUTHOR

Laura L. Zimmerman lives in a suburb of Charlotte, North Carolina with her husband, three daughters, and four adorable kitties. As a child, she became convinced she was a mermaid, which she still believes to this day. Being a mythological creature, she caught the traveling bug at an early age and spent two-and-a-half years with a missionary organization roaming the world.

During her travels she met her Mr. Darcy, and they married soon after. Recently, she and her family moved across the country twice in a ridiculously short amount of time, but she's happy to report she plans to stay put for a good number of years, thank you very much.

Laura is currently a stay-at-home mom and home educator by day, drinker of coffee by night. Besides writing, she's passionate about loving Jesus, fangirling over anything *Star Wars*, and singing loudly. An avid reader, she often has overdue library fines and a TBR pile as tall as Trump Tower.

Her favorite form of writing is flash fiction, so check out her blog to read some of her most recent work! You can catch her in a bookstore, coffee shop, or being a taxi driver for her teens.

Laura loves to hear from her readers! Follow her on social media, check out her website, or drop her a line to let her know what you thought of Lament. *Happy reading!*

———

www.LauraLZimmerman.com
Facebook: @AuthorLLZimmerman
Twitter: @LauraLZimm
Instagram: @LauraLZimmAuthor

REVIEWS

Did you know reviews can skyrocket a book's career? Instead of fizzling into nothing, a book will be suggested by Amazon, shared by Goodreads, or showcased by Barnes & Noble. Plus, authors treasure reviews! (And read them over and over and over . . .)

If you enjoyed this book, would you consider leaving a review on:

- Amazon
- Barnes & Noble
- Goodreads

. . . or perhaps even your personal blog? Thank you so much!

~The L2L2 Publishing Team

PRONUNCIATION GUIDE

- Caoine (keyn)
- Saoirse (SEER·shuh)
- Clíodhna (KLEE·uh·nuh)
- Aibell (ee·BOOL)
- Laoise (LEE·shuh)
- Raghnall (RAHY·nuhl)
- Faílenn (FEE·luhn)
- Eithne (ahy·NUH)
- Einin (ahy·NEEN)
- Elan (EE·luhn)
- Marfóir (mahr·FYA·ruh)
- Mairéad (muh·RED)
- Oísin (oh·SHEEN)
- Neamini (nuh·MEE·nee)
- Seamus (SHEY·muhs)
- Bean-nighe (ben·NEE·yuh)

More from L2L2 Publishing
Don't miss the first book!

Half-faerie Caoine has no control over the banshee lament she sings each night, predicting the death of others. A senior in a brand new high school, she expects the same response she's received at every other school: judgment from fellow students over her unusual eyes and unnaturally white skin and hair. However, for the first time in her life she finds friends. Real friends. Life spins out of control when her lament comes out during the day, those whose death she predicts die right in front of her, and a dark faerie known only as the Unseelie prince blames Caoine. Her curse is not supposed to work like that. In a race against time, Caoine must uncover the Unseelie prince's identity and stop a spell before it unleashes hell on earth, all while trying to control her banshee song and finding a place among her peers. Senior year just got real.

LAURIE LUCKING
Common

More from L2L2 Publishing

Don't miss the first book!

Brenna James wants three things for her sixteenth birthday: to find her history notes before the test, to have her mother return from her business trip, and to stop creating fire with her bare hands. Yeah, that's so not happening. Unfortunately. When Brenna learns her mother is missing in an alternate reality called Linneah, she travels through a portal to find her. Against her will. Who knew portals even existed? But Brenna's arrival in Linneah begins the fulfillment of an ancient prophecy, including a royal murder and the theft of Linneah's most powerful relic: the Sacred Veil. Hold up. Can everything just slow down for a sec? Left with no other choice, Brenna and her new friend Baldwin pursue the thief into the dangerous woods of Silvastamen. When they spy an army marching toward Linneah, Brenna is horrified. Can she find the veil, save her mother, and warn Linneah in time?

WHERE WILL WE TAKE YOU NEXT?

Enjoy *Keen,*
Relish *Common,*
Sink into *Drifting,*
Discover *Spark,*
and Devour *Silence the Siren.*

All at
www.love2readlove2writepublishing.com/bookstore
or your local or online retailer.

Happy Reading!
~The L2L2 Publishing Team

ABOUT L2L2 PUBLISHING

Love2ReadLove2Write Publishing, LLC is a small traditional press, dedicated to clean or Christian speculative fiction.

Speculative genres include but are not limited to: Fantasy, Science Fiction, Fairy Tales, Magical Realism, Time Travel, Spiritual Warfare, Alternate History, Chillers (such as vampires, zombies, werewolves, or light horror), Superhero Fiction, Steampunk, Supernatural, Paranormal, etc., or a mixture of any of the previous.

We seek stunning tales masterfully told, and we strive to create an exquisite publishing experience for our authors and to produce quality fiction for our readers.

Lament is at the heart of what we publish: a riveting tale with speculative elements that will delight our readers.

Visit www.L2L2Publishing.com to view our submissions guidelines, find our other titles, or learn more about us.

And if you love our books, please leave a review!

Happy Reading!

~The L2L2 Publishing Team

CPSIA information can be obtained
at www.ICGtesting.com
Printed in the USA
LVHW022249110121
676219LV00009B/1710